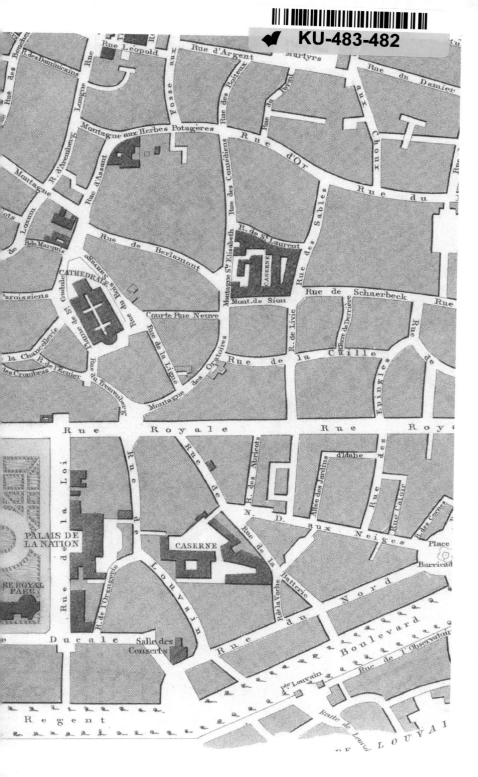

Charlotte Brontë's Secret Love

Jolien Janzing

Charlotte Brontë's Secret Love

Translated from the Dutch by Paul Vincent

World Editions

Published in Great Britain in 2015 by World Editions Ltd., London

www.worldeditions.org

First published as *De Meester* in the Netherlands in 2013 by
De Arbeiderspers, Amsterdam

British Library Cataloguing-in-Publication Data
A catalogue record for this book is available on request from
the British Library

ISBN 978-94-6238-059-2

Typeset in Minion Pro

The translation of this book was funded by the Flemish Literature Fund
(Vlaams Fonds voor de Letteren—www.flemishliterature.be)

Flemish
Literature
Fund

To Paul

To Serge and Alessandra

'Experience is simply the name
we give our mistakes.'
OSCAR WILDE

Characters

CHARLOTTE BRONTË: *daughter of an English parson, pupil, governess and talented novice writer*
EMILY BRONTË: *sister of Charlotte, pupil, genius, poet and novice writer*

HAWORTH England

PATRICK BRONTË: *Anglican parson, widower of Maria Branwell and father of Charlotte, Branwell, Emily and Anne*
BRANWELL BRONTË: *brother of Charlotte, problem child and only son of Patrick Brontë*
ANNE BRONTË: *sister of Charlotte and youngest daughter of Patrick Brontë*
AUNT ELIZABETH: *sister of the late Maria Branwell and sister-in-law of Patrick Brontë*
TABBY: *the elderly maid at the parsonage*
MARTHA: *the young maid*

BRUSSELS Belgium

PENSIONNAT HEGER

MONSIEUR CONSTANTIN HEGER: *teacher of French literature at the Athénée Royal and the Pensionnat Heger*
MADAME CLAIRE HEGER: *headmistress of the Pensionnat Heger and wife of Constantin Heger*
MARIE, LOUISE, CLAIRE, PROSPÈRE AND JULIE-MARIE HEGER: *their children*
LOUISE DE BASSOMPIERRE: *pupil, special friend of Emily Brontë*

CAMPAGNE CLARET

ARCADIE CLARET: *very attractive daughter of Major Charles Claret*

HENRIETTE CLARET: *mother of Arcadie and wife of Major Charles Claret*

CHARLES CLARET: *major in the Belgian army and treasurer of the Fund for Widows and Orphans of the Belgian Army, at the Ministry of War*

JOS: *the Claret family's coachman*

CHÂTEAU OF KOEKELBERG

MARY TAYLOR: *English pupil and bosom friend of Charlotte Brontë*

MARTHA TAYLOR: *younger sister of Mary*

VIEUX MARCHÉ

EMILE: *Flemish workman attending evening classes in French with Constantin Heger*

ROYAL PALACE

LEOPOLD I: *first king of the Belgians since 1831, widower of Princess Charlotta Augusta of Wales and husband of Louise-Marie of Belgium*

LOUISE-MARIE: *daughter of the French king Louis Philippe and Queen Marie Amélie of Bourbon-Sicilie, first queen of the Belgians and wife of Leopold I*

JULES VAN PRAET: *private secretary to King Leopold I, first king of the Belgians*

I

The bells of the church of Saint-Michel and Sainte-Gudule strike twelve and you find yourself in the year 1842: a time when ladies' taffeta dresses rustle, the streets are illuminated by gaslights, the seed of married men must not be spilt and penniless girls sell their long plaits. You will witness a love story; a forbidden romance. Piles of letters bound with yellowy ribbons bear testimony to this clandestine love, this passion which was illicit, but could not be simply extinguished. The story takes place in a kingdom so small and absurd that it is difficult to believe it does not exist purely in the imagination: Belgium. The name seems to come from a fable, but indeed Caesar mentioned the Belgians and wrote that they were the bravest of all the Gauls. However, this tiny country, a louse in the coat of Europe, is particularly fertile, with lush meadows and fat cows and geese so big you can scarcely lift them. Although most farmers and labourers have only just enough to eat to keep the flesh on their bones, the gentry are plump and sturdy and the ladies have luxuriant hips and breasts and oval, rosy faces. The good people of Belgium cannot all understand each other, since the king likes to express himself in German, the aristocracy and the bourgeoisie speak French, the common people in the south of the country use a French patois and in the north they speak Flemish—a rich dialect of Dutch. So much Babylonian twittering brings confusion and disunity. If you come across a specimen of the repressed Flemish working class, note the strong but obstinately shrugged shoulders: the head thrust a little forward in an attitude of eternal suspicious attention, the eyebrows set in a frown above a look of silent rebellion. Belgium: where division reigns. And although it is a ridiculously small country, it has a capital that is growing at frightening speed: Brussels! A city with a heart of spacious squares and wide avenues that intersect at right angles, of palaces and mansions and a splendid park with shady walks—a worthy domicile for the rich and the bourgeoisie. From the edges of this heart wind the streets of the common people overripe with increasingly numerous damp alleyways. And through the canals of the city, between the houses of both noblemen and paupers a narrow river flows, muddy green in colour and stinking fearsomely.

But before you travel with the heroine of this story to the rampantly growing Brussels—by steamer across the North Sea and by stagecoach through the Flemish countryside—I shall give you one glimpse of her future there.

*

See how the young teacher wanders restlessly through the streets of Brussels. The day has been exhaustingly hot and darkness has still not fallen. She does not want to return to the boarding school yet. A booming of bells catches her attention. It is the hypnotic voice of the church of Saint-Michel and Sainte-Gudule calling the faithful to vespers. She does not know what possesses her, but she hurries towards it, along the rue de la Chancellerie and up the many white stone steps to the church. Next to the porch a beggar puts out his hand towards her and she gives him a coin, not for his salvation, but for hers.

How cool it is in the church. A few women are sitting praying with rosary beads between their fingertips. She wishes she could sink down onto the flagstones, but she goes and sits at the side to wait until evening prayers are over. In a deserted corner of the church, confessions are being heard. Confession! She is a sinner and she must tell her story. Someone must listen to her. A working-class woman approaches the confessional; she tidies her greasy hair by smoothing it against her skull and straightens her apron. Can the priest see her then? Isn't confession anonymous?

She can still change her mind: she can go back to the streets where no one knows her. However, she remains seated and waits. The woman emerges from the confessional with the trace of a smile on her lips.

She gets up, scarcely knowing what she is doing. The tradition is alien to her: how should she address the priest? She creeps into the confessional, lets the red velvet curtain fall behind her and is almost overpowered by the smell of incense, pipe tobacco and old sweat. Just enough light enters to be able to vaguely make out the face behind the wicker grille.

'*Mon père*,' she says and the blood rises to her head. 'I have sinned.'

'Are you a foreigner?' asks the priest severely, obviously surprised by her accent.

She answers in the affirmative, and adds that she was brought up as a Protestant. He wants to know if she is still a Protestant and she nods, which he appears not to see, so she clears her throat and whispers: '*Oui, mon père.*' He says that in that case she cannot confess. Tears well up in her eyes. If he dismisses her without letting her tell her story, she will be close to despair. She tells him this and begs him to listen to her.

'*Ma fille*,' says the priest tenderly, making her almost choke on her tears. 'Confess and let this be your first step towards the true Church.'

She tells him everything, at a furious tempo. About the safe but oppressive life in her father's house and how she escaped from it. How she thought she would be able to enjoy freedom in Brussels, but allowed herself to be shut up in a boarding school. The priest's face comes closer to the grille: she feels his breath on her cheek.

'Tell me what your sin is.'

And she tells him. She tells him everything.

THE JOURNEY

II

Cast an eye over England and look for the windy, treeless hills of West Yorkshire. There, in the small, but overpopulated industrial town of Haworth, at the top of the steep, blustery main street and behind the church with its careless draughts board of mossy tombstones, lies the parsonage, where a young woman of twenty-five is taking her white petticoats down from the washing line in the back garden. Her name is Charlotte Brontë and she is, as yet, unaware of the fame that will one day be hers— and of the passion that awaits her in distant, dissolute Brussels.

*

Charlotte is busy with the washing, which gives us the opportunity to observe her at our leisure. She is not beautiful, that should be made clear at once; she is not exquisite, rich and spoilt like Blanche Ingram or seductive like Ginevra Fanshawe—characters from her later novels. No thick golden hair falls in waves over her shoulders; no rosy mouth waits to be kissed. But isn't the importance of physical beauty greatly exaggerated? Sit with me at the window of the White Lion or the Black Bull, two popular taverns in Haworth, or even a random café in a metropolis like Paris, and let us watch the passers-by. How many beauties are there among them? How many women with completely symmetrical features and noses without the least bend in them, how many classical athletes, muscular and with a healthy head of hair and perfect skin? We can sit there for hours without seeing one—and then all of a sudden, a pearl. They are rare, beauties, and how ridiculous it is to get worked up over prettiness when it is simply not given to most people.

She may not be beautiful, this Miss Brontë, but she is certainly not unattractive. Her rich, soft hair (rabbit brown, mixed with a drop of fox red) has a severe centre parting, and two braids fall over each ear in a low loop which is gathered at the back with the rest of her hair. Her face is an almost virgin canvas, on which the only colour is supplied by the lively, dark eyes and sensitive mouth. There is a certain charm in her features, and the way she moves is feminine. She takes the wooden peg from the line and bends gracefully to put the petticoat into the basket. She stretches to catch hold of the second petticoat and reveals her ankles—in her haste she has forgotten to put stockings on, and is wearing only wooden gardening clogs—and her ankles are slim and elegant. What a delicate woman; the wrists of her white hands are scarcely broader than those of a child. Although it is only February, spring is in the air and for a moment Charlotte turns her face towards the sun.

'Emily!' she cries in the direction of the open kitchen door. 'Come here a moment.'

Her sister does not come, and Charlotte takes her leave of the geese by herself, and when Keeper, Emily's dog, pushes his head against her belly and growls softly she scratches his neck and gently tugs a fold in his skin. Is there still time for a walk on the moor? The melancholy she feels about leaving her home tomorrow is greatly tempered by her impatience to depart. There won't be time, she knows, and she puts down the basket and goes to the front garden: a lawn with a couple of overgrown brambles against the low wall, a lilac and a few rough pines.

A gap between the pines affords a view of the church of St. Michael and All Angels, and she has never known any different: it is the church where her father preaches and in her childhood she thought the tower was the highest in England.

Since she has seen York Minster, the church tower has come down in her estimation and its brown colour reminds her of a rotten tooth. Between the church and the garden wall is an extension of the cemetery; there are a few standing tombs here and there, but most stones are flat on the ground, as if the living want to prevent the dead from creeping out of their graves. Charlotte's mother and her older sisters Maria and Elizabeth are buried in the family vault near the altar in the church. Her mother was thirty-eight when she died—not that young when you consider that most inhabitants of Haworth die at a much younger age. Maria and Elizabeth were only eleven and ten when they succumbed to typhus.

She opens the garden gate and in the look that scans the view there is a certain affection, although she cannot wait to put as great as possible a distance between herself and the town. She will not return; if she has her way she will never return.

*

'I hope the mild weather continues.'

She turns and there comes her father, a clergyman in the Church of England, holding his Bible and prayer book for the evening service. At sixty-four he is still an impressive-looking man: slim and handsome, his coarse red hair almost completely silver-white now. He still takes the same long steps, but recently a touch of hesitancy has crept in. The northern blue of his eyes is increasingly troubled by cataracts.

'Daughter, are you taking your leave?'

When she hears his deep, calm voice the emotion wells up in her and she cannot answer. He puts his hand on her shoulder and seems to lean on her for a moment, although she is small and delicate.

'This is a bad moment for me to leave my congregation,' he says. There are grumblings about church taxes, which are supposedly too great a burden for many people. She feels she should say something about the poor in Haworth—about how terrible she finds it that people have to endure so much. She lacks the courage. In the last few weeks she has put much time and energy into collecting money and subsequently distributing clothes, blankets and the fifty pairs of clogs, a hundred sacks of oats and two hundred loads of coal. She has seen so many grey faces, so many thin, trembling hands... And then there is the coughing, the clearing of the throat and the sneezing in all those dark cave-like rooms! She is ashamed of the discomfort she feels in her dealings with the poor and of the resentment she harbours against the mothers who despite their penury give birth to a child every year. A child who in turn will grow up to become a badly-paid labourer in one of the textile mills on the river, will spend long days at a hand loom or combing wool in a stuffy upstairs room. She wishes that she could muster more sympathy, but she is unable to forget herself. During a visit to a dying father—she was bringing the family coal, bread and eggs from the geese at the parsonage—she suddenly felt the slimy hand of a child sliding into hers. The toddler was wearing a grubby nightshirt and green snot was running out of his nose, and in pure disgust she had tugged her hand free.

Disease is everywhere in Haworth. The workers' cottages are overcrowded; often various families live in one hovel. Along the street are the wooden privies that are shared by various families, and their contents flow downhill in an open sewer. Her friend Ellen once remarked that the air in Haworth was bound to be good, since the town lies high in the Pennine hills; but it is a chilly, windy place where it often rains and snows.

Although Charlotte has never been out of the north of England and apart from a few years at boarding school has spent all her time in Haworth, in her imagination she has fled almost daily. When she sits at the table in front of the fire and takes up her pen, distance and lack of funds are no longer obstacles and she can travel wherever she wants. Then come the images of Mediterranean coast with olive groves, palms and vanilla-scented flowers. Or she loses herself in the lanes and alleys between the churches and mansions of cities like London and Paris.

'Tomorrow evening we'll be in London, papa,' she says, louder than intended, and resolutely turns her gaze from the brown church and the graves, walks past her father and goes back in through the kitchen door.

*

Although it is not yet anywhere near morning, Charlotte cannot get back to sleep. The bed is too hot for her; she sits up carefully and throws back the bedspread on her side. Emily's breathing ends in long squeaks, like the wind whistling in through the broken pane of glass in the church tower. It was a bad idea to share a bed with her again. She is like an old maid in bed with her sister. There should be a man lying beside her; her husband.

There is a restlessness in her legs and she wants to get up, but the floorboards tend to creak so terribly and she will wake Emily. She turns onto her back and takes it into her head that she wants a husband, but without children. Without the sour smell of milk, the measles and the croup and the eternal, irritating crying in the night. She has seen enough fresh young girls in the first year of their marriage turn into nervous drudges with a cotton cloth tied carelessly round their heads and a whining baby on their arm. But there is no way of escaping the responsibilities of motherhood and the household if you join with a man in marriage.

Charlotte runs her fingertips along the fringe of the blanket and pulls two tassels apart so hard that it causes a tear in the wool. She must sleep, because tomorrow the first leg of their journey awaits her. Her father will accompany her and Emily, first to London and three days later on the packet boat to Ostend. He wants to be sure that they arrive safely, although there is not really cause for concern, since her friend Mary and her brother John will accompany them and they have made the crossing several times already.

By the first dim light of morning she can see their travelling dresses hanging from the wardrobe. Is simple Yorkshire clothing suitable for a worldly city like Brussels? Emily refuses to leave behind her dresses with their enormous puff sleeves, which are completely out of fashion; she does not give two hoots about her appearance, but does not realise that there they will be judged by it in the first instance. Come to that, there are a number of reasons why their stay in Brussels could be a difficult one. The bourgeoisie speak French, a language she herself can write quite reasonably but has spoken only with teachers who have never set foot on the continent of Europe. Emily can read some French, but cannot conduct a conversation in it. In addition, Belgium is a Catholic country, where different morals and customs apply.

Suddenly Emily starts coughing. She sits up and coughs against the sleeve of her raised arm.

'Are you all right?' Charlotte piles up both their pillows, so that her sister can lie in a more upright position.

'Em, are we doing the right thing going to Brussels? I'm suddenly not sure.'

'Do you want to be a governess again then?'

She knows how to put her finger on the sore spot.

'Do you want to work like a slave again and be bossed about by someone like Mrs White?'

Charlotte looks at the contours of her sister's body: her long thin legs pulled up and her profile like a ship under sail, her nose the full sail, her chin the stubborn bow.

'No, no, you know I don't. And what will happen with papa?'

'He will miss me.' Emily clears her throat. 'He's used to having me to look after him, but he's got Aunt Elizabeth and Martha. And we'll be back in six months, won't we? You promised. We don't need to stay away longer than that.'

'You'll be coming home in any case,' says Charlotte. 'I may stay a little longer in Brussels, but I'm not sure yet.' She gives a halting sigh. 'Am I a fool?'

'Not a fool, no.' Emily peevishly tosses one of the pillows over the foot of the bed. 'Your plan will bear fruit in time. We'll learn French and German and I'll brush up my piano playing. With all that knowledge we'll soon be able to open a school. Anne can teach the girls to embroider. That way we'll never have to leave.'

Charlotte listens to her own arguments. Strange how her sister intones them almost verbatim, as if in an attempt to convince herself.

'Perhaps Branwell can help out too,' she suggests.

'Branwell is a wastrel,' says Emily sternly. 'He'll never amount to anything.'

'I miss him, though.'

'What do you miss? The smell of drink?'

Emily rolls onto her stomach, facing the other way.

III

Charlotte drinks her coffee and enjoys a growing feeling of excitement. It is time: she is leaving.

There is a knock at the door of the dining room and her father's curate comes in. He shivers and rubs his hands together, because the night-time cold is still persisting outside.

'Well, well, Mr Weightman,' says Charlotte, 'Up so early?'

She likes teasing the young clergyman, because there is something about him of a puppy jumping around wanting to play with you. With a face finely modelled by the Creator, lively eyes and long, shapely legs, he is an attractive man. On this, all the women in Haworth are agreed. William Weightman is aware of his physical beauty, like a child that takes for granted the fact that he is perfect and sweet; there is nothing presumptuous about him. Charlotte is immune to his charms, which for her are too feminine; but she knows that Anne has a soft spot for him.

'Davy from the Black Bull is here.' Martha wipes her hands on her apron and starts noisily stacking the plates from the table. Her milky-blue eyes are full of tears.

Aunt Elizabeth helps Emily into her cloak and ties the ribbons of Charlotte's bonnet. She throws a shawl hastily over her shoulders and follows them outside.

'Time to go!' says Patrick Brontë firmly. He takes his sister-in-law by the elbows and kisses her on the cheek.

'I'll be home in a week or two.'

Elizabeth strokes his hand and then reaches out to her nieces. Charlotte kisses her with affection, but Emily's embrace is wooden and absent. Elizabeth has looked after the offspring of her sister Maria for over twenty years, and she knows the children through and through. Anne, the youngest, is her favourite, an angel, and Branwell, the only son, still seeks out her company when he is at home. However, the two oldest sisters seem to see her increasingly as a conventional, stupid woman. In Charlotte the disdain is tempered by her warm feelings, but Emily sometimes makes fun of her openly. The children are truly fond of her, she does not doubt that, but they have never come to love her as a mother and that is one of the great disappointments of her life.

At the time she left everything behind to support her brother-in-law: her home town of Penzance in Cornwall ('The sun shone so beautifully, Patrick!') *and* her chance of having a family of her own. There was no other solution, since as a widower with six young children Patrick Brontë could not find a respectable woman to marry him. In the first years in the parsonage Elizabeth fell deeply in love with her brother-in-law and she watched him fighting his growing desire. Like that day in the kitchen when she stood at the draining board and he put his hand on hers—and left it there for minutes on end. Until, with a grimace of frustration, he ran out of the kitchen and emptied one of his pistols into the fence. There was no future for them as man and wife, since the law forbade a widower to marry the sister of his dead spouse. Gradually their love gave way to affection, and it is consequently with warmth that she hands him the basket of sandwiches and tells him to button up his coat.

Aunt Elizabeth sees Charlotte look round one last time as the horses start moving, to take her leave of the parsonage, the church and the graves. She calls out to her, but her niece is already far away in her thoughts, in a world where she cannot follow her. She stands and watches till the carriage has disappeared over the brow of the hill.

*

Davy and the curate are sitting on the box as the horses cautiously descend Main Street. The town is waking up in twilight. Mabel, the butcher's daughter, is sweeping the pavement in front of the shop. When she sees the carriage she rests the broom handle against her shoulder and waves at the travellers. On the other side the grocer is lugging a basket of red cabbages and calls out: 'Reverend, you'll be comin' back, won't you?'

Joseph—father of eleven children who always has some problem or other—runs breathlessly after the carriage and cries: 'Reverend, will you be gone long?'

Davy pulls up the horses, because Patrick Brontë tugs hard at his trouser leg. The questions of the congregation must not go unanswered! He stands up in the carriage and tells them that he is accompanying his daughters on their journey overseas to Brussels, the capital of Belgium, where they will go to school. Mabel's docile cow's eyes are wide open: Belgium, what sort of country is that? And are the young ladies not exposed to danger there? There is a growing throng of people wanting to wish their parson and his daughters a good journey. That makes Charlotte smile. Emily seems deaf to the good wishes shouted to them. She does not shake hands or smile; that is her reputation in Haworth. Charlotte can understand her sister: she wants nothing to do with the inhabitants of Haworth, since they are coarse in everything they do. Even the great landlords are scarcely more than gentlemen farmers and in their free time engage in hunting or in giving vulgar parties. The really rich people in Haworth, the owners of the mills down on the river, may think that they are gentlemen, but they drink too much and organise cockfights. In the midst of this desert her parents had transformed Haworth parsonage into an oasis for the mind: here with her sisters and Branwell she was able to nourish herself with beauty and wisdom. Her mother read fairy tales and legends and after her death their father ensured there was always something to read and study. Outside, life was hard and the wind fierce, and so they huddled together like young foxes. At the table in front of the fire they created their own ideal world in inspired verses. Her father had to venture into the outside world, but he liked his ministry.

He is a good speaker and every Sunday his church is packed full. It is amazing how easily he talks to people! Although she has to admit that, big man that he is, he looks down his long, delicate nose at his congregation, like a university professor at a group of as yet ignorant students. Her brother is the only one in the family who has a talent for mixing with the common people, but it is a pity he does so mostly in the tavern. She has not seen Branwell for six months, as he is working as a clerk on the railways. What does he have to do—sell tickets at the window? And to think they all had such grand dreams for him! He was given the best opportunities. In his earliest childhood he was taught at home by her father, including Latin, while she and her sisters were sent to boarding school. He could have studied at Cambridge or Oxford, but he did not want to. He was permitted to go to London to take the entrance examination for the Royal Academy of Art, but did not even turn up. He was given a studio in Bradford and all the necessary materials to set up as a portrait painter, but came back home surly and defeated. And then there is his literary talent—which he definitely has; according to their father he is the most gifted writer of all of them, but manages to make a mess of everything. He is her brother, her brilliant, but oh-so stupid brother. 'Charlotte, I've done it!' he cried when he had just read the letter with the news that he had been appointed as assistant clerk for the station at Sowerby Bridge. Lots of young men dream of joining the railways and the line from Leeds to Manchester is a pioneering project, but Charlotte could not understand his elation. In his enthusiasm he lifted her up, twirled her round and ruffled her hair. His whole thin body celebrated. The creases had gone from his trousers and he seemed slightly drunk, but his long face and conceited nature gave him the air of a young aristocrat. He is her brother and she misses him, but she will have to leave him behind in England too.

Below, at the edge of Haworth, William Weightman jumps off the box, and when he has recovered his balance, takes off his hat with an exaggeratedly deep bow.
   'Adieu!'
   Emily cannot help smiling for once.

*

Yorkshire, Yorkshire, you relentless land.
   Charlotte slides her hands into the sheep's wool muff in her lap and the road to Bradford continues through the hills. Bleak hills with low walls built of stones that shepherds and farmers have removed from the fields. Acid, boggy land where only flax and heather will grow. In September the moors are foaming purple, but in October the bushes run to wood. The ground is now brown: pale brown like bread and patchy brown like a bird of prey, rough brown like bark, brown—almost yellow—as the

droppings of a dog, or green as moss and sometimes black. She is leaving before her heart fades into something brown.

*

Mary Taylor is standing on the platform stroking the large, hairy dog belonging to another traveller, and when she sees Charlotte coming she jumps to her feet in delight. Rarely were two friends so different. The frail Charlotte, underdeveloped and with a waist that a big man could circle with his two hands, in a rather too loose grey-blue dress and smelling vaguely of violets. And the proud, well-filled figure of Mary, a head taller than Charlotte and with a blush on her cheeks, elegant in a slightly faded but still beautiful travelling dress and a bonnet with red ribbons. Charlotte and Mary met when they were fourteen at Roe Head, Miss Wooler's boarding school in the town of Mirfield. Charlotte greatly admires her friend, because she has an independent nature and goes her own way. With her sister Martha she is studying in Brussels at the château of Koekelberg and she is making plans to emigrate to New Zealand later. Her brother John, a young man with a frank expression and full black hair cut off level with his chin, shakes Patrick Brontë's hand. This is their first meeting and the parson surveys him suspiciously, as he does with every man who comes close to his daughters.

Nothing will be the same again. The moment has come and Charlotte is seizing her chance. Her life, like the locomotive, is starting to move. Today, at this moment, at Leeds station. She hasn't remained a governess, but has mapped out an alternative route for herself.

'Oh Mary, Mary,' she says, 'We're going to London.'

'And to Brussels,' says Mary, squeezing Charlotte's hand.

'Tell me about London,' says Charlotte.

'We'll be there this evening. Then you can see it all for yourself.'

'It will be dark,' replied Charlotte, pouting.

'It's never dark in London,' says Mary. 'There are more and more gaslights, and in dark streets you can hire a boy with a lamp to light your way.'

'Tell us about the packet boat,' says her father to John and the young man embarks enthusiastically on a detailed technical exposition about the ship, so dreary that Charlotte gets up and starts walking up and down the carriage.

She has to hold on to the seats, the train is jolting so, but she is too restless to sit. The stench of coal and oil nestles forever in her memory as the smell of adventure. She looks at the landscape and is carried along on the rhythm. The train thunders through Yorkshire, and soon they will reach the Midlands, on to London and further and further away from her past. Away from the sad memories! Her dead mother and the sour smell that hung in her room, her hands folded around a bouquet of wild flowers that Elizabeth and she had picked for her. The thin, feverish body of her oldest sister Maria and the way she, Charlotte, had slept in her dear arms. How wise and good Maria was—an angel. The hills, the eternal hills, and how hard her father's face can sometimes become. The train tears a path for itself and to the right and left of the tracks are ravines, which divide her from the fearful child she once was. She sees her standing there, the child Charlotte, on the verge beyond the cutting: a delicate girl with blue smudges under her eyes in a waving white nightdress. She blinks and the child is gone.

IV

They say London never sleeps, and though after midnight no respectable person ventures outside and the city is the realm of burglars, whores and privy-cleaners, who for a bottle of gin will come and empty your cesspit, at ten o'clock it is still bursting with life. Smart bourgeois stroll along the pavements; carriages depart and arrive. The performance at the opera house in Her Majesty's Theatre in the Haymarket is still in full swing, in the music halls acrobats are swinging on the trapeze, pretty women are singing racy songs and in the restaurants, tables are being prepared for supper.

On this rainy evening in February it is just the same. In Euston Square station the peace is disturbed by the arrival of a train from the north, with at least twenty or thirty carriages. The iron and copper locomotive, with its churning drive rods and the champing sound of the cylinder strokes, hisses and puffs and blows out a dark grey cloud of smoke. The doors are pushed open and the platform is a scrum of shouting and pushing. Men call for porters, a mother looks for her child that in its astonishment at this spectacle had let go of her hand; travellers stamp their feet on the ground to warm up after the cold journey, and coachmen for hire loudly extol their services. All this beneath a roof of glass and cast iron.

It is into this chaos that Patrick Brontë and his party land, and when John Taylor sees the parson looking around him in bewilderment, he immediately takes control. He negotiates with porters, who scarcely listen and speak a weird language of their own—they seem to gnaw their English. A porter with a nose like an enlarged strawberry and eyes glassy from gin, starts tugging at Emily's case, but she urges him to take care by squeezing his arm with her long, strong fingers.

'Whoa there, Missy!' cries the porter, and spits a gob of phlegm on the ground next to him.

At the exit to the station the porters start arguing with the coachman with whom John Taylor has just come to an arrangement. Only when Patrick Brontë gives each of the men a shilling are the cases put on the cab and are they able to leave. Emily discovers to her horror that her palms are black; she stroked the horses, but the animals are obviously covered in a sticky black powder.

'From the coal, missy,' says the coachman over his shoulder. 'They work in a coal mine a couple of days a week.'

When the cab frees itself from the commotion in front of the station and they are driving along a stately, wide avenue, our travellers regain their composure somewhat. Emily complains of cold hands, but Charlotte is spellbound by what she sees. When she spots a statue or a special building her impulse is to shout something in her enthusiasm, but her father is sitting with his eyes closed and Mary, with a hairpin between her lips is trying hastily to refashion her bun, which has come loose. At the corner of an alleyway the coachman cries 'Ho!' From here on, only pedestrians are allowed and so the cases are unloaded. John goes to the inn to find an errand boy. This is Paternoster Row, it dawns on Charlotte, and she goes arm in arm with Mary to the Chapter Coffee House. Over there must be the firm of Longman which published the poetry of the Lake Poets! She is excited, but the rest of the company is tired, as it is late, long past bedtime.

*

In the boarding house (next to the huge cathedral, whose existence she does not even suspect in the dark) the young woman from Yorkshire lies in bed wide awake. Last night she was still at home in her father's parsonage and now she is here in London, the metropolis. Her friend is fast asleep beside her, all plump warmth. In the bed against the wall lies her sister, most probably wide awake like her. The room is small and shabby, with—if she remembers correctly—yellowed flowered wallpaper and musty quilts. About half an hour ago she blew out the candle and she can still smell the smouldering of the wick. A familiar smell, but apart from that everything is strange. When they arrived she was so fearless and it is strange how her fears return in the depths of the night. How quiet it is here. Of course not as quiet as the hilltop where the parsonage stands and where at night you occasionally hear an owl hoot, but surprisingly quiet for a city with almost two million inhabitants. She hears the rattling of a carriage and the hoof beats of a horse on the cobbles, but it ebbs away. The other noises of the city form a distant, dull rushing sound like a watermill. Oddly enough it is this silence that alarms her. Perhaps it is what her father once said and what she refused to believe: that there is more loneliness in the big city than in the village.

This frail young woman has embarked on an adventure of which she cannot foresee the consequences. Tonight London, and in a few days Brussels, the capital of a bizarre foreign country. How will she cope there if the English of London already sounds different from the English of her own region? In Brussels they do not speak English, but French and Flemish, which seems to be a dialect of Dutch. The wild plans she has made, how thoughtlessly! A woman is nothing without a father or husband, without a protector by her side. And worse still: she is not plunging into this adventure alone, but is dragging her sister along with her. What she had not thought possible happens after all: she misses the parsonage. The house with its cold stone steps, but with the warm stove in the kitchen. She even misses the fields where no trees will grow, because there were sheep on them, and she misses Keeper loping ahead of her. The tears come and that helps; they roll down her cheeks and damply into her neck. She does her best not to make any noise and wipes them with the sleeve of her nightdress. What made her think that she is special, that she has been created to make a difference in the world? Her face is not oval and her intellect is limited, and she is no more than a lump of limestone by the brook or a bone for the dog: drab and futile! All that scribbling with her brother Branwell, their poems and stories about the imaginary world of Glasstown and Angria. How could she ever have told herself that there was a great writer in her? A woman is predestined for marriage, for the care of husband and children. She is reminded of Henry Nussey, the brother of her friend Ellen. He appears to her mind's eye as clearly as if he is entering the room. A young clergyman, only four years older than her: straight-limbed, with white hair, white eyelashes and a skin as bluish as buttermilk. Three years ago he proposed to her in a letter as cold and insistent as a bailiff's summons. She could not possibly believe that he loved her, and he did not pretend to. He spoke of respect and friendship. She refused his proposal, simply because he felt no passion for her. Fool that she was! Who was she to spurn such a chance? Henry was an honest, virtuous man. He offered her a house and asked her to manage the village school. A school of her own! What a fool she had been to expect more from life than it had to offer—more than a safe haven, a husband, children and a school. In addition Henry suggested that his sister, her dear friend, might live with them. But no, she of course had to dream about passion.

She wipes her wet nose with her sleeve, but just as she is about to turn on her side, the church bells start chiming. It takes her by surprise, this pealing, deep and full and divinely beautiful. Again and again and the reverberation travels through her body. She forgets to count the strokes, but it must be midnight. These of course are the chimes of St Paul's—yes of course, the inn is next to the cathedral! She listens with her whole being and as the last stroke dies away, she is at peace with herself and her presence here.

V

Saturday 12 February 1842, early morning, and Emily is standing with Charlotte, her father and the Taylors amid a throng of people waiting on the quay of the London Bridge Wharf. They are just about to board the packet boat. When they arrived on the quay a downy darkness, with here and there a misty patch of gaslight, had made this whole adventure seem like a dream, as if at any moment she could wake up in her familiar bed in the parsonage. A daylight as unpleasant as a mouthful of cold tea now dissolves the night and she begins to make out details. The irritating snuffling of someone who has a runny nose and has forgotten his handkerchief, turns out to come from a thick-set, uncouth woman with a red, swollen nose. She not only sniffs, but also spits on the ground. And there are the children Emily heard crying. Look at that poor London family over there: father, mother and five little ones, all equally pale, emaciated and blue-eyed. As long as they keep away from her. She wants to be left in peace during the crossing, as for four days now, she has been constantly surrounded by people. This is her first trip on a boat, but it holds no charms for her.

'How can you write about travelling if you've never done it yourself?' Charlotte asked yesterday evening over their meal in the Chapter Coffee House. Her cheeks had been red with excitement. But what does Emily care how the cabins in the hold of the boat look or how it feels when there's a storm at sea? Unlike Charlotte she is inspired by the Pennines with an unreasoning love. In her thoughts she can travel wherever she wants, and she will decide for herself what she wants to experience. It worries her that she will have no time in Brussels to write poetry about the magic island of Gondal and its inhabitants, that Anne and she created from nothing when they were young. She will think of little except Gondal and Keeper and the moors.

As they go aboard, Patrick Brontë takes the arm of his daughter Emily, as he suspects what is going on inside her. He knows her better than Charlotte does and she is his problem child, but now she is going somewhere where he cannot protect her. Emily finds it difficult to make friends with strangers. Still, he has to let go of her; it has to happen one day and after all, she is already twenty-three. If she does not become ill and die (for that is a sad possibility that he takes into account since the death of his wife and his two oldest daughters), she will return to him. She is like a dog that when it is left somewhere far away will walk for days to find its home. With Charlotte it is different; with her he runs a different risk. It is quite possible that she will find a husband there in Brussels and settle down.

*

The *Ondine* is a splendid white ship, not very big, but comfortable. Charlotte is delighted when she sees the restaurant: the dark varnished floor, the gleaming brass portholes, the carefully laid tables and the waiters in white aprons. John jokes that Charlotte and Emily can get home in a trice if they feel homesick, since the British mail boats make the crossing between London and Ostend four times a week. Emily's mouth twitches a little at that remark. Later that day she is seasick and sits greenish and miserable on a folding chair on the deck. They have not reserved cabins in the hold, as the boat will reach Ostend before midnight, but John Taylor suggests arranging a cabin for Emily after all—which she refuses, because she hates being molly-coddled. Neither does she want company, so the others go inside for tea. Mary pours the tea and Charlotte enjoys one last time her favourite meal of toast and marmalade. The boat is rolling considerably, but it does not trouble her much. She drinks her tea and is almost completely happy. It is lovely being on board the *Ondine*; for a whole day there is nothing useful for her to do. She submits to fate and at this moment could not even return to England if she should want to. She has to surrender control, and that makes her unexpectedly light-hearted. Life really cannot be that bad if it is in your nature to submit to what others decide for you—if you are married off to a rich old man or sent to a convent and meekly endure your fate. Her father is not an easy man and she had to defend her plan of going to Brussels tooth and nail, but now he is loosening the reins to some degree, it is precisely that freedom that worries her. But she is a traveller and has not yet reached her destination. Tonight they arrive in Ostend and remain there until Monday, as papa is loath to spend the Lord's Day in the stagecoach to Brussels.

Although she is beginning to enjoy the adventure, she does not find it too hard to postpone their arrival in Brussels a little. Once there Emily and she will take leave of their father, who after a week's tour through Belgium and Northern France will return to England. They will not see him for at least six months—and perhaps, whispers an inner voice, never again. Mary will leave for the château of Koekelberg and Emily and she will be left alone in the Pensionnat Heger.

*

How often do you have the opportunity to sail the North Sea? Don't for heaven's sake stay with Charlotte sipping that over-strong sweet tea in a restaurant where the greasy smells of eggs, toast and fried meat mingle with tobacco smoke. We're going to get a breath of fresh air on deck where Emily is standing at the railing. She is looking out over the waves, which are rather agitated. The deck is wet and if a kind lady had not grabbed her by the arm just now she would have slipped. But the salt air seems to be doing her good and does she not look a little less pale?

Emily is attractive in an unusual way, as she stands there breathing deeply. Her body stretched in one fluid line, no bosom or other curves, her features relaxed and open. There is something androgynous about her: if you were to cut off her brown hair level with her chin, she would be an engaging young hero.

However much she feels she is untrammelled in her thinking, she is still a child of her time. This is the age of Queen Victoria, and personal happiness is of secondary importance. Duty is the highest good. What you want for yourself is of no importance: the welfare of the family takes precedence. This conflicts with Emily's need for individuality and her innate disdain for the world, but on this occasion she gives in. The die is cast, and she will do what is expected of her. She will study in Brussels, for six months, or even a year if she has to, and then she will take her newly acquired knowledge home with her.

Suddenly her father's hands appear next to hers on the railing. Slim, strong fingers and a pattern of freckles and liver spots.

'You can still change your mind,' he says. 'You can simply come home with me.'

She shakes her head and they remain there in silence until John Taylor joins them and declares with a wink that he can already see the Belgian coast.

VI

That night the parson and his daughters not only reach the European mainland, hitherto unknown, but are immediately introduced to the stronghold of another social class. On the quay a number of young fishermen clamour to be allowed to carry their cases. John Taylor points to two of them and gives the address of their lodgings. The toughest of the two, a wiry chap in a dirty smock and trousers that are kept up by lengths of string as braces, sneaks a look at him from under the brim of his cap, with a sarcastic trait round his mouth. His mate brings the pushcart, repeats the name of the lodging with a scraping guttural sound and grins benevolently. Charlotte smells their clothes and unwashed bodies—a strong odour of fish, sweat and cabbage soup—but she finds them young and brave and not totally repulsive. She wonders whether the men will take their boats out to sea towards morning. And do they rush to the harbour every evening when a packet boat comes in the hope of earning a little extra? With her arm through Mary's and her shawl prickly warm round her head she follows the cart. The cobbles are slippery, as if sleet has fallen, but it is good after all those hours on a bobbing ship to have firm ground under one's feet again. The jetty is already behind them and here there are no more lamps alight. Even if those young fishermen were to lead them directly to hell, they would follow as meekly as lambs. The moonlight makes the sea glow like an antique silver platter; the fishermen clump along on their clogs and somewhere a horse kicks against its stable door.

They halt at a large, tall house—with a flag waving above the door. The night porter lets them in by the side doorway and having cast a glance at the new guests he leads them, mumbling all the while and lantern in hand, up a spiral staircase so narrow and windy that Charlotte feels as if she is making pirouettes—and right up to the attic floor. They are given two rooms under the eaves, scarcely bigger than broom cupboards, but they are too tired to protest.

*

Only the next morning does Patrick Brontë realise that he has made a serious blunder in the dark. While John is still getting washed and shaved, he goes in search of the breakfast area and descends the spiral staircase a few steps. One floor below he sees an Oriental carpet on the floor and at the end of an stylishly lit corridor a marble staircase leads down to a spacious hall. The Hotel des Bains is not a modest boarding house at all! He wonders what the servants' rooms upstairs will cost and regrets having listened to John Taylor who knew of 'clean and civilised lodgings' where there was always room. His impression that John is a frivolous young person is now confirmed. Just as long as he does not take it into his head to pay court to one of his daughters.

He is a thrifty man, Patrick Brontë, and on occasion downright mean. So much so that he fed his children as toddlers on nothing but potatoes, vegetables and milk. He was firmly convinced that such a sparse diet would toughen them up physically, but it also benefited the family budget. Yet he is definitely a man to derive pleasure from comforts—but only when someone else pays, which unfortunately seldom happens. It is not very probable that John will settle the bill and so he is hopelessly trapped.

Breakfast is served in a long room at the front of the hotel, with wide, tall windows looking out onto the beach. The sea has retreated, but there is still a strip of rolling water on the horizon. How flat this country is: no cliffs and no hills. The beach is bare and two boys in blue and white race across the wet sand with sticks and hoops.

Let me just order coffee, thinks Patrick Brontë, walking over to a table that seems suitable and nodding politely to the other guests—and some toast and butter perhaps. He sits down and looks outside. Later they can walk on the beach; that's completely free. This brainwave cheers him up and he tries to enjoy the exceptional view. There is nothing blue about the sky, but a blanket of cloud sailing past, grey and yet lively (like the seals they saw on the voyage across) suits the North Sea better than a jolly blue. Seen from below, the winter sky is exactly the same as the sea, not only in tint but also in form, with the clouds as waves.

At the moment a maid brings him coffee, his daughters and Mary Taylor come in. They linger for a moment between the doorway and the dresser with the fruit dish before they venture further. In the parson's eyes Emily, Charlotte and Mary are three attractive young ladies, soberly but tastefully dressed. What does it matter that Emily's lace-up boots are on the worn side? They have been polished, so there is nothing to be ashamed of.

Let us leave the old father with his conviction, but it is interesting to see what the other guests think about the three young women, two of whom are obviously awed by the grandeur of the hotel while the third exudes a proud indifference. To be quite clear: the guests of this establishment form a select company. They may not belong to the high aristocracy, but country squires have a few days' rest here with their families and the clientele includes a number of barons and even a viscount. Senior officers also feel at home here, but the majority of the guests belong to the well-to-do bourgeoisie. *Well-to-do*, because if you are not well-to-do you do not take a room here (unless you are as stupid as John Taylor). The hotel was previously always closed from November to April, but this winter it reopened just after the New Year celebrations. According to the wife of the manager it is fashionable nowadays to be seen at Ostend in the cold season too. It is questionable whether she is right, since it is not really busy in the breakfast room this morning. If you let your eyes wander, you will see a corpulent granny in a mourning dress who is trying to feed her troublesome grandson a soft-boiled egg; a delicate young man with the beginnings of a moustache who was sent to the coast by his mother to recover from persistent bronchitis (and who is thoroughly bored); two old maids who have pushed away their breakfast things and are sitting knitting; and a major in uniform with his wife and daughter. There is genteel conversation: even the young man exchanges a polite word with the grandmother when she inquires in a friendly fashion whether he has had a good night's rest. Of course they speak French—what else did you expect? It is true that rich and poor once spoke Flemish in these parts and Flemish was even the lingua franca in Brussels, but slightly less than fifty years ago the French occupied the territory. Anyone who wanted to be someone had to speak French, and Flemish was for the rabble. After the defeat of Napoleon at Waterloo (and the major present can tell brilliant tales about it) the country was included in the United Kingdom of the Netherlands, but scarcely fifteen years later Willem of Orange-Nassau was ousted by the French bourgeoisie. Since then Belgium has been an independent kingdom and it is *bon ton* to speak French, even if one is of Flemish descent—which one preferably keeps quiet about. But that is not simple if your name is Van den Broeck or Michielsen, as is the case with the old maids with their knitting things.

One old maid gives the other a tap with her knitting needle to draw her attention to our English young ladies. Curious as hotel guests usually are, the breakfasting ladies and gentlemen have noticed the three young women out of the corner of their eye, and immediately form an opinion of them. The girls do not belong in their circle; that judgement is unanimous. The plump young lady with a face in which there is not one hard line (the charming Mary Taylor) could be one of them if it were not so apparent that her light-blue travelling dress was cut for a lady with a slimmer figure and is too tight for her under the armpits. The other two young ladies—although the smaller one could pass as a child from a certain distance—are clearly not in the habit of moving in polite company and their clothing is really depressing. Even the chamber maids in this hotel are better dressed! The major's wife—a rather brash lady with bright blond hair, blushing cheeks and an impressive bosom—surveys them from their sad bonnets to their boots, which seem eminently suited to trudging along the beach.

When the young ladies sit down at Patrick Brontë's table, she leans over to her husband and says: 'Oh yes, what do you expect, they're the daughters of that English parson!' Not even in whispered tones, as she assumes they cannot speak French.

The remark leaves Emily cold, but Charlotte blushes deeply—bright red as far as her neck. She wishes she had put on her dress of cream-and-blue striped calico, but she had wanted to keep it clean for her first day in Brussels.

'Look at the view!' says Patrick Brontë enthusiastically and louder than is fitting in these surroundings for a man in a black suit that is shiny with wear. His Irish accent sounds harsher than usual. Just at that moment a coffee spoon falls on the floor from the major's table and Charlotte looks unwittingly into the eyes of his daughter and with a jolt realises that this young girl has everything she would so much have liked to have.

It would be entirely uninteresting to describe the major's daughter if Charlotte were never to see her again after this morning in Ostend, but she will crop up again regularly in this story. So it is worthwhile taking a closer look at her. She is seated perfectly for an appraisal: at the table by the window, since in the daylight you cannot hide your complexion and your true nature. Charlotte thinks she has never before seen such an attractive girl, but she also sees at a glance how spoilt and self-centred she is.

The girl feels wonderful: she is fifteen and perfectly happy with herself and her life. She smiles vaguely and slightly mockingly at Charlotte, but immediately forgets that strange Englishwoman again. She stirs sugar in her coffee and eats the triangles of buttered currant loaf that her mother puts on a plate for her. Her luxuriant light blond hair is in a loose plait—a hairstyle that on any other woman would have looked slovenly, but with her fresh appearance the effect is one of natural gracefulness. She eats eagerly, but with relish, like a child eats an ice cream, and whispers something into her mother's ear that she herself has to giggle about. Her face is more beautiful than attractive, and her lips are so full and pronounced that it is almost improper; and to make it worse they are not diffidently pale, but red and juicy as the flesh of a watermelon. Lips that suggest vice, Charlotte judges, but she would be prepared to give the girl her own modest attractions and her talents in exchange for her complexion, her head of hair and her lips.

*

During their walk along the beach the Brontës and the Taylors have not much more to say to each other. Their lives are on the point of changing and each one is wrapped up in his own thoughts. Patrick Brontë is thinking of how after Ostend and Brussels he will return to his parishioners in Yorkshire. He will carry his case into the parsonage, the big house that has always been full of life. He has known it all: the sound of children's feet on the stairs and in the hallways, the laughter and chatter, serious little faces over open books that they are actually too young for. The moody outbursts of Charlotte in dissatisfaction at her humdrum appearance (her pleasant face with its serious chestnut brown eyes and her slight, petite figure do not accord at all with what she wanted for herself in her ambition) and the volatility of Branwell. Anne's calm presence, the way she stares ahead of her with the tip of the pen against her bottom lip when she is looking for the right title for a poem. The clear sounds of the piano under Emily's dancing hands and that much coarser musical tone: Emily whistling on her fingers for Keeper like a street urchin. That has all gone; it will be a silent and lonely house. A house in which only an old man, his sister-in-law and the maid live. None of the children will be waiting for him, but he is expecting a visit from Branwell soon. Hopefully the lad can keep his job on the railway.

John Taylor walks along the beach next to the parson, with his top hat in his hand (since it has already twice been blown off his head by an eager wind) and is thinking of the reunion with his sister Martha that will take place in the château of Koekelberg on Tuesday morning. He feels responsible for the welfare of his sisters and does not want them to have to seek employment anywhere as a governess or companion. That means he will have to earn money, lots of money, and he intends to make his fortune somewhere in this world. The gentlemen walk at such a pace that the ladies fall behind a little. Mary, strong, sunny Mary, walks between Emily and Charlotte and looks forward in silence to the adventurous life that awaits her.

The reflections of Charlotte and Emily are familiar to you, dear reader, so you can walk on ahead with the gentlemen to the fishing village of Middelkerke. It does not matter if you do not have a scarf with you: it is a grey day, but not icy cold. Anyway, that grey sky is typically Belgian.

In a modest establishment the Brontës and their friends have a lunch of sole, chicken and *rijstevlaai*, a typical Flemish rice pie. Emily sits pricking at her sole with a certain distaste, since as an inhabitant of a village in the hills she is not used to fish. The waiter pours brown beer from a jug which makes them cheerful and sleepy. So dozy that father Brontë nods off to sleep after the dessert and only Emily dares to wake him.

They walk back and are about halfway when they see the riders. Proud horses and proud riders: a slightly older man in a military uniform who sits very upright in the saddle, accompanied by several younger men.

He is in conversation with two ladies who were obviously out walking and one of them wears a bonnet with an abundance of silk flowers—slightly ridiculous at the seaside.

'Horse-riding on the beach, that must be marvellous!' says John, spreading his arms out wide and rocking to and fro as if he is a seagull riding the wind.

When they come closer, Charlotte sees that the ladies must be a mother and daughter and oh, it's the girl from the breakfast room! She wears a simple straw hat with red ribbons and her hands are bare. The man remains in the saddle, but speaks very intently to her, and her sparkling eyes and lively blush reveal how delighted she is with this meeting. He must be her indulgent uncle, thinks Charlotte, who overloads her with presents. The girl lifts up her skirts slightly and twirls round playfully. She is wearing soft calf leather boots and Charlotte hates her.

VII

We find our company the following morning at about six-thirty on their way to Brussels, in what the hotel porter calls the '*diligence*'—a very elegant word for this rattling cart of a mail coach. Two greys and two bays pull the contraption along, and Charlotte Brontë sits between her father and a common-looking woman with a sizable posterior and opposite a tall, tart-looking lady, who begins the day by peeling a bowl of prawns, her taciturn husband, and a young monk. There are eleven passengers, which is three too many, and that does not include the coachman and his assistant on the box. After some hours a small, naughty boy, who cannot be controlled inside, is placed among them. And then there is all that luggage! Charlotte's feet are on a box with a rope round it and Mary is wobbling on a postbag full of letters, her head almost touching the roof. The big leather sheet that is stretched over the luggage rack is like a waistcoat over an enormous belly that may burst at any moment. Though before their departure the doors of the coach stood open to air it, it is anything but clean. Obviously the passengers on the previous trip were cracking walnuts, as there are shells among the velvet cushions. But the railway between Ostend and Brussels is not yet complete, so there is nothing for it but to take the stagecoach. The parson is quite happy about this, as train tickets would definitely have cost more.

The journey—over a hundred kilometres—will be an ordeal for most passengers, but not for Charlotte. The woman on her right falls asleep and in this state of complete abandon her buttocks seem to spread even more. Charlotte does not mind; she rests her hands on her knees and looks left and right out of the windows. Now and then she is shaken up and the plump wench threatens to squash her—but how strange the landscape is here! The polders look so neat, the fields fringed with lines of pollard willows. And there is so much water. Narrow canals, flowing slowly by the side of the road, and meadows that are green, so green, and here and there boggy. She is amazed by the large numbers of cows and the grunting pigs that jog along with the coach for a while, and roll roguishly in the mud. And then those big, solid cart-horses with their long blond manes! This is the first time in her life that happiness seems close at hand. But there's more to come, because she has great expectations—expectations which she knows are rash. What was it she wrote to her friend Ellen before she left? *Belgium is my Promised Land.*

The passengers find it difficult to travel on after lunch in Ghent: they are bored, tired and slightly nauseous, and looking forward to their arrival in Brussels, but that won't be until long after sunset. But never fear: you will not have to board that musty stagecoach again. The interior with its salty smell of prawns is familiar to you by now. Without that boneshaker weighing you down you have greater freedom of movement and you can travel swiftly through the panorama. Cast your eye over the land. This wintry landscape with bare fields and whitewashed farmhouses. A farm labourer lifting full churns of milk onto a cart; a few boys in school uniform chasing each other playfully; a man and wife in a chaise, he with an imposing moustache, she with a dainty black hat and a veil. Anyone who looks closely, also sees what can scarcely be hidden behind the picturesque windmills and the pollard willows: the bitter poverty of the tenant farmers and farmhands. Behind the couple's chaise two ghostly young children appear for a moment: girls who are dressed like old frumps and who already have something dead in their eyes. They are barefoot and have been working in a flax mill since the break of day. But come, let us talk about more pleasant things. After all, Charlotte has come to Belgium to escape the misery of Haworth. Seen from above, the fields and vegetable gardens in all their tints of brown and green are just like remnants of material made into a huge patchwork. The countryside is charming, slightly hilly and we have almost reached our goal: down below are the bell towers and abbeys of villages and hamlets with curious names like Kobbegem, Bekkerzeel and Zellik. And over there is Brussels! The town ramparts and their ponderous towers were demolished years before, and so they do not block the view of the churches. A wide boulevard with elegant flower beds circles the city, but we have no time now to wander around. Before it gets dark and the rain clouds yonder burst, I want to show you the Royal Palace. It was built in the days when Willem I of the Netherlands was still in power here, and consequently has a severe Dutch front which is not to the taste of the people of Brussels. The building was scarcely finished when the Belgian Revolution broke out and Willem had to flee to the north in all haste. The new monarch, Leopold I (the first king of the Belgians!), opted to spend the summers in the château of Laeken and the winters in the Palace in Brussels.

As it happens, the king is present this evening, and you can actually see him through the fourth window from the left, the one with the simple white curtains. He is standing at a high lectern with his fountain pen—a novelty in these days and the thing is still on approval—poised over a document and looking slightly fretful. In December he turned fifty-one and he looks it: there are deep wrinkles in his high forehead, his nose is sharp and gleams, and his hair—black as a gypsy's and with locks stuck to his temples in a curl—turns out on closer inspection to be a wig. Once Leopold was known to the ladies as an excitingly handsome prince and he has led a dazzling life. Shall I lift the veil a little? He is of Bavarian origin, born in the mighty fortress of Coburg in a wooded, mountainous region. At the age of eighteen he travelled to Paris with his oldest brother Ernest to meet Emperor Napoleon Bonaparte and his entourage. The Parisiennes received him delightedly in their salons and Empress Joséphine took him under her wing. Her daughter Hortense remarked after a tea party with the prince that she had never seen such a handsome man. He was tall in stature, with a proud bearing, a head of dark hair and good skin—and that at a time when most men were thick-set and pock-marked. On his way back to Bavaria he did the rounds of the European royal houses, where he was worshipped by the ladies. How young and powerful he had felt then! But in the eyes of the fathers of all those princesses Leopold was not a desirable match. As the younger brother of a duke he was not particularly wealthy. Oh, how much has changed since then!

However, you will have to wait for the numerous secrets of the Belgian monarch to be revealed to you, since the present demands our attention. The king is bouncing a little from one foot to the other, since he is tired and has cramp in his legs, which has been afflicting him increasingly recently. But he forces himself to deal with his correspondence standing. The documents are handed to him by Jules Van Praet, his affable and highly competent private secretary. In his black coat, carefully buttoned, and with his exaggeratedly tall stand-up collar, you might take Mr Van Praet to be a stiff, unpleasant man. But as he thanks and nods to the king, his piercing eyes show great benevolence and a desire to please. The pile of documents is signed and Van Praet withdraws with a slight bow. The king goes over to the window to look at the rain, and it is remarkable how proud his posture is; he seems to be standing at attention, straight as a die, with his arms at his sides and his heels together. He comes so close to the glass that you can almost count the pores on his nose. And indeed, that was very observant of you: he is the man whom Charlotte Brontë saw last weekend with that attractive girl on the beach! The question immediately rises: what was he doing there, and who is the young lady? Patience, patience, all in good time. The king looks at the wet Warande Park and wishes he were elsewhere. Once he was a man of promise, but now he is just a man who is bored. The same cannot be said of Jules van Praet, who has already appeared down below at the cast iron gate, the collar of his coat turned up against the rain and a leather writing case under his arm. He does not go into the park but takes the pavement on the left side of the square and at the marble statue of General Belliard descends the wide stone steps to the lower, older part of town that dates from the period of Spanish domination. Plumes of smoke snake out of the chimneys of the rue d'Isabelle, a narrow street with solid houses and sound paving slabs. Once at the foot of the steps Jules Van Praet has a view of the sober yet distinguished white house front, two storeys high, of Madame Claire Heger's boarding school. The lady in question happens to be standing in the doorway and he doffs his hat gallantly to the charming figure. '*Bonsoir*, monsieur Van Praet!' she greets him cheerfully. She came to check whether any secret rendezvous had been made here in the street between her pupils and the boys of the adjacent Athénée Royal. Let us slip inside quickly before she shuts the door! Jules Van Praet may be an indispensable man for the young state of Belgium and the meeting in Hotel Ravenstein to which he is hurrying is undoubtedly about matters of great import, but we must let him go on his way, for it is Claire Heger who will play such a leading role in the lives of Charlotte and Emily.

*

In the household of Claire Heger and her husband Constantin there is no time for arguments. Within the high, whitewashed walls Claire has created in her boarding school a small, well-functioning world. A charming globe that rotates on its axis to a rhythm determined by the ringing of the brass school bell: Lessons begin! To chapel for mass! Lunch! The end of the school day! The *Pensionnat Heger, maison d'éducation pour les jeunes Demoiselles*, as Claire advertises the school, is her creation, there is absolutely no doubt about that. Her aunt—a prosperous, dapper nun—previously ran a boarding school on these premises, but this in no way met the high requirements of the well-to-do families of Brussels. Claire Zoë Parent—this was Madame Heger's name before her marriage—took over her aunt's institute without, however, purchasing the property. With her impeccable manners, the effortlessness with which she moved in the circles of the rich and her shrewd teaching methods, Claire transformed the school into an establishment for which mothers from the bourgeoisie and lesser nobility queued up to enrol their daughters (charging a servant with this task is unthinkable, since no one would dare insult the headmistress). The boarding school was already a success when Constantin Heger, a young teacher, began courting Mademoiselle Parent. He had met her at a gathering hosted by Zoé de Gamond, a lady with innovative ideas about education. Claire seemed to welcome the advances of Constantin, which those around her could not understand. At twenty-five he was no less than five years younger than Claire and had not a penny to his name! During the Revolution of 1830 he had manned the barricades as a nationalist, which was of course heroic, but also pointed to a stormy and rebellious character. In that same memorable year he married, but his wife and child had died three years later in a cholera epidemic. It is true that Constantin Heger was a gifted speaker and taught French literature, mathematics, geography and Belgian history both at the veterinary school and at the Athénée Royal, but it was well known that teaching was badly paid. Malicious tongues were soon maintaining that he was after Claire's money. If he had been a handsome fellow into the bargain—yes, that might have explained her soft spot for the man, but that was not the case. In the company of the tall, slim and interestingly pale young men of the Athénée, the muscular, squat and easily blushing Heger seemed like a farmworker.

It is still a mystery to the teachers and young ladies of the boarding school why their headmistress has chosen Constantin Heger as a husband, but that is what has happened, and when we meet them they have been married for six years and have three delightful daughters: Marie, Louise and little Claire. The nursemaid has taken the children to bed and Constantin Heger is sitting reading in what the pupils call *le salon de madame*, a cosy room with a piano, a sofa, two comfortable armchairs and a chiffonnière. The stove is roaring and Constantin is smoking his pipe. He looks up when his wife comes in, at the ripe rounding of her belly—she is seven months pregnant. There appears to be harmony between them, as is almost always the case. They cannot argue at any rate, since otherwise there would be chaos and if there is anything that Claire hates it is chaos. Not that things never go wrong in the school. It can happen that a spoilt *demoiselle* fails to report to the gate before bedtime on Sunday evening after visiting her family or friends. Or that there is an outbreak of flu or diarrhoea in the house. The headmistress can cope with all that, as long as she manages to preserve harmony in her marriage. Constantin Heger is quite choleric by nature, but in the presence of his energetic wife he becomes as docile as a fat French poodle. He is resigned to the fact that she is the boss and holds the purse strings. She has made her husband a gift of several small houses further up the street, but her generosity extends no further than that; she is saving in order to be able to buy the school building in a few years' time. Since Constantin plans to remain married to Claire all his life, it does not matter to him what is hers and what is his, but there is one thing that annoys him. It has done so for years, though yesterday an incident made his irritation flare up again.

'I'll come and sit with you for a moment,' says Claire, 'but then I have to go back for evening prayers.'

'Good, good.' Constantin takes a good pull on his pipe, as if to pluck up courage. 'Let's discuss something then, *chérie*. I must tell you I find what happened yesterday particularly unpleasant. You're avoiding the subject, but we really must talk about it.'

'You mean what happened with Mademoiselle Marie?' Despite her pregnant belly Claire sits with her knees slightly aslant and her legs crossed at the ankles.

Constantin nods earnestly and massages the beginnings of a double chin with thumb and forefinger. 'Yesterday Marie was standing waiting with Blanche and Sophie in the big drawing room for the wages to be paid out. You were otherwise engaged and would come later than usual, so this new teacher expected me to arrange it. But the strong box was not there and you always lock the drawer with the register in it.'

'That's right,' says Claire breezily.

'None of that is too bad, but after all these years you still expect me to stand in line with the ladies to receive my wages. So that they can see that I am not paid one franc more than the others. And you make me sign the register.'

'Yes,' says Claire. 'It's always been like that, hasn't it, Constantin? Why are you raising the issue now?'

'I don't want to do it anymore,' he says, his voice trembling with emotion. 'It's humiliating.'

She gets up and rearranges her black, stiff silk frock. 'I'm very sorry you see it like that, *mon amour*, but don't forget that I am the headmistress.'

He goes red, or rather: he was already red and now takes on an alarming plum shade. He moves forward in his chair and holds up his right hand with the pipe in it as if about to make an important pronouncement, but does not do so. This man who is known for his irascible temperament, this dark creature with his lively eyes and over-wide side-whiskers, half rises, but sinks back wordlessly as his wife leaves the room with great dignity.

By the time the mail coach from Ostend clatters into Brussels, a storm has begun and when passengers get off at the stop by the chapel of Sainte-Marie-Madeleine, the rain is lashing their faces. At that moment the Hegers are asleep in their large, old-fashioned bed. Both are naked. Claire is on her side, her cheek resting on her palm and Constantin lies against her, with his hairy hand on her belly under the blanket.

VIII

It is questionable whether Charlotte would have embarked on the whole adventure if she had known what awaited her. She still has no idea how different this city is from her village in Yorkshire, how different her life will be here and how it will be required of her (of her, a daughter of the Church of England!) to adapt to Catholic manners and habits. Yet it is here, in this mysterious city so far from home, that she will first become a real woman.

Charlotte wakes in a downy bed in the comfortable Hôtel de Hollande, roused by the jubilant, resonant peal of bells from the church of Saint-Michel and Sainte-Gudule. Emily is already up and brushing her light-brown hair, in which penetrating sunbeams create soft-red strands. Her face is grey and her large round eyes exude melancholy. Charlotte watches in silence as she puts on her woollen stockings and steps into her petticoats. One can only hope that that stubborn sister of hers will not fall ill with melancholy in the Pensionnat Heger, as she did seven years ago in Roe Head. She herself had gone to school there and when she returned as a teacher Emily had come with her as a pupil. Oh, there is that old feeling of guilt again! If only she had paid Emily more attention then. She was busy teaching all the time and as a teacher she did not sleep in the dormitory. Emily did not complain, extremely self-contained as she is, but immediately started pining away. She refused to eat and virtually stopped talking. One rainy afternoon she had found her in a deep windowsill with a view out over the hills. The moor, so dry in the summer, had come to life and formed waves in a vibrant, vital purple. She had realised that Emily was not made to live with twenty boisterous girls and recite the conjugations of French verbs in a cold classroom. She had to be able to wander through nature in complete freedom and give her imagination free rein. Her sister had become horribly thin—so thin that it raised the spectre of the two dead sisters. Emily had to go home and in the farm waggon that was sent from Haworth to collect her, sat their younger sister Anne, aged sixteen. She would take Emily's place and graduate with good marks. Emily, Emily! Charlotte pins up her braids and sees that her sister has gone over to the window. A huge carriage thunders past and a women is hanging out of a window on the other side of the street airing a blanket. There is no moorland in the big city and the horizon is made up of roofs and smoking chimneys. I'll look after you, Emily. Nothing bad will happen to you here in Brussels.

Mary comes in and has such a fresh blush on her cheeks that Charlotte passes her fingertips over her own. She looks fleetingly in the mirror and the sight of herself disappoints her: she had thought that in Brussels she would be someone else—that not only would the décor change, but she too.

'Come to breakfast quickly,' says Mary. 'You're going to the school at nine-thirty, so I can show you something wonderful first.'

*

Emily leaves the other two women behind, so briskly does she walk. Her coat hangs open and a strand of hair that has come loose tickles her neck. She is wearing flat brown boots with brown laces. She has thin but straight legs and shapely knees, she knows, and big feet, which her father teases her about.

To the careful observer her appearance has something aristocratic, despite the indifference she displays towards her appearance. She could be a distinguished, eccentric English lady going into the garden to cut a few green branches from her shrubs. Her ears are small, perfectly shaped, and in her haste her bonnet falls onto her back, but the ribbon is still firmly round her neck.

She does not care two hoots about that Grand-Place; she does not care two hoots about the whole of Brussels, but the morning air is freezing blue and tingling. She wishes she were alone. The passers-by do not matter—they do not appeal to her anyway—but her sister and Mary are following her. She walks down the street where their hotel is and hears Mary cry that they must turn into the rue de la Madeleine. A street full of shops. At Vandoren's you can buy *moutarde*, which to judge by the stone jars must be mustard, at Dooms' shoes and at Meulemans' spectacles and opera glasses. Names that do not seem very French. She hears a language that must be Flemish, and there is the Grand-Place.

My God. She stops, but there are so many people streaming about the square that you are automatically pushed into the middle. She looks around, twirls round a few paces: this square is a jewel box from a long-vanished age. What riches, what splendour! Gables decorated with gold leaf, a grey stone swan that proudly spreads its wings above a doorway, a bas-relief of Romulus and Remus being fed by the she-wolf, and at the top of a gable a phoenix arising from its ashes. And more, more: festoons of blossoms and fruits and a dapper gold fox. She hears Mary talking, but does not listen; she wants to quench her thirst for beauty. There is a street seller with a basket on her arm containing pieces of soap in the shape of sea horses. The girl comes closer with a sea horse in her hand and wants to let her smell.

Her sister grabs her by the arm.

'Emily,' says Charlotte, 'Calm down. Stop. Come to your senses.'

She shakes off the annoying hand and escapes. She stares at the stone statue of an old king of Spain.

'We must go,' says Charlotte, and Emily just wishes she had the courage to put an end to her existence as a hostage and could return home with her father.

BRUSSELS

IX

Madame Henriette Claret, *née* Neetesonne, hurries to the house of her neighbour a little distance away in the Etterbeek Fields. She takes short, rapid breaths, with her mouth slightly open, like a lapdog panting enthusiastically when his mistress gets out the walking gear. She has difficulty controlling her impatience, like yesterday during the long ride from Ostend to Elsene. In their landau she had been dying to speak to her daughter Arcadie, but Charles would not fall asleep as he usually does. He kept talking politics. And no, he really must not know anything yet—since she has no idea how he will react.

Now Henriette is on her way to her neighbour, Babette Claeskens, and hopes she will be able to spend at least an hour telling her story and enjoying the expression of utter surprise and admiration on her face.

Henriette (short and quite plump, but with a pronounced waist thanks to an ingenious whalebone corset) has just left the grounds and tall oaks of the old country house Campagne Claret. She walks down the country road; though 'waddles' might be a better word to describe her gait, since her shoes are too high-heeled for this bumpy lane and she is not a good walker. Henriette is a woman who prefers to stroll along a level path through a flower garden, skip around indoors or lie full length on a chaise longue with a plate of cake on her belly.

The country road leads to the village and here and there are a number of elegant, spacious houses under construction. Although the municipality is located just outside the Porte de Namur and the centre of Brussels, it is still very rural. In recent years it has been *en vogue* among the bourgeoisie to reside in

Elsene, mainly because the violin virtuoso Charles de Bériot has a country house here. Six years ago the famous opera diva Maria Malibran, his late wife, actually spent a whole summer in their pavilion. But alas, a few months after her summer in Elsene the Parisienne was killed in an accident. She travelled a lot and one day an escaped pig ran under the hooves of the pair of horses pulling her coach. As a result of the jolt, the pregnant Maria was hurled from the coach. A tragic death, but nonetheless a splendid story, which was told with relish to visitors in the salons of Elsene.

Henriette is not from this area either. She is a typical product of Ghent, and although she was brought up in French, she can speak a comic Flemish dialect. Henriette speaks French with Charles and the children, but outside the tall beech hedges of the Campagne Claret she is in the habit of exchanging the odd word of Flemish with a market stallholder, a driver or a seamstress. She strikes a benign tone to make it clear that she as a distinguished lady is prepared to converse with ordinary working people.

A farmer comes past with his workhorse on a coarse length of rope and greets her by tapping the peak of his cap, but Henriette does not return the greeting—either in French or in Flemish. She is deep in thought and suddenly feels a tightening in her chest. *Mon Dieu, mon Dieu!* Here comes another hot flush. She stands still for a moment, opens her small mouth as wide as possible and waves her fleshy hands about. A drop of sweat runs between her breasts and when the farmer is out of sight she unbuttons her cape so that the morning breeze can cool her bosom. There is the fence of the Claeskens residence: the front garden with the impeccably pruned rose bushes and the low house with the thatched roof. Certainly very neat and utterly charming, but not comparable with the spacious country house-cum-estate of the Claret family. Babette Claeskens is consequently not exactly a woman with whom Henriette would want to be seen arm in arm. She is quite simply not chic enough to pass as a good friend. When all is said and done Henriette is the wife of a major (treasurer of the Fund for Widows and Orphans of the Belgian Army, no less) and Charles might even become a lieutenant-colonel. Oh, just imagine, what a celebration! And in those circumstances you just cannot be friends with the wife of the postmaster, can you? Henriette does not hide the fact that she socialises with her neighbour, but dismisses it purely as artistic interest in Babette's work. Since her neighbour is an artist; she embroiders—not colourful flowers or songbirds, but scenes and places that are not normally embroidered. Recently she has had a weakness for cemeteries. Her most recent work shows the grave of La Malibran in Laeken cemetery, with a wreath of lilies and her husband standing mourning in shades of grey. A little dated, since Charles de Bériot has recently remarried and definitely does not look so sad any longer.

'Magnificent!' Henriette had exclaimed. 'And so atmospheric.'

But to her husband she declared that Babette had a lugubrious streak and that she herself would never ever hang such a piece of embroidery on her wall, not even in the cloakroom. Oddly enough, Babette is successful with her embroidery and a lot of Elsene ladies commission her to immortalise the grave of their departed husband, child, father or mother. Henriette actually brings her customers, but she herself values other qualities in her neighbour, since Babette is an excellent listener and loves meaty gossip.

Henriette pulls the bell and waits. She knows that it may be a little while before her neighbour opens the door, since if she is absorbed in creative work, she cannot immediately tear herself away from it.

'Well, there you are, Henriette.'

Babette steps over the threshold to push a strand of ivy back into the latticework. She has elegant hands, but Henriette sees with a certain satisfaction that Babette's skin is already starting to exhibit those ghastly liver spots. Oh, *Seigneur*, if she ever has that problem she will wear long gloves morning, noon and night!

*

They are sitting in what Babette calls the 'orangerie': a semi-circular bay with tall windows. Babette next to a palm, and behind her—in cross-stitch on the wall—a scene of cows being led to the gate of the slaughterhouse. Henriette has Babette's obtrusive greyhound at her feet. She drinks a hasty mouthful of her coffee and puts the cup on the wicker side table.

'He came,' she says emphatically.

'Nooo,' says Babette.

'He really did.' Henriette places a fat, ringed hand on her heart to add solemnity to her words and leans forward. 'He was in Ostend, on the beach; he kept his word.'

'Is he handsome?'

'A god, Babette, really, without exaggerating. Not all that young anymore, but as I say to Arcadie: "He's a real man, and those young chaps of your own age cannot compete."'

'Does he not wear a wig?' After each sentence Babette's mouth closes into a fine line, and yet her face has an amused expression: this is conveyed by her violet eyes.

'No,' Henriette lies. 'But do you understand what I'm saying,

Babette? He travelled all the way to the coast for my daughter. The king, in love with my Arcadie!' Now she is really getting too hot, with the winter sun on all that glass and then the emotions. She undoes the top three buttons of her blouse.

'If you'll permit me, *ma chère*.'

'We're all girls together,' says Babette reassuringly. 'Would you like a glass of water?'

'A drop of brandy would calm me, I think. You have no idea, these are such exciting days.'

'But Arcadie,' says Babette, 'she's still so young. The old lecher! And he's married, which you mustn't overlook. What…'

Before she can finish her sentence, Henriette sits up and snaps: 'Old lecher? He is the king after all. The king! And he has a soft spot for my daughter. What mother would not welcome that? Anyway, Arcadie will be sixteen in May.'

'I don't know, Henriette. When I think of my own Mélanie.'

Your daughter is as skinny as your greyhound, thinks Henriette. She does not like the fact that her neighbour is starting to raise objections. She knows she can expect such hypocritically prim reactions from her posh friends; she must consider how to break the news to them. But her neighbour, her neighbour with her loud cut-glass earrings and her tiny little house! She had at least expected her to gawp in awe.

Babette wants to stay on good terms with Henriette, because Henriette is important for her embroidery business. And so she offers the bowl of pralines, goes over to the drinks cabinet to pour a glass of brandy and says soothingly: 'I simply meant, dear friend, that not even the king of Belgium is good enough for Arcadie. She's such a pearl.'

Henriette's face brightens and she claps her hands with delight.

'Oh, Babette, I'm so excited! I can scarcely wait to know what's going to happen. But she's still young, it's true and it would be best if we kept quiet about this until she is old enough to appear in public as his official mistress.' She pronounces these last words almost trembling with ecstasy. Then she sinks back in her armchair and pops the praline in her mouth.

'He's had lots of mistresses, Henriette.'

'Not one of them is as special as my daughter,' says Henriette with chocolate on her front teeth. 'After her he will never yearn for another woman. Arcadie will be the only one.'

'That German actress must have thought the same.' Babette gives her neighbour a stiff shot of brandy. 'What was her name? Karoline Bauer, poor girl! He was even secretly married to her and still he dumped her.'

'Actress!' Henriette wrinkles her nose, which with its round tip resembles the end of a Viennese sausage. 'Slut you mean. She wasn't right for Leopold at all.'

'Leopold? Oh. Are you on first-name terms already?' Babette blurts out, and it sounds so sarcastic that she could kick herself.

Henriette squeezes her eyes into narrow chinks and drinks some brandy.

'Let's talk about something else.' She points to a piece of embroidery peeping out of the wicker basket under the palm. 'What are you working on—Mademoiselle Jacqueline's dead poodle in petit point?'

*

A little before midday Henriette is back in the Campagne Claret. Her oldest sons are at boarding school in Lille and Marcel and Cédric are staying with her mother in Ghent, but her three girls are at home. At this moment they are having a piano lesson in the large drawing room. She peeps round the corner of the door, and oh, how proud she is! Her daughter Henriette, aged nine, is sitting at the grand piano—the stool up as high as it will go—and playing a simplified version of *Für Elise*, far from faultlessly but with a touching childish seriousness. Then Henriette sees how the eye of the piano teacher (an impecunious, but talented and conceited young man) is caught for a moment by her daughter's paunch. Has he noticed the rolls of fat under the ingeniously fanned-out pleated skirt? Yes, it's true: the poor child shows a tendency to run to fat. Not charmingly plump like herself, but definitely puffy. It is time she was put on a diet. A shame she cannot wear a corset yet, but according to the doctor that is unhealthy before the age of fifteen. However much her mother's heart goes out to Henriette, she sees the child's broad jaw, almost broader than her forehead, and her sturdy calves. No, she is forced to conclude, her Henriette is not an attractive girl—for that she is too like her father. Yet Charles is not an ugly man; he is robust, that's true, and when he slumps into his leather armchair after dinner he is like a cake bulging out of its tin, but he has a pleasant face and mischievous eyes of the clearest blue. Little Henriette has exactly the same eyes, but while boys are admired for their strong calves, girls are jeered at. Nevertheless, in a few years' time she will have to find a husband for this daughter. For the man, Henriette Claret is convinced, represents the future of the woman; in him resides her only chance of safety and prosperity.

Pauline, just seven, is sitting at the table copying a sheet of music, biting her lower lip as she does so. She is pretty as a picture, with a slight curl in her blond hair, but Henriette detects in her too something of her husband's broad jaw. Fortunately there is Arcadie! Arcadie, her pride, her glory, even more important to her than her sons. She stands at a table covered in art books and looks at prints of paintings. Her lesson is finished, but her mother insists that she makes sure her sisters do their exercises as they have been told. Henriette is pleasantly surprised that Arcadie has not escaped to the stables or to see Chloé who lives nearby. But then she sees how the eyes of the young piano teacher and her daughter meet. Does Arcadie feel attracted to this young chap? She herself finds him insufferable and has only employed him because his references are so good. But she now realises that with his single blond lock on his forehead (which he regularly sweeps aside with a jerk of his head) and the boldness of his behaviour, he might constitute a pleasant diversion in Arcadie's eyes. Just imagine Arcadie allowing herself to be seduced by such a nincompoop, poor as a church mouse!

'Monsieur Jacques!' It sounds cheerful and cordial, and she trips into the drawing room with hands fluttering, but she has already decided to dispense with the dangerous young man very soon. *Für Elise* grinds to a halt and the piano teacher retreats one pace.

'I'm terribly sorry to interrupt your lesson,' says Henriette and with her outstretched fingers she gives the piano a playful tap.

Her mischievous smile makes the young teacher stiffen for a moment like a mouse looking into the yellow eyes of a languorous but cruel cat. Just for a moment, after which monsieur Jacques pulls himself together. He casts a sideways glance at Arcadie, gives madame a stiff nod and hurriedly gathers his things together.

That afternoon Madame Claret goes shopping in Brussels with her daughter, since it is high time Arcadie's wardrobe was adapted to her new status as the king's favourite. If she is to retain his attention, she will have to be at her most delightful: blushing, blond and coquettish in elegant gowns of supple worsted cloth and airy muslin, swirling petticoats made of organdie and bonnets with long satin ribbons. Charles will grumble when he gets the bill, but she can use the excuse that it is about time that they started looking for a husband for Arcadie. 'And admit it, Charles: a girl in cottons like that and home-knitted woollens won't be able to attract much more than the son of a country doctor.' No, their daughter needs a pearl necklace with at least three rows of pearls and gloves in various shades. Someone who wants to catch a chicken, strews maize, but someone who wants to lure a pheasant must mix aniseed with the grain.

'*Mon trésor*,' Charles will bluster, 'What are you talking about? Arcadie is still far too young to get married.' But she will pinch his cheek and rub noses with him, and then he will usually become as docile as a fairground horse.

Mother and daughter take the coupé to town. Jos, the coachman, has washed and polished the carriage; the brass gleams and it is splendid weather, pure, the sky almost blue, and freezing cold—just like winter in Switzerland. Arcadie wears her navy blue school coat and although adorable, she does look very young. They are going to Brussels, mother and daughter, to achieve a metamorphosis. Henriette has her nicest hat on and looks out through the window. She is sorry that the streets of Elsene are deserted, as she would have liked to meet a couple of acquaintances. She feels wonderful; her glory days have arrived! Actually it is time for a new coupé and the family carriage should also be replaced. But Charles does not think their budget will run to this and it will be better if she is reasonable for now. Arcadie's wardrobe comes first and she needs a new gown herself. As mother of the *king*'s mistress—the king, oh, oh *mon Dieu*, how oppressive it is in the coupé! But it's true, isn't it? As the mother of the king's mistress you must be presentable. Leopold must be able to be proud of them. She can see him say to his entourage with eyes shining: 'Look, there come mademoiselle Arcadie and Madame Claret!' And she sees him whisper in the ear of a good friend that he has seldom met such beautiful women.

*

Henriette takes her daughter to the dressmaker who it seems makes the wardrobe for the very chic dowager d'Ydeweel. The atelier is on the first floor of an exquisite mansion in the rue de la Montagne and the dressmaker is nothing like the fat, rural seamstress from whom Henriette usually orders their dresses. She is tall and as thin as a poplar; no longer a young woman, but so smartly turned out that her visitors are impressed. Henriette introduces herself and her daughter and talks of her friendship with the dowager, at which point she starts to stammer and rosy red apples appear on her cheeks. In reality she has seen madame d'Ydeweel once, fleetingly, namely at a meeting of Les Dames de Charité d'Ixelles. But the dressmaker seems to be scarcely listening. She observes Arcadie closely and then rolls sunflower yellow cloth out over the table.

'*Et voilà*,' she says. 'This will look beautiful on your daughter.' Her voice is hoarse and carries a certain authority.

Yellow is an unusual shade for a dress, and Henriette would never have thought of it herself.

'The Parisiennes like to wear yellow in the summer, madame,' says the dressmaker, holding an end of the fabric against Arcadie's cheek. It looks very colourful, but Henriette realises that next to the figure of the dressmaker her daughter suddenly appears rather too luscious. That bosom, that derrière, there is so *much* of them. She reminds one of a peony with an abundance of silky leaves. Charming, but don't peonies belong in a farmyard?

They decide on a sunny yellow dress, and Arcadie is handed a crêpe de Chine shawl that would go nicely with it.

'Does the young lady need new petticoats?' The dressmaker drapes a remnant of pale cotton around Arcadie's waist.

'Fashion prescribes dresses that almost trail on the ground and the petticoats really must not be too short. My petticoats are made of first-class material and of course I decorate the top layers with valenciennes.'

The maid brings coffee and pours three cups. What's the world coming to, thinks Henriette rather sourly, when even dressmakers have their own maid? She sits down and accepts a cup. The taking of Arcadie's measurements may take quite some time, since anyone claiming to be as good as the best of the Paris *couturières*, of course works very accurately.

Jos the coachman is allowed an afternoon nap, since after the visit to the atelier madame Claret and her daughter walk to the rue de la Madeleine. They wander in and out of shops and at Swan's Arcadie is given a cashmere shawl and an embroidered purse and at Soeurs Mylas a lace blouse. The assistants display their finest wares for them and the girl is in seventh heaven. But what a childish taste she still has! She likes meringue colours and lots of ribbons. Henriette would like to see her a little more grown-up: she must not emphasise that naïve side to her daughter. Oh, if only the child were two years older; if only she had reached the landmark of eighteen! Although it is of course precisely her youth, her virginally white skin and her innocent blue eyes that please Leopold so much. In fact, he is not the only one who is charmed by her. In the street Henriette sees lots of gentlemen looking with scarcely concealed interest at her daughter. Interest—is that the word? Or is it desire? At Delvaux's the shopkeeper has a hungry look in his eyes when he helps Arcadie choose a suitcase. And the errand boy at Mesdemoiselles Clara stares at her open-mouthed when she disappears with an assistant to try on a corset.

'Your daughter is a beauty,' says the saleslady whom Henriette pays for the corset. This compliment from a woman reassures her. Arcadie is all strawberries and cream, and while that may not look so distinguished, it is seductive. No wonder that Leopold prefers her blushing girlishness to his sickly wife; after all, Queen Louise-Marie will be thirty at the beginning of April. If she herself were a powerful queen—Cleopatra—she would definitely take a youthful lover. A slave with fiery eyes and a body black as ebony. What a magnificent vision! Thirstily she drinks the glass of lemonade the errand boy has brought her. Her husband Charles is a fine chap, but that heavy paunch of his… His best years are behind him, although it has to be said that he is still virile—something she cannot complain about, since it seems that healthy urges go hand in hand with healthy ambitions.

Ah, there's Jos! The coach is outside the door of Mesdemoiselles Clara and Jos takes all the packages and boxes from them. Henriette and Arcadie cross the street and enter a patisserie where one can also eat something. At the table, Arcadie takes off her muff and sighs. Her cheeks are deep pink with excitement, because so many things are happening in her life! It is certainly exciting, but on the other hand she feels like just going riding with Chloé. Of course it's nice to be spoilt by her mother, but all those suggestions about a romance with King

Leopold! And no, she cannot keep quiet any longer.

'I'll never be able to marry him, *maman*.'

Henriette looks up in surprise. 'No darling,' she says, placing a gloved hand round her daughter's fingers. 'But it's better to be the king's mistress than the wife of an impoverished nobleman. You won't be short of anything, you know; you'll be a lady and be received in the best salons, you'll…'—she looks for something with which she can tempt her daughter—'… live in a splendid house, and you can invite all your friends, as he won't be there that often.'

'Yes,' says Arcadie and her smile reveals a row of perfect white top teeth. 'That sounds fun.'

The waitress brings a trolley piled with exquisite cakes and mademoiselle Claret is allowed to choose the petits fours.

'What a nice coffee house,' says Henriette. 'And what a splendid city we live in.'

Arcadie runs a wet fingertip over her plate to pick up the last crumb of the sweet cake—bad-mannered behaviour that is censured with a peevish growl by her mother. She does not care, since her disquiet has vanished. That thing with the king won't happen that fast and *maman* has just told her that she does not have to go back to the boarding school in Liège, but from now on will be taught at home. She will learn German and be given time to devote to her piano playing, since nothing is so charming, says *maman*, as a young lady able to coax sweet sounds from an instrument. It is wonderful to be relieved of the boarding school! Brussels is *her* city and she feels like a squirrel in a pinewood here. She would like to run across the squares and bridges. All that energy in her young body! She wants to walk with her handsome young piano teacher through the park in front of the Palace. Perhaps he would touch her hand. ('Why don't you call me Jacques?' he whispered in her ear that morning.) She would make eyes at him from under the brim of her new bonnet, the one with the blue irises.

*

Strange that for mademoiselle Claret, Brussels is a true home, and that the very name evokes a warm feeling, while for the younger of two English sisters who have just arrived it is a place of exile. Strange how one person is familiar with a city; how he has a dog there that wags its tail, and a whistling kettle on the stove and a lump of sugar in his coffee. The streets and tolling bells are familiar to him, a hand is raised in greeting and in the stable is a horse he knows will not rear up. But in the same city a traveller stretches out exhausted on his bed in a rented room and thinks of home: a home that is a long journey by train, ship or coach from this city. How homesickness gnaws at one in this strange place, where the bread smells different and prayers have a different sound.

Emily Brontë unpacks her trunk in the dormitory of the Pensionnat Heger in the rue d'Isabelle, just a few hundred metres from the patisserie in the rue de la Madeleine. She is alone with her sister in the dormitory, and it is just as well that Charlotte is wisely silent, since otherwise Emily would definitely snap at her. The sleeping area is long and narrow, but as a concession to Charlotte and her, a private corner has been created at the back by the wash room with the aid of two screens. There are eighteen other beds, but there are only twelve other boarders. The girls are at present downstairs in the refectory eating their evening meal.

Up here it is cold. There is a wood-fired stove in the middle of the room, but according to Gertrude, the concierge, it is lit only for an hour after prayers. At ten o'clock everyone is supposed to be in bed. Emily hangs her dresses in the wardrobe. She feels like kicking the cupboard or knocking over the chair next to her bed, but she has learned to control her wild impulses. That does not mean that her frustrations have been overcome, and she shrouds herself in disgruntled silence. And then to think that Charlotte and she are expected at table shortly with madame Heger and her family!

That morning she said goodbye to her father. In her usual way: her palm on the lapel of his coat, a fleeting kiss on the cheek and that was it. Charlotte embraced him, but she always shows off. After his departure madame Heger said something in rapid French: they must have been words of comfort, but she did not understand a thing. Madame's French sounds so different from what Charlotte tried to teach her in the parsonage. Actually it would be better if they said as little as possible until they have a better pronunciation, as their accents are abominable.

'You can put your stockings on my side,' says Charlotte cautiously. 'There's a basket here.'

Emily does not answer and abruptly pushes her woollen and linen stockings in to a corner behind her scarves and knitted waistcoats.

*

The stove is burning in the Hegers' dining room. A large, good-natured dog with a golden coat lies on the rug in front of the hearth and Emily kneels down beside him. She tickles him behind the ears and for the first time that day the features of her narrow face relax. On top of the dog, like a saddle, lies a little girl who hides her face in his coat, so that only her dark bunch of curls is visible. When the dog, wagging his tail, tries to rise, the child stands up. She is still only a toddler, but has the eyes of a street urchin about to get up to mischief. A younger daughter stands hugging her doll and sucking her thumb.

'Tell our English guests your names,' says madame.

The smallest girl takes her thumb halfway out of her mouth and says: 'Louise', but the other girl just looks at them stubbornly. Louise nods in the direction of her sister and says, still sucking her thumb: 'That's Marie.'

The girls are wearing powder blue tunics, with a ribbon at the neck, over white breeches—simply cut, but made of light, supple wool.

More expensive wool than I have ever worn, thinks Charlotte.

The dining room is as richly decorated as the salon in which madame received them this morning. The wooden floor is shining with the many layers of plain varnish, the heavy curtains are mint-green and on the walls hang paintings of Biblical scenes in gilt frames. On the hearth are two statues, and because Charlotte does not know how to conceal her embarrassment, she examines them with feigned attention. One represents a woman with red shoes and a puppy jumping up at her, the other one shows charming angels fighting with a billy goat.

'Old Parisian porcelain,' says madame, and suddenly she is very close by. Her smile hovers between benevolence and playfulness. 'We'll be sitting down to eat very shortly. I expect you're ravenous.'

She looks from Charlotte towards her sister, but she is still squatting by the dog.

'What's his name?' asks Emily scarcely audibly.

'Ulysse,' replies madame indifferently. The door opens wide and a young maid brings in a carafe of water. The room immediately fills with the delightful smells from the kitchen. Fresh butter melting in the pan, roast meat with rosemary being taken from the oven, steaming milk with sugar and saffron strewn in it.

Madame summons her daughters to table, as *papa* will be here at any moment. Charlotte takes Louise by the hand. The delightful creature is the spitting image of her mother, but her eyes have a softer expression.

'*Asseyez-vous*,' says madame Heger with an elegant gesture of her hand. 'Make yourselves comfortable. Don't forget that this is now your home. All the pupils here are my daughters to some extent.'

I'm too old to be your daughter, reflects Charlotte, but she does not mean it in a curt way. She wants to do her best to make a favourable impression on madame Heger. This is her new home, she is quite prepared to believe that. But what will monsieur Heger be like? Will he like her? He teaches French literature, the most important subject for Emily and herself. Madame Heger has already made an impression. She runs her school with great insight and the boarders look healthy and content. In addition Charlotte has never before seen a woman approaching forty who has had children and yet is so undeniably feminine. Madame is fully a mother and yet exudes a certain sensuality. Her neckline is too low by English standards of decency, certainly for a pregnant woman. It reveals the beginning of her breasts, the full bosom of the breast-feeding mother—or of the mistress?

Marie crawls onto the chair at the end of the table, where her mother would surely normally sit. But madame sits down at the side of the table and lifts Louise onto the chair between her and Marie. It is, by the way, highly unusual for little children in the better circles to have supper with their parents. When Charlotte was in Upperwood House as a governess with the White family, her pupils always took their meals with her in the schoolroom. And her own father used to eat only breakfast with his children, though that was mainly for a dietary reason. At the time his stomach was very sensitive and he could not tolerate cabbage, eggs, spicy foods or vinegar. So as not to be tempted he had a tray with a sparse meal on it taken upstairs. As housekeeper, Tabby was not supposed to join the young Brontës, so they had only each other's company at table.

Charlotte has to admit that it is quite jolly with Marie and Louise there. She saw little Claire this morning, but she must be in bed by now. The girls know how to behave properly, but how could it be otherwise with madame as their mother? She seems the kind of woman who can silence a class of girls with a single quiver of her nostrils.

'Lord, bless us and this food,' murmurs madame, closing her eyes. 'Given to us by your benevolent hand. Through Christ our Lord. Amen.'

A short grace, and Charlotte, head bowed, sneaks a look at her sister. Emily is deep in prayer and her lips are moving soundlessly. Charlotte closes her eyes, but the words of her prayer will not come. She is in a Catholic house and the Roman Catholic faith is smiling invitingly at her. The tense silence is broken by Marie's suppressed giggling.

And there is the maid, with the soup tureen, because: *Monsieur est arrivé.*

Madame Heger takes a small round mirror out of the pocket of her skirt and shakes her head firmly, so that a few curls come loose. Strange, thinks Charlotte, because you want your bun to sit securely, don't you? Madame licks her forefinger and rubs her eyebrows into shape.

He comes in, and Charlotte is disappointed. Strange—did she have particular expectations then? She had assumed that monsieur Heger would be a gentleman, and that he definitely is not. He is respectably dressed, but that seems to be more thanks to his wife. There is a smudge of chalk on his coat, but the coat is taken off and thrown nonchalantly on a chair against the wall. The man looks like a farmer, a tenant farmer. Coarse nose, coarse build and a deep groove running up between his eyebrows to the lowest wrinkle on his forehead.

He bends over Marie and Louise and kisses them.

This is the kind of man who beats his wife, thinks Charlotte. She recognises fellows of that sort, since she has seen enough of them in Haworth. The villagers came to her father to complain about the noise caused by marital quarrels and sometimes a wife sought protection in the parsonage. Monsieur Heger is muscular, she can see that at once, his upper arms are taut in his shirtsleeves and he has a thick neck. All that vigour, that male fire, must have an outlet.

He sits down and bends over to kiss his wife, on the mouth, which makes Charlotte look down at the napkin on her lap in embarrassment. He pours himself a glass of beer from a jug and drinks a couple of mouthfuls. Only now does he indicate that he has noticed Emily and her.

'Well, well, the English ladies. How does it feel to come back to school at your age?'

Charlotte does not dare look up and knows that Emily does not either.

'Come on, Constantin.' Madame unexpectedly throws her head back with a peal of laughter. 'Don't tease so! Be nice to the

Miss Brontës. This is Charlotte and that is Emily.'

He springs half to his feet—his napkin is tucked into his belt—and extends a firm hand with broad fingers to Emily.

'*Meess* Emily,' he says teasingly and with a thick French accent.

She puts out her hand, but does not look up. Charlotte pushes the toe of her boot against Emily's calf, but without result. Monsieur shakes her hand too and she forces herself to look at him. He has the kind of weak mouth one would be more inclined to expect in a mason or a fruit-picker than in a literature teacher. A mouth that quickly starts pouting sullenly—and is doing it now, since Emily's behaviour has obviously spoilt his humour. Monsieur Heger kicks off his shoes and, without getting up, roars at the maid for his slippers. She must have heard his order through the closed door, because it is immediately carried out. He puts on his slippers without even nodding to the girl.

Madame ladles the soup with imperturbable calm and monsieur bends deep over his plate to eat, with his left elbow on the table. Charlotte is flabbergasted. How can it be that madame Heger, a woman who must be financially independent, who runs her own school no less, has wanted to associate herself with this character?

'Tell me, *mademoiselle* Charlotte,' says madame, 'can I call you that, *ma chère*?—what your first impressions of Belgium are.' She obviously wants to get a civilised conversation underway. 'Yesterday you drove all day through the Flemish countryside.'

Charlotte does not know what to answer. During their meeting this morning she had been able to restrict herself to polite formulae. Conducting a real conversation in French is something quite different.

She stammers something about the meadows, the farmers and looks for the French word for 'tower' or 'citadel', which she simply cannot remember. She drinks another spoonful of soup, but chokes on it. First she has to clear her throat and then she coughs. She goes red and wheezes. That seems to cheer monsieur Heger up somewhat, since she can hear him sniggering. He pours her a glass of beer and thrusts it into her hand.

'Come on, drink!'

'No beer,' Charlotte manages to say with difficulty.

'Drink!'

Later she is to think back so often to this moment. To the way she brought the glass to her mouth, although she had so firmly resolved not to drink any more Belgian beer, which according to her father was too strong for their constitution. Three words from monsieur and she had abandoned her resolution. His voice is deep, male and dominant: there is no arguing with him. She drinks the beer, which is brown and sweet, and he pours a glass for Emily too, but Charlotte knows that her sister won't drink even a mouthful.

The maid brings some roast meat and monsieur takes the dish out of her hands. He carves the meat, humming as he does so and his smile makes the rather loose skin of his cheeks wrinkle in the direction of his ears. His wife serves him and he puts his hand on her belly.

'The young ladies will certainly have noticed that my wife and I are going to have an addition to the family?'

'You are undoubtedly hoping for a son,' says Charlotte, but she already regrets those words when she sees madame Heger's face freeze.

'A son? That would be wonderful, but I think a daughter is just as sweet,' says monsieur Heger. 'Women are the most beau-

tiful thing on earth. They make a man's life worth living. Ha!'
He throws an arm rather too firmly round his wife's shoulders
and she gives him an indulgent pat on the hand.

Charlotte tries to relax. Perhaps it is good that monsieur Heger is not distinguished; that means that she does not need to
be ashamed of her modest background.

The food smells divine. The dishes keep coming. There are
mashed potatoes, yellow with butter and egg yolks, red cabbage
with apples and carrots strewn with parsley.

Emily takes only some mashed potatoes, although she ate
scarcely anything during the journey. Charlotte does not want
to go to bed hungry and takes something from every dish she is
offered. Marie pushes her plate towards Emily, as if she expects
her to cut her meat, but Emily is blind to that kind of thing and
finally madame pulls the plate towards her.

There is pudding too, a pudding full of cream. Monsieur
Heger asks for a jar of jam and everyone gets a spoonful of
strawberry jam in his dessert. When monsieur tips the jam
into Charlotte's dish, her attention is caught by his firm, broad
wrist, which is slightly hairy.

After the meal monsieur pushes back his chair and lights his
pipe. He does not withdraw to his study, he does not go to the
drawing room. No, he sits here smoking, contentedly, like a pa-
sha after a visit to his harem.

'The girls must go to bed, Constantin.'

'Come, come, Claire, I have so little chance to play with
them,' he says and lifts Louise onto his knee. He plays 'horsey,
horsey' and 'hanging from the washing line', holding up Louise
and Marie in turn by their feet.

'The pudding will soon be coming out again!' says madame,
her voice shrill with irritation. Instantly monsieur puts Marie

on the ground. He gives her a pinch on the bottom and growls: 'Now then, off you go, to bed! Listen to your mother.'

Madame wishes the English ladies good night and gently closes the door of the dining room. A model of affability, this lady, a model of piety and restraint, although her décolleté and the sparks in her eyes make one suspect that a corset of conventions is necessary to keep her passions in check. She is the result of the Catholic upbringing enjoyed by girls from the better Brussels families and which she in turn gives to her daughters and her pupils. Charlotte and Emily go down the corridor with the refectory on their left and find themselves in the large square hall that madame calls the carré: this is where the wide staircase to the upper floor begins. A double glass door and high windows look out onto the garden. The crystal chandelier will certainly give the space a magnificent aura when it is lit, but the sisters are too tired to notice much about the interior. Emily lets go of Charlotte's arm and hurries towards the outside door.

'Em,' says Charlotte weakly, 'we're expected upstairs.'

'I need air—*air.*'

Emily pushes the handle down. It gives way and she looks at her sister, wide-eyed with relief as if she were expecting to be shut up here. Supple and swift as a cat she slips out.

Charlotte knows it's better if she gives in. Outside she remains on the bluestone terrace and watches Emily walking among the old, hardy fruit trees. The bare branches sway slightly and it is not clear whether rain is still threatening or whether it is just evening that is making the sky so dark. While Charlotte descends the four steps into the garden and follows the path among the trees, she breathes in the fresh air deeply. What a strange garden this is: surprisingly spacious and full of growth in the heart of a big city. A secret garden, in the summer definitely a Garden of Eden, protected from the world outside by high walls. Later it will strike her that the walls hide the outside world and although by then she will have tasted the fruits of the garden, the sweet pears that melt on the tongue, she will experience it as a prison. It starts raining and she throws her shawl over her head and shoulders. Full, cold drops. Emily walks quickly ahead of her and disappears among the trees; surely she won't take it into her head to leave the garden? Her sister's body is too tall and her legs too strong for a demarcated area of land, however big this garden is. She is like the sheepdog walking circuits round its cramped kennel with its tongue hanging out. She should be on the moors, striding rapidly through the landscape.

'Em,' she calls out softly, and hurries on so that she can touch her sister's hand. 'I need you, Em. I cannot do it without you.'

'We're so far from home,' says Emily. She has stopped and starts coughing. The shawl almost slips off her shoulders, but she makes no move to arrange it better.

'You are your own home,' says Charlotte. 'You think you cannot do without the moors, but in reality you take them with you everywhere.' Emily is as boundless and inaccessible as the treeless hills, and Brussels with its potpourri of strange sounds, smells and faces is so different that no bridge can span such a ravine.

'Help me in this, Emily.' Charlotte does her best to sound determined. 'We'll show the Hegers and the girls from the boarding school what we English can do.'

This is the right tone. Emily wipes the drops from her cheeks with the end of her shawl and nods scarcely visibly. The damp air, the wet, black leaf mould and then those tall trees—so different.

My sister, thinks Charlotte. Her English transparent skin, the stubbornness flowing through her blue veins. She is a complex soul, an impressive stranger under the Brussels sky.

By the time Emily is able to breathe a little more freely again, she is very tired and leans on her sister's arm. The garden is a jungle of bushes and trunks, branches reaching out and slippery leaves. Above, at the window of the oratory, candles are alight, giving it an inviting look, but absurd practices take place in that room. Those white ghosts are the pupils, dressed in wide nightdresses, and they are murmuring their popish prayers.

Here and there in the school Emily has seen statues of saints. In the refectory there is a St Francis in an oatmeal-coloured habit with two white doves in his cupped hands. In a niche in the first classroom, where Charlotte and she are to have their lessons, a shiny wooden saint looks at his bare feet. However, the most impressive of all the saints' statues is that of the Virgin Mary. She is of course the mother of Christ, but to worship her so fanatically! She stands enormous, in fragile milky white biscuit ware, on a pedestal in the dormitory. Her cheeks are pink as if they have been powdered and she is enveloped in a gown with a painted, sugar-blue edging.

How strange this Catholic house is. Emily asks Charlotte to wait with her in the carré until prayers are over. Madame Heger has given them permission not to attend this service, but not all teachers may be aware of this. It is shadowy in the carré and they have no candle. The heavy dark branches of a huge pear-tree wave behind the tall windows.

The creak of stair treads alarms them. There is madame. She is wearing a peignoir and her chestnut-brown hair has been gathered into a braid. Only when she holds up her candle to light her way does she see them standing there.

'Oh, are you here?' She smiles in amusement, although her tone is a little reproachful. 'You need not pray with us, but please sit in the refectory in future! It is still warm in there and there is always something lying about for you to read.'

Upstairs in the corridor they are given a lecture by mademoiselle Blanche. 'I saw you wandering in the garden,' she says curtly, opening her mouth just sufficiently to let the words out. 'On the path by the wall of the Athénée Royal! That is out of bounds, because the boys can look into the garden from the windows above. Count yourselves lucky that you are new, because otherwise there would be a punishment.' She turns rapidly, lifting her skirt to descend the stairs. There are three teachers living in at the school: Sophie, Marie and Blanche, a woman who must be over forty. With her wide brown eyes, slanting nostrils and pinched mouth she is reminiscent of a hare staring at one in fright.

A pupil comes over to Charlotte and whispers confidentially: 'Don't worry. She's always in a bad mood before bedtime. Tomorrow she'll have forgotten all about it.'

The girl has an appealing, heart-shaped face and Charlotte would like to say something in reply, but gets no further than a scarcely audible: *Merci*.

Emily leads the way to the dormitory; in the doorway she stops and lets her sister go ahead. Charlotte makes her way cautiously among the young women thronging the aisle between the beds. It strikes her how tall and sturdy most of the girls are. The English ideal of beauty—the young woman as delicate as a rosebud—is here crushed like an inferior insect by the Belgian *beauté*: the healthy young woman with a figure that is a model of fertility. The goddess of the earth, of wheat, of milk and the fruits of the orchard! The Belgian girl has a face as oval as a mirror. Her plaits have more colour than those of the English-woman (whose hair always tends to light-brown, even when it is supposed to be blond or black). The hair of the women here is a lighter blond with gold streaks, or a shiny hazel or chestnut.

'*Bonne nuit!*' says Charlotte, and she had forced herself to speak so loudly and clearly that her voice resounds though the whole room. She lifts her head slightly and deliberately meets the gaze of one of the pupils so that no one can suspect her of exaggerated timidity.

'*Bonne nuit!*' she hears a few pupils say, but the girl with whom she happens to have eye contact starts giggling behind her hand.

*

Once hidden by the screen Charlotte is no longer brave. A paralysing tiredness overwhelms her. She wants to sleep and gather strength. Stupid that she and Emily did not wash before retiring.

Emily is already undressing. Her dress goes on a hanger, but the petticoats are folded up carelessly. She tries to put on her nightdress on with almost all the buttons done up and Charlotte gets up to help her.

There is laughter in the room—no longer giggling but open laughter. There is a hubbub and whispering in sing-song, mysterious French.

'*Seigneur*, how ugly they are!'

There are guffaws. A soft voice seems to take issue with this assertion and it is quiet for a moment.

Ugly.

And then another voice. 'So what, they cannot understand us anyway! They don't speak a word of French. Come to that what have they come here for? Let them go back to England, those Protestants.'

Charlotte sits up to look at Emily. Her sister is lying on her back with her eyes closed and hands folded like a dead body that has been laid out.

Charlotte turns onto her side and pulls her knees up high. *Laide.* Ugly. *Moche.*

'*Bonne nuit!*'

They imitate her pronunciation, with the Irish accent that she has obviously unwittingly adopted from her father.

*

Later that night Emily needs to relieve herself. She neglected to go and get a chamber pot and is now being punished for it. For a while she lies there, but there is nothing for it. Unless she wants to wet the bed, she must come out from behind the screen. She goes into the room in her bare feet. The night candle is out, but not all the curtains are closed and surprisingly bright moonlight is shining on the beds. Mademoiselle Blanche must be sleeping in a neighbouring room and she will have to go and ask her for a pot, however humiliating that may be. But suddenly she feels a cool hand slide into hers.

'Come on,' she hears a voice whisper, and the hand pulls her towards the washroom, where there are a couple of chamber pots.

X

Constantin Heger is intrigued by the English sisters. What unusual young women! Particularly the taller one, what's her name—Emma, or is it Emily? She is undoubtedly the most eccentric young woman who has ever attended the school. A few days before, the two ladies had been invited to dinner at his house. However, when he got home, he was so preoccupied with worries that at first he had not paid them much attention. That afternoon a pupil of the Athénée Royal had been caught stealing from the kitty for the pancake party. In itself not such a shocking incident, if it were not for the fact that the thief was one of his favourite pupils. Not some conceited *fils à papa* whom he would have been happy to see expelled, but a hard-working, bright student. It was his intention to recommend the young man for a university scholarship and he envisaged a successful future for him, but after his misdeed that was out of the question. The lad had stolen no more than a handful of centimes and half-francs from the kitty! Even after one of the feared fire-and-brimstone sermons from the headmaster, which had moved many a young sinner before him to tearful repentance, he refused to confess what had happened to the money. In all probability he gave it to his mother. The woman was recently widowed and has to feed a number of children with a scant pension. The boy was expelled, but appeared not to be that worried. Presumably he went in search of a job as a clerk the next day. Perhaps he may even have offered his services as a labourer in one of the factories. A regrettable business, about which Constantin still feels angry and sad. He had been looking forward to talking the matter over with his wife, but on that evening of all evenings, those two odd English-women had joined them for dinner. The taller one—he will call her Emma in his mind for now—stared fixedly at her plate, as if expecting to see a vision in it. He saw only her elegantly shaped eyebrows, her pale eyelashes, long nose and full lower lip. Her narrow hands, with fine, over-long fingers, lay on either side of her plate. She reminded him of a performer in the Grand-Place who occasionally stands on a folding chair next to his barrel organ and pretends to be a statue. This young English lady breathed, even coughed now and then; she ate, though very frugally, and wiped her mouth with her napkin. Her gestures were measured and most of the time she simply sat still. Occasionally she looked up, but he did not manage to catch her eye. Her older sister is not really like her. Both have a vague red sheen to their hair, it is true, like the blush on an apple. But while the younger averted her gaze radically, the older sister sought hesitantly to make contact. She did not speak much, but when she said something her charming, clear voice rang out like that of a young girl. He immediately saw through her. Although she is the strictly brought up daughter of a Protestant parson and makes the impression of being an intellectual, she cherishes the hope of exerting attraction. During the meal she did not wear glasses, but one can see at a glance that she is short-sighted. She came very close to dipping her fork in the soup. This Charlotte—and what was the surname again? Brontë? Why those two dots? Strange—suffers from vanity, so much is clear. But well, you must forgive a woman that.

Anyway, according to Claire, Miss Charlotte is more an elf than a woman. Most people would agree with her, but his ideas on female beauty depart from the prevailing norm. He is not the type of man to swoon over the majestic females of Rubens or the light-footed Graces of Raphael. He feels attracted to the rather forgotten woman; he likes the flower modest in colour and size: the daisy, the buttercup rather than the proud tulip or the rose. He is aware of his own physical shortcomings, but also of the fact that he is no less a man for that.

*

When he enters the classroom he sees immediately that Charlotte wears glasses. However, the things disappear immediately from her nose and are placed next to her inkwell. How amusing! That coquettishness won't last long, since without glasses she certainly won't manage to read a word.

'*Votre grammaire*,' he says drily.

Most girls have the textbook out already—they know what to expect—but the English sisters disappear behind their desk lid.

'When the ladies are ready,' he says, and sits back in his desk, with his hands folded over his belly. The lid closes and it strikes him that the sisters look less sickly. The waxy complexion was mainly due to the tiring journey, because now they have a simple English pallor.

'*Le subjonctif.*' Constantin stretches his legs in front of him and crosses them at the ankles.

Well I never! He sees Charlotte casting a worried look at that strange sister of hers. So that Emma not only cannot manage to speak one word of French, but obviously knows nothing about grammar either. *Bon*, he will go easy on her and not question her in class today. He does, however, intend to make the pair study hard, for it seems an aunt is paying for their stay in Brussels, and only in that way will the lady get value for her money.

*

Charlotte is bent deep over her book and her nose is almost touching the page. The characters are dancing in a thick fog. Monsieur Heger lights his pipe and briefly explains the rules of the subjunctive to refresh the memories of pupils who have been studying French grammar for years. As soon as he starts dictating exercises, Charlotte cannot manage without her glasses and puts them on again. She has only realised here in Brussels that round lenses are considered frumpish. Obviously oval lenses are the fashion here. A warm caramel smell circles upwards. The pipe! Monsieur has got up, although it had looked as though he would sit like that for ever. He appears to be exceptionally lazy, and suddenly he springs to his feet, like a predator that has smelt blood. He prowls the classroom. There are only twelve pupils in the first class, and of course he comes to her and Emily, the new girls. She feels his presence behind her and he leans over her shoulder. Although the subjunctive holds no secrets for her, she starts doubting the correctness of what she has written. The man is so close! The smell of the starch in his shirt and also a vague odour of sweat. She makes a blot on her work. Unbelievable—she who is always praised for her neat handwriting. He moves on to Emily, but her sister goes on writing and his presence does not seem to confuse her in the least.

There goes Constantin down the steps with the exuberance of a healthy cart-horse. He is relieved that this part of the lesson is over. What Charlotte does not know, but what she—shrewd as she is—will soon start to suspect, is that he thoroughly dislikes grammar. 'Grammar,' as he sometimes expresses himself to friends, 'is the mathematics of language.' He teaches the subject dutifully, but what is it actually good for? He cannot understand how some can need dry rules, when French is so melodious, so poetic, that you can surely hear a false note immediately? Anyway, he slips the book into his desk with pleasure and takes out the pile of essays that the girls handed in last week. A soft murmur goes through the rows (*'Oh non!'*) but it is so brief that it cannot affect Constantin's humour.

Charlotte closes her eyes for a moment and feels her heartbeat calming. What a relief: she and Emily have not yet had to do this assignment. Monsieur stands next to his desk, clears his throat and in a firm voice starts reading an essay that has obviously won his approval. There is a blue fug around him; his pipe is lying smouldering in the ashtray. The pupils look sideways at each other. Who wrote this essay?

It is about motherhood and how through it a woman undergoes a metamorphosis as it were. Not the transformation that Charlotte has witnessed scores of times in Haworth: the young, fresh-faced girl changed in the space of a few years by all the slaving and toiling for her family into an exhausted woman. No, in this essay the young mother is depicted as a model of devotion and serenity, although monsieur Heger makes the words roll so sensually that she acquires the charm of a celebrated courtesan. He sounds relaxed like a man taking his ease by the fire with a glass of red wine. Charlotte does not think much of the text; it ends with a comparison (so obvious if you are Catholic) between the young earthly mother and her infant and the Virgin Mary and Baby Jesus. But what a pleasure to listen to monsieur Heger! She is reconciled there and then to the fact that this man will be the master from whom she will learn everything about the French language.

He stops dramatically and gives the essay to a pupil at the front with the panache of an actor. It is one of the less attractive girls, to whom Charlotte could almost bring herself to grant this happiness. She herself has sat up straighter, as if she shares in the pride, as if monsieur is going to read an essay of hers too. How wonderful it must be to have an audience and hear your text being read with such conviction. Indeed, the girl looks as if she would like to kiss monsieur Heger.

But he has returned to his desk and unearths an essay that as one can see from the look on his face stinks of cow dung.

'Renate Piessens.' He holds up the folded sheet. In the second row a young lady lets out a cry. She is summoned to the front of the class. It is one of the girls who have an extensive wardrobe and expensive linens and also belong to the group of beauties.

'What is *this, mademoiselle?*' asks monsieur Heger. 'Shall I read out your work?' His voice is full of sarcasm.

'Oh no,' she begs, 'please don't, monsieur.'

'I'm sure you don't want me to.'

He does so anyway, the devil. The essay is bad, but monsieur's declamation—the ironic tone and the raised hand, palm upward—makes it much worse than it is.

'"The prince stuck a dagger in his heart,"' says monsieur and sinks to his knees. '"Farewell, *mon amour.* And he died with the white rose in his hand."'

It is deathly quiet in the classroom. Monsieur Heger makes a bow. Renate stands there convulsed, a puppet whose strings have become entangled. He takes her right hand and plants a kiss on it like an Italian suitor, whereupon she bursts into tears and runs back to her place. She cannot control her sobbing and her round shoulders are heaving. Monsieur appears upset by these woman's tears, and is already standing by Renate's desk. Charlotte is surprised by the remarkable change that comes over him. The demon seems to leave him and his aspect becomes that of a tame, faithful pet. A lock of fluffy hair hangs over his eyes from the passionate reading he has just given.

'Come, come,' he says and lays a comforting hand on her shoulder. 'You mustn't cry about it, *mademoiselle*,'—he looks for her name on her work—'Renate!'

He makes tut-tutting noises and the outbursts grow less. She accepts his handkerchief and dabs her eyes. 'Look at my notes in the margin and then you'll know how to do it next time. And, my dear girl, don't read any more romantic literature, understood? Stick to the titles I give you.'

'Y-yes,' she manages to say.

*

At five on the dot the bell goes for supper. In winter Gertrude closes the curtains in the dormitory at this time. The pretty working-class maid not only watches over all the comings and goings in the school, but also keeps the dormitory and the washroom clean and tidy. Charlotte lays her nightdress ready on the bed and together with Emily follows the other girls downstairs. She is hungry and is looking forward to the meal. Mary had told her that the Belgians eat well and that wasn't an exaggeration. The delicacies that are served to the pupils! The breakfast may be sober—coffee and a plate of oat or barley porridge—but the other meals are copious. Yesterday at midday there was marinated herring on the table and to follow chops with funny sweet little cabbages called 'Brussels sprouts'. But she prefers the five o'clock meal: thick slices of fragrant white bread with pâté, cooked ham or *breughelkop*, a cooked meat dish in jelly that tastes wonderful with mustard. And as if they have still not had enough to eat, at about eight o'clock the kitchen maid puts out a tray of rolls and two jugs of warm milk and honey in the refectory. For those who still feel like it! The abundance is such that there are girls who pour themselves a mug of milk, and forget to empty it, and half crumbled rolls are left un-eaten. From the sum that madame Heger spends per week on feeding her fourteen young lady boarders, all the pale children in a Yorkshire orphanage crammed to the rafters could surely be given gruel and soup for a month.

Once on the staircase Charlotte sees monsieur below in the carré. He is holding his hat in his hand and seems to be waiting for someone. For madame? She did not see her upstairs. Monsieur waves away some pupils impatiently, until Emily and she have come downstairs.

'Ladies,' he says, putting his arm round Emily's waist. 'Can I invite you to accompany me? I am going to Vieux Marché, where I occasionally give French lessons to a group of Flemish workers. This seems to me a good opportunity to show you something of the city.'

'Oh,' says Charlotte, 'interesting.'

'We won't see anything of the city in the dark,' says Emily, freeing herself from monsieur's grip. 'Could I, by the way, point out that my name is Emily and *not* Emma as you called me yesterday in class.'

'You can soak up the atmosphere,' said monsieur imperturb-ably, 'and meet some Flemings. My wife generally does not like me taking her pupils to the back streets of Brussels, but she is prepared to make an exception for once.'

'You'll have to excuse us,' says Emily. 'We're still rather tired from the journey and in addition I have a cold on my chest.'

'Stay here,' says monsieur, 'but you're coming with me, *meess* Charlotte.'

'Without my sister?' Charlotte begins, but he rises up on tip-toe and breathes heavily in and out.

'Get your cloak and shawl,' he says imperiously. 'It's time, we must be going. You needn't bother about a chaperone—Gertrude is coming with us.'

Charlotte turns and runs upstairs, not in a position to resist his will. Emily will certainly feel abandoned, and what is to happen now: her poor sister, alone among strangers? But it is monsieur whom she must obey: she is his pupil and he is her master—they each have their role.

Constantin Heger runs his fingers quickly through his hair and puts his hat on. There is Charlotte! She has thrown a woollen cloak round her shoulders and as she comes downstairs she ties the ribbons of her bonnet under her chin. What a petite, attractive figure she makes. Charming! Her lively eyes seem to be searching for something. Constantin holds the door into the garden open for her. At that moment Gertrude emerges from her porter's lodge, that dark little office under the stairs. Constantin starts every time she suddenly appears out of nowhere. Gertrude's blond hair is worn untidily up and her gloves are threadbare around her wrists, but he holds the door open for her too.

*

The damp air kisses Charlotte's face and she feels young and healthy. Hopefully monsieur Heger will step up the pace, because she feels like running. At home she likes taking a daily walk. Emily, Anne and she are used to walking fast, since the moors are not boulevards even in summer. There is no strolling there, because apart from the occasional shepherd you see no one and no one sees you; you walk through the bare hills to empty your head and let the blood flow through your veins. Here in Brussels it looks as though she will not be getting much physical exercise. In the morning break and again at lunchtime pupils may stroll in the garden for half an hour and after five they can stay there for as long as they like. But however big that garden may be for a town house, Charlotte feels like a toddler being restrained by its mother with its lead. Consequently she is relieved when monsieur shuts the gate behind them.

He sets a fast pace and she follows close behind him, but Gertrude has difficulty from the start in keeping up with him. She is lugging a wicker basket that is filled to the brim, but Charlotte does not feel like helping her. In monsieur's company she definitely does not want to be too familiar with the domestic staff; after all, she is a writer in the making, an intelligent young woman, and when you're that you don't go carting baskets about. But when monsieur turns round and sees that Gertrude is ten metres or so behind, he says with one eyebrow raised: 'Damn, what's that? Give her a hand.'

Crestfallen, Charlotte stops and waits and grabs the handle of the basket.

'Pretentious little madam,' sneers Gertrude, just audibly through the woollen shawl that she has thrown high round her neck and mouth.

It has rained all day. In the classroom it was so dark that afternoon that mademoiselle Blanche had lit candles. Chilly tears made lines on the panes. Now the sky is empty and there is not a breath of wind. Monsieur leads the way and his bearing cannot be called particularly straight. It expresses a certain nonchalance, a *je-m'en-foutisme*, as he calls that kind of attitude himself. This morning there was definitely still a crease in his trousers, but now the material flaps around his sturdy legs.

Our party leaves the rue d'Isabelle, where the well-to-do intellectuals live and the houses and gardens are so smart. They do not go upwards, via the steps of the library to the avenues and squares where the palaces of the rich are situated. You would recognise the Place Royale even with your eyes closed. You can smell them as they pass, the rich. The perfumed powder on the ladies' skin, which at every movement of their bodies, swathed in silk, soft wool and fur, releases a marvellous odour; and the gentlemen's pomaded hairdos, the chest sprinkled with eau-de-cologne, the shoes polished with beeswax. Up there the gas-lights will soon be lit and the brass of the carriages will shine. But our party takes another hilly flank of the city, crosses the square in front of the high court and descends into a less salubrious neighbourhood.

'The hospice of the Alexian Brothers!' Constantin Heger's voice is directed like a lash at his two female companions, who are toiling with the basket slightly further up the hill. This is the master at his best, the cicerone, the guide of the ignorant. A boy carefully crosses the cobbles with an earthenware pot undoubtedly containing the evening meal for a sick family member. At the blue-painted gate of the hospice stands a blind young man—in his shirtsleeves despite the time of year, and he returns Constantin Heger's greeting by lifting his stick off the ground in front of him for a second.

A street further on Heger calls out, shamelessly loud and tauntingly: 'In this area there are still a few adherents of Calvin hiding, *meess* Charlotte!'

'Is it really true then?' Gertrude stops abruptly, and the content of the basket is almost emptied onto the street.

Charlotte sucks in air and breathes out heavily in irritation.
'Is what true?'

'That you and your sister are Protestants?'

She does not deign to give an answer and does not even feel aggrieved, she is so absorbed by the sight of the city and the image of her master walking ahead of them. They are descending into the underbelly where the common people live. The workers' houses are like the heads of impoverished old men: the wooden panels pulled askew and subsiding; the small inset windows tired, matt and disappointed; the doors like brown toothless mouths. From the chimneys comes the greasy smoke from all the combustible rubbish that is thrown into the stove.

Monsieur has disappeared round the corner and Charlotte gives a tug on the basket, so that Gertrude is obliged to quicken her step. The concierge is now softly singing a song, not in her juicy French, but in that mother tongue of hers which in the school she is only allowed to speak with the errand boys who come to deliver their wares. Gertrude cannot be really stupid, since her job requires a certain knowledge of the alphabet and the abacus, but she belongs unmistakably to the working class.

'Lift your skirts up, *mam'selle*,' says Gertrude good-naturedly, since she cannot sulk for long. 'The city gets dirty here.'

Charlotte wraps her shawl round her nose and mouth, as the neighbourhood is not exactly sweet-smelling. In the alleyway they pass the grey washing hanging outside, although it will almost certainly freeze tonight. Somewhere a woman is crying. Not rebelliously or passionately, but full of humility, as if she knows that no one will come and console her. Her sad weeping cannot suppress Charlotte's feeling of excitement. It is magical wandering through this foreign city—without any fear, as there is a man to protect her.

Monsieur is waiting for them by a narrow wooden bridge and they move aside to let a horse and cart pass. The driver holds the reins in one hand, indifferently, shoulders low. The bridge creaks under the weight of the cart and the river stinks like a damp dog. They follow the bank past a row of hovels, but monsieur seems to be in a hurry and no longer looks round at them. When he is out of sight, Charlotte swallows her pride and asks: 'Are we nearly there?

'It's here,' says Gertrude. 'Just round the corner at the Vieux Marché.'

XI

The parish hall is long and narrow and has only a ground floor. The outside must have been whitewashed in the distant past, but the colour has faded to the grey of a dirty mop.

In the doorway stands a young worker with his hands in his pockets. He wears a faded hat, pushed to the back of his head, and is leaning with his upper arm against the doorpost. When monsieur Heger approaches he looks at him, his chin almost touching his chest, his light eyes full of suppressed tension. For a moment it looks as if he will not move, but then, with a certain reluctance, he takes a couple of steps outside to let the company pass. This is the first Flemish worker with whom Charlotte has come into contact, and she cannot resist subjecting him to scrutiny. His light-brown hair urgently needs cutting and he has not shaved, but his skin seems as fresh as a child's: he must have scrubbed his face before he came to class. He takes a ball of wound rags out of his pocket and starts tossing it up like a young rascal not wanting to hear the school bell. Charlotte feels Gertrude pushing the wicker basket in her back and crosses the threshold.

Inside there is a languid murmur of voices. About thirty workers are standing together talking rather wearily. Boys who seem scarcely to have been untied from their mothers' apron strings, but also worn-out men with hunched shoulders and vulture-like necks. There is a penetrating smell, which almost makes Charlotte recoil: the smell of stained coats and smocks, of beer, greasy hair and teeth that have grown mossy with chewing tobacco. Monsieur goes to the front, the hats and caps come off, and are turned meekly round and round in their hands. The men look for a place at the rough wooden tables which have been carelessly arranged. Charlotte looks around feeling rather lost, since monsieur has not told her what to do, until Gertrude gives her a sharp tug on the sleeve.

'For goodness' sake come here!' she hisses, and points to a couple of chairs at the back against the wall.

So there they sit, and the concierge puts her right foot on the basket as if wanting to protect the contents from thieves.

'Why he takes us with him to the slums, *mam'selle*, I wouldn't know. I have to go with him every time, but I don't like it at all. All those common people.'

But when a tough-looking chap at the table in front of them winks at her over his shoulder, she starts giggling and nudges Charlotte as if they are friends.

'That's Jef,' she whispers. 'He fancies me.'

The fellow turns round and tries to grab Gertrude's foot, but she pulls it away and holds her chin up haughtily. Oh, how expert she is in this age-old game of attraction and repulsion with which women drive men mad. Jef looks better dressed and fed than most of those here and must be a foreman or something. He has a broad nose and a heavy pale head like a bull's. Gertrude may be a beauty and feel quite a lady, but these are the kinds of lads she grew up with, and undoubtedly there will come a day when she will succumb to the advances of one of them.

Charlotte knows the workers: she knows them from Yorkshire. These men are not all that different. The same unhealthy skin, boorish manners and hungry eyes, cunning as a fox's. She sits up to look for the young man who was standing in the doorway just now. Her eyes scan unwashed necks, a dirty neckerchief, a head that is almost clean-shaven (most probably to get rid of lice) and then there is the back of a head with long, caramel-coloured hair that rests heavily on the shoulders. There at the end of that table; it is almost bound to be the young man. But he looks straight ahead and her attention turns to her master.

Monsieur stands in front of his odd class and is so much more serious than when he teaches at school. On their first meeting Charlotte thought there was something of the work-man about him, and here, among working men, the similarity is striking. He does not have the tall figure of a gentleman, but is as stocky as a boat hauler. His clothes make the difference: the black suit, the white shirt with the stiff collar and the top hat that he has placed on his lectern. In the boarding school his clothes look old-fashioned and even a little shabby, especially compared to the dandyish elegance of monsieur Chapelle, the music teacher. But among the shapeless trousers, baggy shirts and stained smocks of the workers his dress has the mark of distinction. He explains something, is serious, runs a thumb pensively across his lips. She no longer hears what he says, she sees only his mouth.

At the end of the lesson monsieur waves to Gertrude and she sets the basket on her chair.

'Help me then, *mam'selle*,' she cries, 'or they'll tear everything out of my hands.'

There are slices of rye bread, hunks of pungent cheese and sweet wrinkled pears from the previous harvest from the school garden. The workers surround them, but Gertrude snaps: 'In a line, otherwise you get nothing.'

Although her French is far from refined, it sounds particu-larly presumptuous here.

The men continue to push and shove, and the very dainty

face of the concierge goes beetroot-red with agitation. She repeats her command, but only when she is beside herself and starts cursing in Flemish do the men form a queue. There is a wave of mocking laughter, because although they may be hungry and tired, there is still life in them.

Then Charlotte sees the young man she had noticed before. He seems to be in doubt whether to join the queue and is already holding his hat by the dent in the top. His eyes are clear: light and innocent in their striking beauty and resentful in their expression. He pushes his hat on his head, nods briefly to Charlotte and leaves.

'God Almighty,' says Gertrude, who has followed Charlotte's look. She wipes her hands, which have become greasy from distributing the cheese, on the cloth in which the bread was wrapped. 'Emile actually said goodbye to you. Don't think that chap will ever accept anything, he's far too proud for that.'

*

What an unusual trio makes its way through the night. Gertrude's basket is empty, yet the concierge is just as slow as on the way there. She falls behind and Charlotte refuses to walk beside her any longer. Monsieur walks fast; even at this late hour he has the tread of a farmer who wants to get his grain in before the rain. The lace is loose on one of her boots, but she ignores the inconvenience and hurries so as to be able to walk next to her master.

'Monsieur,' she says once she is alongside him. 'Are you pleased with this evening's lesson?'

She cannot help looking at him obliquely, but his figure is enveloped in darkness. Yet she knows exactly what he looks like—his face, on which there are no right angles in evidence, the nose, the chin, the cheek bone: all in rounded, earthy forms.

'*Meess* Charlotte,' he says emphatically, as if surprised to find her next to him. 'But of course—yes, yes, I found the lesson satisfying. The Flemish workers are my favourite pupils. So much more eager to learn and brighter than my pupils at the boarding school. Oh, the young ladies aren't very studious. That never ceases to amaze me. Literature or history does not interest the girls. They want to learn a few German and Italian sentences, as it is so distinguished to weave them into the conversation. Music lessons also go down as easily as hot chocolate, because they give them the opportunity to try out their budding charms on Maurice Chapelle. How intently he guides their fingers over the keyboard in an elegant melody! And as the ultimate challenge in the boarding school there is, aha, the embroidering of handkerchiefs. Italian, music and embroidery are the key to the highest goal: snaring a rich husband.'

Charlotte, dismayed, looks to the side and sees monsieur appear in a patch of yellowy gaslight. His mouth forms something resembling a lop-sided smile, a grin, his eyes narrow to chinks and the laughter lines in his left cheek spread to his ear.

'That's what you've come here for, isn't it, *meess*? A husband?'

Charlotte stops and shakes her head desperately.

'You're under a false impression. For my sister and myself education is of the greatest importance.'

Constantin Heger is again shrouded in darkness, as if he were a slide from a magic lantern.

'Is it really?'

He stands before her, broad and threatening as a huge bat.

'I think nevertheless that you are also in search of a husband. Perhaps not a rich man, no—a woman of your modest background will not cherish such foolish aspirations—but at least well-off, is that not so? You have come to the right place. Here in Brussels there are definitely more young doctors, school-masters and merchants than in your remote village in *York-sheerr*.'

He pronounces the name of her native region with as much disdain as if he were talking about the land of the Hottentots. Charlotte feels a constriction in her chest and to avoid him seeing her rebellious tears, she kneels down and ties her boot laces.

'*Meesss!* What are you doing, I'm only teasing you a little.'

He puts his hand on her shoulder, or rather, he grips her shoulder. She feels the pressure of his fingertips on her skin through leather and fabric and remains kneeling longer than is necessary. There is only his hand and she is only the skin beneath his hand. When she stands up, he taps her on the cheek with a gloved finger.

'There, there, that's better. A real Englishwoman, so over-sensitive.'

They enter an alley so narrow that the two rows of houses almost touch, like fat thighs. In daylight you can find your way here, but now there is only the vague glow of a couple of oil lamps. There is an empty beer barrel in the way and a rat runs along the wall. In Charlotte's eyes rats are the most disgusting of all animals. Somewhere a gong sounds and drunken laughter echoes through the alleyway. Something is lying on the ground—rags, no, they are the decayed remains of vegetables, from a market or a kitchen. Monsieur Heger kicks his way through and Charlotte lifts her skirts. What is that brushing her leg? Oh my God! She screams.

'A pig,' says monsieur Heger. 'Unknown to you in England?'

She expects him to burst out laughing, but he does not. He stays very close to her, and for a moment she has the feeling that he will offer her his arm. Which is of course out of the question, since a master cannot walk arm in arm with his pupil, can he? The closeness of Constantin Heger deprives her of the ability to think clearly. Her breathing is shallow and her whole being waits. She thinks of his firm wrists, of the movements he makes with his hands to add force to his arguments. The air is full of stench, and yet she believes she can smell his pure male scent.

People are foolish. At the height of rapture they instinctively want to return to normality. They cannot stand the heat of the flames and shrink back. And that is exactly what Charlotte does. To shake off her timidity, she suggests with a certain vehemence:

'Let us wait for Gertrude, monsieur. Where has she got to? Who knows what may have happened to her!'

Not long after the concierge comes round the corner, hand in hand with a man.

'Gertrude seems to have met a friend,' says monsieur Heger. 'We mustn't spoil her pleasure. Take my arm, *ma chère.*'

Charlotte slides her arm into his and feels the firm grip with which he greets her, but the magic has gone. It suddenly seems unremarkable that a master and his pupil should be walking arm in arm: he full of paternal concern, she full of trust and admiration. Such a bond between the master and his student can withstand the brightest glare of daylight. If madame could see them like this, she would cast a gentle, benevolent eye upon then and feel no jealousy, since this is just a gallant gesture by her husband. Oh yes, Charlotte is sure of it: if monsieur had been walking here with another young woman from the boarding school this evening, he would have offered her his arm too.

'You cannot keep a child away from its people,' says monsieur, and it does not immediately dawn on Charlotte who he is talking about. 'If you have an Indian papoose grow up with a rich, white family, its roots will still tug at it. Gertrude is and will always be a Fleming.'

His thoughts are not with her, but with as insignificant a creature as the concierge.

*

Let us take a little distance in order to assess the situation better. You were most probably swept away by all those overheated reflections of a woman who should have been married long ago. It would be better if Charlotte Brontë were to lie at night in the firm embrace of a lawful wedded husband, because she is far too passionate by nature to go on living alone. And far too naïve for a city like Brussels. Those English adventuresses obtain permission from their fathers and uncles to travel to Belgium as easily as to visit a cousin in Sussex. Without an accompanying male from home at their side they simply fall prey to the womanisers here. Belgian men do not, thank heavens, have the bad reputation of Italians, but there is more opera in their blood than in that of the English, whose emotional life resembles that of a lizard. The gentlemen of Brussels tend rather more towards the Parisians, although they can never quite equal the latters' eloquence, refinement and cunning. While haughtiness is the birth right of the Parisian, who wears his airs and graces with as much panache as his silk scarf and gold monocle, the conceitedness of the man of Brussels gives the impression of being unearned and inappropriate. The different temperaments of the gentlemen, moreover, are splendidly expressed in their way of paying court. In the French capital a man will lavishly fête the young woman of his choice and try to lure her into his bed with wine and compliments. The Londoner proposes to his chosen one—after three walks accompanied by an old aunt—in the same sober tone in which he bids for a healthy mare at the market. The man from Brussels, finally, is known in both business and love for 'beating about the bush' or in the typically Brussels expression *tourner autour du pot*— in this case the honey pot. With vague promises and allusions and the odd glimpse of paradise he turns a girl's head. He offers his heart, but not completely; he courts her, but in such veiled terms that it is not a proposal after all. She lies brooding night after night, as it is not clear to her whether he is actually still a bachelor or what his intentions are, but often he does not even know himself. Many a woman has wound up in the lunatic asylum on the rue du Rempart des Moines because her suitor has driven her to distraction. The man of Brussels is a Don Juan without a compass.

Take Constantin Heger. He was born in Brussels and between the ages of sixteen and twenty was subject to the unedifying influence of the French capital, where he was articled to a lawyer and lost his virginity in the arms of a faded courtesan. Today he is the husband of Claire Heger, on whom he has already sired four children. However, his passion has never been totally fulfilled, since he is continually surrounded by attractive ladies. Teachers and growing girls pass him in the corridors, greet him respectfully and listen wide-eyed and with lips slightly parted to everything he says. His virile nature makes it impossible for him not to notice them. How he enjoys their company! But just as a lanky youngster returns dutifully to his mother after a summer's day spent wandering in the fields, Constantin Heger has always returned to his wife reasonably unscathed.

For your information: the schoolmaster and the English lady have reached the rue d'Isabelle. You can now see them much more clearly in the light of the gas lamps. Charlotte in her grey cloak, too cheap for this boarding school and too thin for the season. And then her hat, her hairdo—hopeless! It does not matter, since Constantin Heger has virtually forgotten the lady next to him. In his thoughts he is already in his warm home. He fancies a glass of liqueur. During the day he allows himself only wheat beer or the occasional *geuzelambiek*, but before bed he likes something stronger. How chilly it is here outside and how warm his bed will be soon. Is Claire already in it or is she still sitting at her dressing table?

At the gate of the boarding school monsieur turns the heavy key in the lock, but waits for Gertrude before going in. There she is, her face so young and so fresh that Charlotte feels a stab of jealousy.

'Well, did you kiss?' he asks and Gertrude whispers: 'Oh, I beg you, please don't tell madame!'

With swishing petticoats, Gertrude hurries through the garden to the carré, but Charlotte waits while monsieur slides the narrow wooden beam across the gate. He looks at her with a question in his eyes and lets her lead the way inside. Her heart is warm; it not only beats as the bodily organ it is, but is alive like a young animal, a cub, a frisky piglet! She goes upstairs and has to be careful not to dance. Her sister… She must tell her sister about this evening.

At the door of the dormitory Charlotte pulls off her boots. The night candle is lit and she sees the outlines of the beds. Through the screen comes the glow of Emily's candle. She is not asleep and is sitting up in bed learning her French words.

'Em?' whispers Charlotte, but as soon as she sees her sister's severe, tight-lipped expression, she knows that she cannot entrust her with this secret. Her sister understands nothing of matters of the heart—more than that: she would condemn her.

'Thank you for leaving me alone,' says Emily grumpily.

'That's your own fault,' Charlotte cannot help saying. 'You could have come too, it was very interesting. But no, you prefer to sit here sulking.'

Even before she has hung her last petticoat in the wardrobe, she regrets her outburst. It happens quite often that she speaks to Emily like this, but her sister is the one who wins every argument, with guilt as her most powerful weapon. She lies in bed and Emily repeats her French vocabulary silently; her lips are moving. She is wheezing again; she obviously needs rest. But Charlotte does not want to think about her anymore and closes her eyes. The sheet is made of strange soft linen and it is soon deliciously warm under the blanket. She lets her hand glide down to her belly under her nightdress. Then she lets it rest on one breast. Monsieur.

XII

We shall take one last look behind the screen. Emily has finally blown out her candle and is lying down. She will soon slip into a deep sleep. She occasionally has dark dreams, this Miss Brontë, about her dead sisters, who crawl out of their graves and come and tap on her window. Their hair full of mud, their faces pale as the moon and as vacant as blank medallions. Her mother's ghost too, like a timid deer among the tombstones. Emily Brontë is not a woman who can live in the future, since she expects absolutely nothing from it. And the present—what is there in the present that can awaken even the slightest interest in her? The endless intoning of French words and grammatical rules is for Emily what the murmuring of the rosary is for a Brussels nun. It makes consciousness so paper-thin that the present dissolves in a mist. But the past she happily allows in. Lying on her back, with her large, thin hands on the bedspread, she thinks of Anne—once her Anne, the sister to whom she felt closest. Of how they wrote the chronicle of Gondal together and were transported to a fantasy world to which only they had access. Anne left her to work as a governess for the Robinson family. She came home at Christmas. 'Dear sisters,' she said, 'I missed you both so terribly.' The reason was that at Thorp Green she had no one to talk to. Anne had reached out imploringly to her across the table with her little hand, but she had withdrawn hers ruthlessly. Anne. Anne, you no longer have any right to my friendship, because you abandoned me.

And then Emily falls asleep, and see how in a dream she levitates from the mattress! The window opens and she floats out, free, free of the continent. There she is, already hurrying with long strides and Keeper at her side through the purple hills.

*

A lot is about to happen in the life of the two oldest Brontë sisters. We shall let them get used to their new surroundings before we visit them again.

Let us skip the rest of the night anyway and see morning break in Brussels. There is nothing as beautiful as the awakening of a city, if you pass over the awakening of the homeless, which is a problem, since they increasingly come into view unasked. Just as you are admiring the way the misty morning light lies like a gauze veil over the church of Saint-Jacques-sur-Coudenberg, you see in the porch—of what is after all a house of God where every person, heathen or Christian, ought to be able to find shelter—a whole family that has spent the night there, wrapped in rags. The mother spits on a corner of her shawl to wipe the dirt from her son's face, which concludes his toilet for the day. The father distributes the frugal breakfast: for each of his three children a piece of a dry hunk of white bread, thrown to him yesterday over a garden gate by the kitchen maid of a fine household. On the quays of the city, where the water of the Zenne (that stinking cesspit!) flows under the bridges, bearded men lie on the stone quaysides, their breath smelling of beer and an empty stomach. Anyone still sleeping will soon be woken by a gendarme's truncheon.

King Leopold stands at the window of his study and looks out over the Warande Park, which is bathed in a light mist.

'Sire?'

His butler pushes in the trolley with his breakfast on it.

'The messenger has arrived. He is waiting downstairs for your missive.'

Leopold cannot bring himself to write the invitation. Or to have breakfast. Usually he takes his meals in the royal family's private chambers, but this morning he came down before it was light. When he woke up he felt restless, so much so that he wanted to leave the apartment immediately. And why should he not breakfast in his study? Almost every morning Louise-Marie sends one of her ladies-in-waiting to excuse her, and then he's alone at table anyway. Oh, he mustn't be too hard on his wife. If he is away from her longer than a few days, she writes him tender letters. But since she gave birth to her fourth child, she has suffered from a malaise. She feels weak and depressed, and her daily walk goes no further than the Moorish kiosk in the park. No physician has been able to help her up to now, which is not surprising, since she has very little natural resilience. As a young girl she already said farewell to the joys of life, as a novice preparing to take her vows. That Catholicism with its superstition and fanaticism! He knows that Louise loves him, but not in the sense that she wants to embrace him, sit on his lap or run her fingers through his hair. Not in the sense that she desires him and invites him into her bedroom, though it has to be said that she has never refused him, since her mother—that noble lady, that *reine des Français* with her morbid predilection for tragic saints' stories—has impressed on her that it is a woman's duty to give herself to her husband and bear his children, however disgusting she finds that intimate contact. During their honeymoon he still cherished the illusion that he might be able to arouse some ardour in his young wife with fondling, caresses, kisses and sweet words. But she lay there in her chaste nightdress, completely frozen, like a stick that refuses to turn into a voluptuous, writhing snake.

123

Undoubtedly it was a relief to her that since her last pregnancy he has no longer paid any evening visits. Leopold goes over to his desk, picks up a pen and holds it above the inkwell. Just as he is about to dip the pen in the ink, he hesitates and puts it down. He is on the point of allowing happiness back into his life. Why is he still in doubt then? Is it so wrong to opt for life? For the time being he does not know whom he can take into his confidence on this matter; Jules Van Praet can obviously not understand the fact that his king longs for the warmth of a woman. Jules, however, does not mind court gossip about illicit love affairs elsewhere in Europe. He even maintains a correspondence with the comtesse Le Hon to stay abreast of the intrigues at the French court. But with his own king Jules is stricter than a sergeant-major! Ridiculous, because since he married Louise-Marie six years ago, he has not had a permanent mistress. His sins have been confined to a few sweet afternoons with rustic beauties in the castle of Ciergnon, the estate he originally bought to please Louise-Marie.

'Oh, Leopich,' she had exclaimed excitedly. 'Everything here is so pure and idyllic!' Like her distant cousin Marie-Antoinette in her artificial farming village in Versailles she would enjoy the outdoor life here, in a simple cotton dress and with a blush on her cheeks. Her fragile health soon made that impossible. She sat for whole days in the smallest drawing room in the castle, swathed in shawls, moaning by the fire.

'It's so draughty here, Leopich!'

'It's so cold here, Leopich!'

He sighs. He is beginning to dislike his wife with her delicate Madonna's face and her weak hands. He is the king. He can decide. But he owes her respect, because she is the mother of his children.

There is no one in his study. No servant is standing spying on him. Thank heavens, the messenger is waiting downstairs. Leopold grasps the edge of his desk with both hands and would most like to overturn it. As so often he feels like shouting, but he never gives in to the urge—not even at night, because otherwise there would be an immediate knock on the door by a worried valet. The shout is locked in his breast.

An eternal shame that Louise-Marie is not a little more like his darling Charlotte. Then true happiness would have been possible. The contrast with his first marriage is stark and painful. He can still see himself at the altar: a young prince, only twenty-five. And beside him Charlotte, Princess of Wales, his glowing, warm-blooded bride! Although she had been previously promised to Willem of Orange, she had chosen him. Not the obvious choice, since though he was a handsome young chap, he was no match for a crown princess. The Duchy of Saxe-Coburg provided him with only a modest income, and at the time there was not the slightest indication that he would ever ascend a throne. It was due to Charlotte's stubborn persistence that her father, the Prince Regent of Great Britain, consented after much protest to a marriage that offered his daughter no political or any financial benefit.

Charlotte and he had met in London at a dinner given by her father in honour of the kings, princes and generals who had banished Napoleon to Elba. She was radiantly healthy, somewhat plump, with a heart-shaped mouth and a narrow nose. Eighteen, uninhibited and untamed, she did not shy away from showing her interest in him. A month after their meeting she broke off her engagement with Dutch Willem without consulting her family. She wanted him and no one else! When his lovely, spoilt Charlotte did not immediately get her own way at home, she started stamping her feet and sulking. Apparently just as she had done as a child when her father refused to buy her a little black domestic servant. He himself had tried to make an impression on the Prince Regent by the patient, tactful and yet steadfast way in which he endeavoured to obtain his consent. Willem of Orange hated him for the theft of his fiancée and later came to hate him even more when he became king of *his* Southern Netherlands. But at that moment at the altar with Charlotte he had as yet no knowledge of what their fate would be. He saw a future for himself in England, at the side of Charlotte, who would become queen of Great Britain.

However, their happiness came to an abrupt, cruel end. Charlotte died a few hours after giving birth to a still-born son. That miserable winter's night shattered his dream of being able to love the same woman all his life, a woman who was also his wife.

His youth and his great love were taken from him. Where are the days when he galloped carefree and expectantly through the woods? Charlotte! He sought oblivion in the arms of a number of noble and especially discreet English ladies. And there was the greedy Karoline Bauer. This was just playing about, nothing more. His marriage to Louise-Marie brought a brief upsurge of hope, but now she is more a precious sister than his beloved. She cannot assuage his needs, and that causes him a problem. A prince can afford a little innocent flirting, but a king cannot even kiss a maid in her neck behind a pillar without his whole court getting wind of it. Oh yes, he's sure of it: even Louise-Marie knows about his country escapades in the Ardennes. Wisely, she does not make too much of it.

Cold, milky light falls through the high windows onto the tall figure at the desk. Lit by a flickering candle or gas lamp the king can still pass as a very attractive man, but the morning is unforgiving. However skilfully his toupee is made, it would not even fool a child. His side-whiskers are dyed a black that is just a little too black, with a bluish sheen. But his abdomen is firm and his calves are hard and his manhood is still the kind that jerks into life when he catches sight of a beautiful woman. He owes his physical condition to his strict German regimen: a frugal diet, stretching exercises in front of the open window and long rides on horseback.

The pen goes into the ink and then across the paper in a restrained hand, with the occasional elegant loop for a 'j', a 'g' or an 'I'. A dab with blotting paper, a vigorous tug on the bell and there is the butler.

'Thank you, sire. I shall ensure immediate delivery.'

He feels hugely relieved. The decision has been made. On the table are sourdough bread, butter and a dish of pears in syrup. He eats with relish and twice orders a mug of warm milk and honey. Fresh milk, still in the udder this morning. There is life in him. *Verdammt*, yes! Since he met that Claret girl at the Théâtre Royal he has been aware of a new vitality in his body: a desire has been awakened in him. *Mein Gott*, he does not want to put the girl out of his thoughts. Of course there will be gossip. Although Miss Claret is voluptuously shaped, she is still a child, not yet quite sixteen. Yet he cannot resist her. Those green eyes, full lips and slightly oblique smile. That narrow waist and that … yes, that bosom he finds so appetising.

He drinks a couple of mouthfuls of milk and wipes the droplets from his mouth with a napkin. The girl's mother is no obstacle; her rather shy diffidence is play-acting and with her cautious nods and smiles she seems to be encouraging him to come closer. She is in no hurry to give her daughter to the king, but it is obvious that she will eventually. She is cunning, this madame Claret, and also has attractive curves (for which he has a weakness in women). If her daughter were not so enchanting, he might consider some light-hearted dalliance with the mother. But no other woman stands a chance beside Arcadie. It is weeks since he last met her, on the coast—in the company of her mother, it's true. No one recognised him, for who expects the king of the Belgians on a grey Sunday afternoon on the beach at Middelkerke?

In the inner courtyard of the Royal Palace a young courier mounts his horse. He looks magnificent in his uniform as royal postman, with gold braid on his jacket and chamois leather breeches. In the saddlebag of his chestnut brown Normandy gelding is an envelope that His Majesty's valet has just handed him and that he must deliver without delay. What an honour to be able to serve the king! A bloody shame, though, that he had to wait so long in the corridor for the message and so went without his breakfast: the wonderful creamy oat porridge that is served up in such generous portions in the scullery of the Palace, and the mug of sweet, hot coffee!

While Leopold chews on the sourdough bread and spits out the pips from a sweet pear, his invitation travels with the messenger in his saddlebag. The ride does not take long, passing the Porte de Namur, where there has been no actual gate for the past sixty years, and taking the highway to Elsene. The Normandy gelding trots past the villa where the celebrated violinist Charles de Bériot is sleeping in the arms of his new wife, and then takes the path where we saw Henriette Claret bobbing along on her way to her neighbour Babette. The wrought-iron gate of the Claret residence is open and the courier reins in his horse, as you never know whether a child may skip onto the path in pursuit of its hoop.

XIII

The invitation is delivered to the Claret residence at about eight o'clock. The maid brings in the envelope, just at the moment when Henriette is tapping the top of her egg with a silver knife.

'Madame, there's a messenger! He's like a prince.'

The girl blushes violently, the more so because she sees that the yolk of madame's egg is not sufficiently hard.

'*Merci*,' says Henriette nonchalantly, as if she receives an envelope with a crown on it every day. 'And take this snotty mess with you, please.'

Young Marcel is standing on tiptoe looking out of the window as the rider remounts.

'He's got fringes on his cap, Cédric,' he says to his brother, who is still too small to reach above the windowsill. 'He must be a knight.'

'Knight, knight,' sneers Arcadie, but still she has pushed her chair back and half stood up to be able to see the rider. For some time she has suffered from an insatiable curiosity about new men, and not that many come to the Claret residence.

'*Silence*,' says Henriette, but she sounds more amused than strict. 'We're eating.' Marcel helps Cédric back onto his chair and sits down himself.

'Who is the card from, *maman*?' asks Arcadie. 'Who is writing to us?'

'Oh.' Henriette fans herself, supposedly casually, with the envelope. 'Just a gentleman friend sending us an invitation.'

A man, not a woman! Arcadie's eyes widen.

'Come on, *maman*, tell me!'

Henriette tucks the card back in the envelope and pushes it under her plate.

'Your father and I have been invited to a concert at the Palace. It is a performance by our own monsieur Bériot.'

'*Maman*, is it really true, in the king's home?'

Arcadie cannot eat another mouthful and is relieved when her mother waves her napkin to indicate that the children can go and play.

'*Maman*, can I come with you and papa? Is the invitation for me too?'

Not that she is dying to see the king again, but she would very much like to see the Palace from inside.

Henriette does not reply and stops little Pauline, who tries to leave the room with a chocolate roll hidden among the folds of her dress.

'Pauline,' says her mother severely. 'We've talked about this before. Do you want be a princess or a piglet?'

'I think piglets are sweet,' says Pauline, but puts down the roll obediently on the table in front of her mother, and trips off.

'You are invited,' says Henriette calmly.

'Oh, *maman*,' cries Arcadie with delight.

Henriette gives her a friendly tap on the hand, after which she digs the centre out of Pauline's roll and with a dreamy smile dips it in her fragrant coffee.

*

How heavenly it is to receive an invitation from the Palace! Such things happen only very rarely to a subject who is not of noble blood. And when the messenger with the gold braid delivers such a letter the envelope is accepted with trembling hands. Ladies who receive a card with a crown on it start dreaming of scenes from the *Arabian Nights* and meetings with noble gentlemen. Then uncertainty strikes. They reach for their hand mirrors and wonder what flowers to wear in their hair. And is their loveliest gown good enough for the occasion?

Henriette is particularly restless that morning. She wraps a shawl round her and goes onto the terrace. The damp dawn has given way to a golden sunlight which is reflected endlessly in the dew-covered leaves. It promises to be a beautiful day. What she would most like to do is to go to Babette's to tell her the great news, but the postmaster is ill in bed with flu and she has no wish to catch it. Nor can she go into town, as the horses are being reshod this afternoon. And so Henriette puts on her outdoor apron in the garden shed and goes to prune the roses, although it is too early in the season for it. She really must do something to calm her nerves. With each breath she tastes the first stirrings of spring. *Snip, snip* go the pruning shears through the rose branches, and that gives a feeling of satisfaction. But then Henriette lowers the shears because the full import of news begins to dawn on her. A miracle, that's what it is! The king is bestowing an exceptional favour on her daughter. This is not a rendezvous on the beach or a limply raised hand and a gentle smile as two coaches cross. This is an invitation to a musical recital at court, during which Arcadie will be introduced into His Majesty's intimate circle. Although hopefully Her Majesty will not be present that evening!

Oh, Henriette will show the king that her daughter is worthy of so great an honour. He has not been mistaken in judging her so positively. *Mon Dieu.* She sits down on the low wall that surrounds the rose garden. This is a test of course! In order to pass, Arcadie will need to project the aura of a noble lady, or better still, of a princess. In last month's *Journal de Mode* there was a delightful ball gown. Pale pink with a pointed waist and a double Van Dyck skirt, richly decorated with white silk roses. Arcadie would be able to wear endless numbers of light petticoats under it, so that they would swirl around her as she danced. Leopold and Arcadie, waltzing under the chandeliers.

Oh, you silly goose, she corrects herself. It is not a ball at all, and of course he would not ask her to dance. Discretion, *discretion* is the code word. She will explain to her daughter that they must both be especially discreet. With a sigh she says farewell to the image of Arcadie in the pink gown. Anyway, she is still too young for a ball and has yet to make her entry into the beau monde. It looks as if nothing will be done in accordance with etiquette. The king has spoken.

She will dress Arcadie slightly older than her actual age. It's nobody's business that she is only just sixteen. Almost sixteen, as her birthday is at the end of May. The gown must not be too striking. Silk seems perfect, in laurel green, the exact colour of Arcadie's eyes. And her blond hair put up for the first time, by Brussels' highly acclaimed hairdresser Frédéric. Her daughter, the most beautiful of all young women, created to be loved by a king. Henriette takes off her apron and hangs it in the shed. She has a task to accomplish. Jos, the stableman and coachman, must simply tell the farrier that he cannot come until tomorrow, since she needs the horses and the coupé.

*

That same day Henriette bribes the tall, thin dressmaker in the rue de la Montagne, by pressing several bank notes into her bony hand.

'Madame, I…'

'You must give priority to a gown for my daughter!' hisses

Henriette in a whisper, with a peevish look at the distinguished elderly lady in black sitting waiting in the drawing room. A girl, most probably her granddaughter or niece, is standing by the window leafing through a pattern book. Naturally she needs a dress too.

'That sunflower-yellow dress is no good.' Henriette's whispering sounds increasingly threatening. 'The shade is far too garish for a visit to the Palace. We need something new.'

The dressmaker towers so far above her that it seems as if the woman is on stilts.

'You are aware, madame, of what etiquette prescribes?' The woman looks down haughtily at Henriette. 'A new gown may be worn only after twelve months have elapsed.'

'As if I don't know that!' Henriette raises her delicate foot, covered in sky-blue satin, and brings it down again furiously. 'But what else am I to dress the child in? A skirt that comes halfway down her calves? She is developing fast and everything has become too small.'

'Well.' The dressmaker tucks the banknotes into the pocket of her apron, without deigning to look at the bribe. 'Just bring the young lady along with you. Do you also want something new for yourself, madame?'

The sarcastic tone does not escape Henriette. No, she does not want anything *new*. She'll make do with something *old*, something that has been hanging in her wardrobe since last spring.

'Madame,' she says to the distinguished lady in the drawing room. The girl and the dressmaker are given only a curt nod. She turns on her heel and goes downstairs with much angry clicking, after which the dressmaker bends her bony knees and runs her fingers over the parquet.

'Well, madame d'Ydeweel,' she says to the lady who is sitting waiting. 'Things have come to a pretty pass when such women are invited to court.'

*

On the evening of the musical recital, in the carriage on the way to the Palace, Charles is troubled by his digestion. He looks rather green and every so often gives a sour burp.

'Highly embarrassing,' says Henriette. Although she has impressed upon her husband that a supper will be served after the concert, he has still overeaten yet again during the evening meal.

As a soldier Charles cannot afford to become really fat and yet recently he has begun to put on a lot of weight around his waist. Henriette likes his large, portly body well enough. Her Charles, so manly and soft. She cannot be really strict on this point, since he has never made a single snide remark about her plumpness. But this evening she would nevertheless have liked him to be a little slimmer and more aristocratic. Just look how ponderously he sits on the seat. His feet firmly planted and thighs that spread out on the cushion as far as his trouser legs will allow. They are like hams.

'I do want to hear our neighbour play the violin,' says Charles. 'but otherwise I would have rather stayed at home.'

What a shame that as a woman you cannot accept a royal invitation, alone or with your children, because she would have been quite happy to leave her husband by the warm fire. Charles does not like going out after dinner. He is too attached to his quiet evenings at home for that: with a pipe and a glass of herb-flavoured gin, his stocking feet on the leather stool, listening to his daughters singing and playing the piano for him.

'It's only a stone's throw away, *chéri*,' says Henriette, pushing up her ringlets a little. The chambermaid has tried for more than an hour to get her hairdo into shape with a hot iron, but there is not much springiness in it. 'We're almost there.'

She turns to Arcadie to look her up and down.

'Keep absolutely still.'

She runs the tip of her forefinger over her daughter's cheeks to make the rouge she has applied vaguer. It must resemble a natural blush, because although almost all elegant women secretly use red on their cheeks and lips, they utterly condemn the practice in each other.

*

Exultant sounds fill the Empire room, the way deer and frolicking rabbits fill a clearing in the woods. The notes tumble over each other like romping young foxes. After the last elegant stroke across the strings, Charles de Bériot raises his bow theatrically in the air for a moment, lets its fall again, then lowers it, with his violin, head and shoulders, in a deep bow. His wavy hair is tousled when he rises; a lock of hair falls in front of his eyes, which leads the ladies especially to clap with even more enthusiasm. Wilfrid de Bériot, the *Wunderkind*, scarcely nine years old, slides cautiously off his piano stool, after which father and son take a joint bow.

In fact, the audience presents just as fascinating a sight as the charming violinist and his son. The gentlemen are in uniform or evening dress and the ladies are wearing satin and velvet robes and such long and multi-coloured feathers in their hair that anyone sitting behind them must behold the musical proceedings though exotic, occasionally slightly trembling vegetation. Noble acquaintances of the royal couple are present, as well as the French marquis de Rumigny (who it is said will be appointed ambassador in Brussels by Louis-Philippe before the year is out) and two generals and their wives. But whoever can that gentleman be with his strikingly large paunch, wonders a viscountess. Judging by the insignia of rank on his uniform he is only a major. And his wife—oh, *Seigneur*—what vulgarity! Her décolleté is so deep that her white, ample breasts threaten to fall out. Then the attention of the distinguished lady is attracted by two lackeys in pink livery who open the great doors. The long tables for supper appear!

Next to the major and madame Claret the charming Arcadie sits and quietly looks around her. The Palace is so completely different from what she had expected. All through her childhood she adored fairy tales, and imagined the Palace as a wondrous castle, with lavish Oriental carpets, a colourful jester playing tricks, enchantingly sweet drinks and a king seated on his throne, wrapped in an ermine cloak. But His Majesty is in uniform, like her father and many of the other guests. His chair and that of the queen are distinguished only by slightly heavier armrests. Although there are no angels hovering about playing on their lyres, she is most certainly excited, since after all she is in the Palace. The same palace at which she has so often looked through the windows of a coach, wondering what life inside might be like. Monsieur de Bériot's playing has made her almost drunk. And with what a grown-up air of concentration that boy plays the piano! But is young Wilfrid not coming in her direction? He shakes his blond curls with a gesture halfway between shyness and conceitedness.

'*Maman*,' says Arcadie softly to her mother. 'Look, there's Wilfrid. Is he coming to fetch me?'

Henriette smiles benignly, although she does not think much

of the self-satisfied brat and would like the king to pay some attention to her daughter. He has not even looked in her direction yet and is conversing with several elderly gentlemen. Every lady present under seventy chatters, giggles and fans herself in an attempt to attract his attention, but he ignores them. And this is the king who is accused of having a weakness for female charms? She can understand why he takes almost no notice of his wife. It is true what is said about her: she is not exactly a picture of health. Her heavy eyelids are like half-lowered draperies and her shoulders seem to be bearing all the world's suffering.

*

Charles Claret empties his second glass of champagne and is pleased as Punch. The golden liquid has settled his stomach and his appetite has returned. What a relief. In addition he is excited at having heard Monsieur de Bériot perform. Jolly fine violin playing. Not that he knows much about this kind of serious music—he prefers a pleasant waltz or a nice song (particularly if it's a melancholy song, the tears will be sure to come)— but Henriette is right: a man should regularly get out of his easy chair and acquire some culture. Monsieur de Bériot must be a great violinist, since otherwise he would not be allowed to play at court. Marvellous at any rate that the man is called Charles and comes from Elsene, like himself.

Aha, there goes Arcadie to the dining room on the arm of the little pianist. What a lovely picture they make! His dear daughter looks so grown up next to the boy and yet she herself is still only a child. A shame that she is not wearing her blond hair loose over her shoulders. Henriette insisted that Arcadie's hair should be worn up, but it is rather too old for her. And there goes Henriette, arm in arm with a tall skinny fellow. Bound to be a nobleman, just look how proud she is! Oh, where has that old frump got to who has been assigned to him as his dinner companion?

'So you've arrived at last, monsieur Claret!' There she sits, an elderly woman with large feet and a prominent nose. She pokes her walking stick almost in his crotch. 'Help me up.'

She hangs on his arm, and the material of her dress feels like tarpaulin. 'Monsieur Claret,' she says emphatically, raising her stick in the direction of the dining room to make it clear that he cannot first go and get another glass of champagne. 'I understand from the king that you work at the Ministry of War. You are treasurer of the Fund for Widows and Orphans of the Belgian Army.'

'I am,' he says, proud and surprised. But also on his guard, since he knows what will come next.

'Then we have a lot to discuss,' she says determinedly, pointing to their places at table. He is given a tap with her stick for not pushing back her seat quickly enough. 'A niece of mine—from the impoverished branch of our family, you see—has been waiting for six years already for the pension to which she is entitled as the widow of a soldier killed in action. He died when he rebelled heroically against the wave of Orangist looting.' Her words were fired at him like projectiles from a grapeshot cannon and he wishes he could flee. During grace he sees Henriette through his eyelashes at the other end of the table, her face all devotion. If only he were with her! Arcadie is sitting with the young Bériot opposite Henriette and the nobleman. At the top table the queen picks up her fork tentatively to try a mouthful of duck pâté. This marks the start of the meal. Charles half listens to his table companion and promises her that he will shortly note the names of the niece and her unfortunate husband. Luckily on his other side he has a fresh-faced young noblewoman, to whom he can tell heroic stories about his years in Napoleon's army. He is just taking his last spoonful of meringue when he notices that his daughter has disappeared.

XIV

'*Mademoiselle* Brontë?' Emily hears a girl's voice ask. She keeps her eyes fixed on her grammar book. Who in the world dares take it into her head to disturb her? She jerks her shoulders slightly like a falcon rearranging its feathers.

'Emily?'

Reluctantly she looks up. Standing next to her is Louise de Bassompierre, a girl of sixteen in the same class as her and Charlotte.

'What is it?' says Emily, and it sounds like the 'Go away!' you shout when you throw a glass of cold water at a cheeky cat. She closes her book because she hates people looking over her shoulder, but keeps her finger on the right page.

Young Louise is undeterred and sits down next to Emily at the table. It is seven in the evening. The dirty dishes from the evening meal have been cleared away and the other young ladies are sitting in the garden enjoying the mild spring evening. Louise takes a jug from the big tray on the table. She pours herself a bowl of chicory.

'Would you like some?'

Emily does not reply. No one has less need of food and drink than she does.

'*What?* What do you want from me?'

Louise stirs her steaming drink imperturbably with a spoon.

'I want to make you a proposal.'

She is a fresh-faced young thing, this Louise de Bassompierre, daughter of a baron, with eyes the colour of brown sugar. Eyes that have a somewhat melancholy expression, in sharp contrast with the rest of her appearance. She holds her head cocked slightly to one side and a dimple appears in her right cheek.

'Emily, you speak perfect English and I speak perfect French.'

'Not perfect,' says Emily. 'It is foolish and conceited to think such a thing. No one achieves perfection.'

'That is true.' Louise kicks off her embroidered slippers and pulls her feet under her bottom. 'But you have something that I don't have, and vice-versa. Believe me, you won't get it from your sister. I've heard you speaking French together.' She wrinkles her nose. 'It was really awful.'

Emily opens her book with a scarcely audible groan. But Louise gets up instantly in her stocking feet and shuts the book again in a rapid movement. There is a smile playing around her mouth and Emily is dumbstruck by such bravura.

'We can talk together, Emily. There's nothing wrong with that, is there? Half an hour of English a day and you correct me. And half an hour of French and I correct you.'

'No,' says Emily and puts her hand up to indicate that the conversation is over.

'Your knowledge of French will come on in leaps and bounds,' Louise persists. 'We'll start tomorrow. I'm not going home this Sunday anyway. Let's say two o'clock, not under the big pear-tree, but in the small summerhouse.' She slides her feet into her slippers and gives Emily's skinny upper arm a friendly squeeze.

'By the way why do you still wear those wide puffed sleeves? Your sister already has a new dress. Clever of her, since those sleeves are really out of fashion here.'

'I wish to be as God made me,' says Emily solemnly.

'Were you born with wings then?' Louise giggles, but there is no malice in her voice. She leaves the refectory with a full bowl of chicory and a big piece of spiced biscuit. Which is against madame's rules, since in order to avoid a plague of mice she has decided that not a crumb of food may be taken into the rest of the house.

*

That Sunday morning Constantin Heger drops in on Charlotte at breakfast. Without any decorum he steps over the wooden bench to be able to sit next to her. This impertinence causes Emily, across the table, to put down her cup with such a brusque gesture of disapproval that a splash of coffee spills over the edge. He does not notice, as he immediately starts drawing a plan with a pencil stump on a piece of brown wrapping paper. Claire has told him that Charlotte wants to pay a visit to a friend at the château of Koekelberg that day. And as sure as his name is Constantin Heger he won't let any of his protégées set out without a proper plan.

'This is the north of Brussels,' he says, 'with the rue de Laeken, you see. But you must go further left, to Molenbeek, look, and then like this to Koekelberg. You'll be passing right through the poorer districts, which is interesting, but not without its dangers. Be sure to take *meess* Emily with you.'

When Charlotte and Emily leave the boarding school to walk to the Protestant chapel for the morning service, Lena, the nanny, is already waiting for monsieur and madame with little Claire, Marie and Louise.

'The Catholics are off to their idolatrous mass again,' says Emily sharply and just a little too loudly. Charlotte casts a fleeting glance at Lena, but knows they have nothing to fear, since the girl does not understand a word of English. Anyway, she is just reprimanding Marie, as the child, squatting by the gutter, is trying to pull charms off her silver bracelet.

*

In the Chapelle Royale the introductory organ music lasts longer than is customary in other Protestant houses of worship. The reason is that King Leopold, as a devout Protestant, occasionally attends the service and as a result the vicar delays the start out of concern that His Majesty might still come in. The Brontë sisters have not yet seen the king and they are not going to that morning.

'Leo is hunting in the Ardennes,' whispers the panting sexton in the vicar's ear, breathless from his hurried walk to the Palace and back. Whereupon the organist can stop playing and the vicar reaches for his Bible.

The spring has driven the draughty chill out of the chapel and the vicar's French is sing-song and amiable, but Charlotte finds it difficult to keep her mind on the service. During the singing of the psalm she just moves her lips because she cannot find the text in her Bible and Emily does not seem to notice. When the Ten Commandments are read out she starts looking restlessly around her. There are a lot of Englishwomen in the congregation, and how badly dressed they are! Floppy capes, yellowy lace on their bonnets and absurdly wide collars, which make their heads look like pasties served on doilies. Belgian women dress so much better: simply, with fitted sleeves and small embroidered collars. In fact, her own dress is very modest and fashionable. At the beginning of March she was untrue to England by having a dress made in Brussels to a Parisian design. What is more, she bought bootees with narrow toes. All in all a considerable expense, and one which Emily has not yet forgiven her. Now comes the ninth commandment, but she does not want to hear. She takes off her gloves. The tenth commandment. She does not want to see the vicar and nevertheless finds herself looking at him. His hands are too white and too smooth to be powerful. His lips too moist, his voice too melodious.

'Thou shalt not covet thy neighbour's house; thou shalt not covet thy neighbour's wife, nor his manservant, nor his maid-servant, nor his ox nor his ass, nor any thing that is thy neighbour's.'

From his mouth it sounds like a children's rhyme, and yet he scans the faithful in the pews with a questioning look. *Thou shalt not covet any thing that is thy neighbour's.* She scarcely dares breathe. *Covet any thing that is thy neighbour's.*

After the service Emily wants to go back to the boarding school.

'I'll come with you to see Mary next time,' she says.

'You promised me!' whispers Charlotte in dismay. 'Are you letting me go all by myself?'

'I have other plans.'

'Other plans, I'm sure you have! You'll be sitting bent over your book all day again, I expect. You'll be getting a hunchback next.'

There goes Emily, stubborn as she is. She crosses the court-yard in front of the cathedral with great strides, her Bible dangling on a grubby ribbon against her skirt. For a moment Charlotte is at a loss what to do. Should she go after her sister or pursue her own plans? Emily looks vulnerable. She is wearing too few petticoats and her skirt sticks to her long skinny legs. Her bottom is as flat as that of a twelve-year-old boy. She has never eaten much, but since she has been in Brussels she has been starving herself.

Guilt softens Charlotte's heart: her sister needs her. But she cannot stand the idea of being shut up in the boarding school on a free Sunday. She has escaped and wants to wander in unfamiliar streets and follow winding country lanes. To go somewhere where she can daydream endlessly. She is more than just someone's daughter, more than just someone's sister.

*

The streets are full of people. It is a superb day at the end of March and it looks as if the whole population of Brussels has taken a long detour on the walk home from church. Charlotte turns her face upwards towards the sun. How pleasant its warmth is! Spring has only just arrived and it feels like summer. How good that she did not go back to the boarding school. Actually she does not mind too much that Emily is not coming with her. Today is a stolen day, a day just for her. She wonders if Anne feels homesick for the parsonage in Thorp Green? She herself does not at all, oh no! In his last letter papa wrote that Branwell is back home, because he has been dismissed from the railways; apparently some money disappeared from the till. It will probably be a nasty situation in the parsonage. No, she would rather be here. She likes Brussels very much. More than that: she is happy! She almost skips down the steps to the rue de la Madeleine. If they were dancing in a circle in a square somewhere, she would join in, round and round, to celebrate the spring, to celebrate the fact that she is not yet old and is being given another chance. In her mind she sees monsieur walking just one pace ahead of her. His broad, muscular neck, his curly hair just a fraction too long. She can almost smell his scent.

Spring has burst out in the rue de la Madeleine, which with

its colourful shop windows and ladies in flowery dresses is reminiscent of madame Heger's garden, full of blossoming fruit trees in white and red with the first tulips at their feet. The gentlemen are more sober, but also carefully dressed, a haven of calm in this explosion of jollity. The children run cheerfully ahead and twice Charlotte has to step off the pavement because a nanny is blocking her path with an enormous baby carriage. Here and there, scarves are removed and capes are unbuttoned.

Her own dress is grey. A softly mother-of-pearl grey, it is true, and for the first time in her life she feels not that displeased with her appearance. Still, she is not of a tall, voluptuous build, like most Belgian ladies. They are beautiful women with round, marble faces, so lacking in any frown or crease that they have almost no expression. Full lips, which Branwell would undoubtedly say are made for kissing. English women are just like starlings, banal in colouring, impudent and nervous, whereas Belgian women can be compared rather with geese, plump and white, their backsides swaying. She wishes she were like that herself. If only there were a bit more flesh on her bones. Perhaps there is hope; perhaps she has a beauty all of her own and can also excite love. Nothing seems impossible when the sun is shining like this. She buys a punnet of strawberries from a stall. Scandalously expensive, but it means she won't have to meet Mary empty-handed. She savours one strawberry as it melts in her mouth.

After the elegant streets she comes to the neat streets. Some families here have a young servant to help with the heavy work, but most people get down on their hands and knees to pull up the weeds between the cobbles outside their front door. It's a matter of doing one's best to maintain one's dignity. Genteel poverty, not so far beneath her own class. Here too there are families out walking. Father with a young child on his shoulders. Mother with her youngest on her arm or in a rickety pram. The older children freshly washed, parting on the right and quiff short. Straight out of church and free of sin. Because if you are Catholic, you can always go to confession. And after confession, you are cleansed. You don't even have to show your face to the Lord to ask His forgiveness. The priest fixes it for you. She feels intense annoyance rising in her. How strange that monsieur is a devout Catholic.

She had thought that it would be quieter in the workers' districts. Poor, silent streets, where misery hides behind bleak walls. But the sun shines here too, and here too the inhabitants want to be outside. Workmen pass her, their greasy hair combed for the occasion. Cheered up by the sunny weather, but with dull eyes and pale lips from last night's gin and beer. Young women walk arm in arm, giggling and ogling the men. She is pleased with her grey dress, her brown cape and her bonnet without silk flowers. She could pass for a seamstress or a primary schoolteacher, or perhaps even for the wife of a local doctor or pharmacist. A respectable woman who as she passes almost merges with the Brussels décor. A city as a stage for a new phase in her life. A new chamber in her heart.

She scrupulously follows the route drawn for her by her master. She does not dare run her finger over the sketch, for fear of erasing the pencil lines. Not that she is frightened of going astray, but she does not want to lose the work of his hands. No one knows her here, no one can guess her thoughts. Her secret is safe. But when a pretty wench, proud despite her clogs and her patched dress, passes her, Charlotte begins to doubt. This is a woman who is definitely cherishing one or more real secrets. A silent admirer or perhaps even a proposal she is considering. But what secret can she, little, short-sighted Charlotte have?

She mustn't delude herself. It is just foolishness, a delusion that came about because she is lonely and her master lives within the same high walls, sleeps and eats so close to her, and even sires children.

*

The moment that Charlotte walks onto the quai des Tourbes, she sees a man some way off standing on the bridge over the Zenne. He is leaning with his back against the balustrade and seems to be lost in thought or waiting for something. It makes a nice picture: the silhouette of a man on a bridge with two flat blue barges moored on the canal behind him. A touch of beauty in an unpleasant area. It is like a masterly painting hung on a grey factory wall. The lighting is exceptional, because the sun is just breaking through a couple of airy clouds, creating a fan of bright rays. The closer she gets to the bridge, she is seized by a feeling of recognition. The man bends forward and seems to be looking for something in his trouser pockets. When he straightens up again, she is sure: it is Emile, the workman she saw at monsieur's evening class. Her hand goes involuntarily to her plaits: are they still in place? She would most like to turn tail and walk away. She can also walk straight on, without crossing the bridge, and pretend she has not seen him. There is bound to be another bridge over the canal further on.

Although she is not as withdrawn as her sister, there is still something introverted about her. It would not be the first time that she pretended not to see an acquaintance or even someone she knew well and walked on by, simply to avoid a conversation. But Emile has noticed her. Out of the corner of her eye she sees him coming to her side of the bridge. She has a momentary impulse to ignore him completely, but she cannot afford such rudeness. Imagine if Emile complained about her to monsieur Heger. A sick, giddy feeling wells up in her.

'What a surprise!' She hears his voice, but looks at his shoes. If you were to give them a rub with some grease they would look a lot better.

'I'm startin' to believe that you 'ave a predilection for dirty parts of town, *mam'selle.*'

That comment makes her shudder, as she hates sarcasm. For years she has been trying to eliminate that bitter humour in Emily, to no effect. The sarcasm of an unskilled worker is really unbearable. *Unskilled, unskilled.* The word is still buzzing in her head when she finally plucks up courage to look him in the face. And then it goes quiet. The man is an angel.

There are yellowish smudges on his shirt, possibly because the soap was not rinsed out properly, and his braces are frayed. Charlotte sees so much that she could disapprove of. And yet. The man seems to emanate light, as only young, utterly pure children can do. His skin is clear and has a shine to it, although there is a dirty smudge in his neck. He takes his hat off gallantly and shakes his long, unkempt hair.

'Oh,' she says. 'Where do I know you from?'

How presumptuous and false that sounds. Of course he knows that she noticed him, not only just now, but also during the evening class. Surely he knows how attractive he is? But then why does he look at the ground in such a cowed way and wipe the back of his hand across his lips? Emile. It's a nice name; it sounds like Emily.

'Emile,' she says. 'How could I forget?'

She realises that she cannot just pass him with a greeting and a dry nod. He obviously wants to talk to her. What is the situation with etiquette here? Surely you cannot just stand chatting in the street with a complete stranger? Of course he is not a complete stranger, that's not the point. After all she met him in the company of her master. Incidentally, monsieur advised her to talk to workers and ask them about their family life and their working conditions. That would not only be good for her education, he felt, but they would enjoy the attention of a cultivated young woman.

Emile rubs some dust from his hat and pushes it back on his head with the flat of his hand.

'Are those strawberries?' he asks in amazement. He comes so close to her that he almost bumps into the punnet. 'So early in spring.'

'They're from a greenhouse,' says Charlotte. 'It's a present. I'm visiting a friend.'

She automatically transfers the punnet to her other hand, but that makes it look as if she is frightened he will steal the fruit.

She gives him a fleeting sidelong glance. He has a generous mouth and his top lip curls slightly upward. She would like them to be together in the Warande Park, sitting on a bench under the chestnut trees. Or better still in the foyer of the theatre, deep in conversation. She wishes he were well dressed, a gentleman. What is an angel doing in such shabby clothes?

'Are you here for your work, Emile?'

'On a Sunday?' he asks mockingly. 'No, *mam'selle*, even slaves 'ave Sunday off. I've come to say good bye to a comrade who's leavin' for Verapas. Perhaps I should go with him.'

That awakens her curiosity, because where in heaven's name is Verapas? But she does not want to be seen as ignorant and says nothing. He sticks his hands in his pockets and kicks a small red beetroot ahead of him that has obviously fallen off a cart.

'Is that friend of yours at school in the château of Koekelberg? There are lots of English girls.'

And when she says 'mm' in confirmation, he asks: 'Shall I walk with you a bit of the way?'

'If you've nothing better to do.' Oh, what a bossy tone she takes. In that way she's bound to give him the feeling that he's no more than a stupid worker.

'I'd like it if you would walk with me,' she says quickly. He runs his finger over his moustache and smiles, which gives his face a tender expression. Does he perhaps think she is making advances?

'Monsieur Heger says that in order really to get to know Brussels, I should also meet a few workers.' She is immediately sorry that she couldn't find anything better than the word 'worker', although that may have a less negative emotional charge for him. 'He wants me to get to know your living conditions.'

'You're not rich yourself,' says Emile, and she stops for a moment in bewilderment. His shoulders are heaving under the faded brown canvas of his coat.

'I mean you're not as rich as the Hegers and their stuck-up pupils. Those girls don't come here, our smell alone makes them sick. Doesn't our smell make you sick, *mam'selle*?'

His voice sounds hard. He hates her.

'Tell me something about your work,' she says, mechanically in the tone in which you talk to a poor weaver or a washerwoman. It is not an unpleasant smell that prompts her to do this, because though she does her best to smell him, she cannot. She has not seen a better-looking man in Brussels than Emile and although he speaks French with a strange, thick accent, he does not sound coarse. What would it be like if he took hold of her hand? If his were warm and firm, would she be able to let go of it?

'I'm in the rag trade.' He does not look away, no, on the contrary, she feels his gaze resting inquiringly on her face. Now she must not pull a face in distaste. 'What d'you want to know about it? One franc and thirty centimes a day. Eight of us live in a workers' house on an islet near the barracks.'

He is not married. He has no children.

'What does your father do?'

There goes the beetroot again, a rather harder kick this time. It rolls under a rowing boat with flaking red paint lying upside down on the quay.

'My father worked himself to death. At the end of the twenties he was earnin' two francs a day in a Ghent cotton mill. A good wage, but when that Leopold came, it dropped to sixty-two centimes. You cannot support a family on sixty-two centimes.'

Emile stops in order to fill his pipe. She would like to know how old he is. Or rather not, as he might be younger than she is.

'My father lives on what my brothers and I give him,' he says. 'There's no future in this country. It was better under the Hollanders.'

'You must learn French, Emile,' says Charlotte, since according to monsieur that is the only way for a Flemish worker to escape misery.

'What are we speaking now then? I follow French classes with Heger to be able to understand the boss, 'cause otherwise I can't be a foreman.'

'I mean speaking properly, without an accent. And writing it fluently. You must learn to write letters without mistakes.'

A hint of irritation passes across his handsome face.

'The language of the oppressor,' he says. 'The language of the men who make us work like beasts. You don't know what you're talking about, *mam'selle*.'

She starts at so much passion.

'Flanders was once a rich and powerful region. What does an Englishwoman know about the Flemings and the French-speaking bourgeoisie?'

'There are lots of sharp-witted, well-read men among the French speakers of Brussels,' she says soothingly. 'The Flemings certainly seem fine people, but...'

He stops so abruptly that she does not dare to continue. 'You really are too intelligent to believe somethin' like that. Does that nonsense come from your master?'

He sounds like a young man from a good family challenging someone who has insulted his honour. Suddenly he jumps onto a bollard, doffs his hat with style and makes a deep bow.

'This is the partin' of the ways, *mam'selle*. But we'll see each other again, you can be sure of that.'

It sounds so loud and theatrical that a couple of elderly fishermen on the other bank look up from their rods.

*

She leaves Koekelberg much too late. Mary and Martha wanted to show her the whole estate and they walked through the grounds arm in arm, with Charlotte in the middle. On the way she was introduced to young women who spoke her native language, but they had to converse in a whisper, since within the domain only French was permitted. A strict rule by which Emily and she are fortunately not burdened in the Pensionnat Heger.

The Taylor sisters provide pleasant company as they stroll with her to the church of Sint-Jans-Molenbeek. It is already nearly eight o'clock before Charlotte is properly on her way. She is disappointed, since she has not had Mary to herself for a moment. They chatted for hours, but she wasn't able to tell her anything about her secret. Monsieur! She must be able to share it with someone. She might possibly also have revealed something about Emile. The image of monsieur Heger that she carries with her—his masculine face in a patch of yellowish gaslight is disturbed by the memory, still fresh, of Emile on the bridge. The sudden appearance of the workman and his equally sudden departure have created confusion in her. But there is no opportunity to discuss this with a friend, and you cannot entrust such delicate matters to a letter.

Charlotte hurries through the fields and the sky has long, dark-grey clouds, not really lowering, and a few violent yellow streaks on the horizon. By the time she reaches the boulevard around Brussels, dusk is falling fast. She hurries through the streets, but is overtaken by darkness. Here and there she finds an illuminated square or a street with a few lamps, but she loses the way. Heart beating, she goes on, with her tread firm so as not to give passers-by the impression that she is lost. A dog follows her for a while, and then a child pestering her for bread in a whining voice. She does not know how much time passes. When she reaches the gate of the boarding school, Gertrude is just coming out with a shawl over her head and shoulders. Her blond hair is in a careless plait and she is not wearing her uniform, which can only mean that she has been called from her bed and has got ready in a hurry.

'*Mam'selle* Charlotte, oh, *mam'selle*,' she stammers. 'I'm going to fetch the midwife—madame's in labour.'

Charlotte walks through the dark garden and hears two girls giggling. She stops for a moment and stares at the trees and bushes, but has no wish to ask who is there. She herself is also back far too late, and she does not want mademoiselle Blanche to hear her. In the carré she sits on the bottom step and takes off her lace-up boots. Her feet are swollen and she massages a painful toe. Wearily she rests her face against the wall. Monsieur is somewhere behind that wall. What do men do when their wife is giving birth? He is most probably pacing through the drawing rooms. She takes her cape off and unties the ribbons of her bonnet. Perhaps she may see him if she waits for a moment. He'll be bound to come and see where the midwife has got to. But then she hears footsteps behind the French windows on the terrace; she takes her cape and boots, and goes upstairs as quickly and silently as possible.

In the dormitory only the night candle is alight and she almost has to feel her way along. For the last few days they have been instructed that everyone must close the drapes around their bed, but Emily's are still open. She's not in bed! Charlotte lights her candle and looks around her. Where in heaven's name is Emily? She really cannot ever leave her alone. Just as she is about to go looking for her, there is a cautious stumbling sound and two ghosts in nightdresses and shawls enter the dormitory.

'Where have you been?' whispers Charlotte in dismay when Emily throws her shawl on the floor in front of the wardrobe.

'You'd really like to know, wouldn't you?'

'Emily!'

'It's all right,' says her sister. 'I've been telling ghost stories on the forbidden path.' She motions with her chin towards the girl who has withdrawn to a bed on the far side of the room. 'To Louise de Bassompierre.'

'The one with curls in our class. How old is that child—sixteen?'

'*Silence*,' hisses an angry, sleepy voice. Charlotte holds up her candle and sees Emily vaguely smiling—which is very unusual.

*

That night Charlotte is startled from sleep by a baby crying. The cries are no more than a wisp of sound, like the whining of a cat on heat. She sits up and listens intently. A new-born child! There are voices downstairs in the carré. A painful feeling constricts her chest. But it is of course possible that madame has died—in fact, the chance is considerable. How many women die in childbirth? And if she is alive, then for God's sake don't let her have given birth to a boy. Let it be a girl. In a sudden movement Charlotte kneels on the bed and puts her hands together. Oh, how wicked she is! How can she cherish such deplorable wishes? O Lord, lead me back to your flock!

Only when she gets very cold does she lie down and pull the blanket round her like a safe cocoon within which nothing can reach her. Her prayer lacks force. It becomes pleasantly warm and she puts her hand under her nightdress, strokes her belly and touches the soft flesh between her legs. Would she be capable of giving monsieur a son?

XV

'This is who I am,' says Emily firmly, and spreads her large, freckled hands in front of her on his desk. 'Don't ask me to play the hypocrite, not even for a *devoir*.'

She pronounces the last word as if it is green and slippery and ignores Charlotte's angry shoe against her shinbone.

Constantin stares at her with growing irritation. The stubbornness of this woman cannot be broken. With another pupil he would fly into an enormous rage, but with this Englishwoman there is no point: she is not afraid. Her intelligence is close to that of a genius, and that cannot be tamed. She is more obstinate than the cat her essay describes. His eyes glide hastily over the sheet in his hand. Where was it?

'"The cat does not tear what it wants from its master's hand,"' he quotes. '"It stretches out a paw, soft as down. But as soon as it has what it wants, it reverts to its role of Timon of Athens. The cunning that goes hand in hand with this is called hypocrisy!"'

'A characteristic you cannot accuse me of in any case,' says Emily.

Her eyes, beneath the white eyelids with ginger lashes, scan his desk with a look full of contempt. Her sharp nose, longer than ever, is like a piercing weapon. It's a mess, he knows that. Piles of homework that still have to be marked, literary French books, the menu of the annual dinner of the Saint-Vincent de Paul Society, a dirty sheet of blotting paper and an inkwell surrounded by stains that have penetrated the wood.

'What's this I read?' He focuses his attention on the essay and makes a movement with his free hand, an empty sweep. '*Par pure affection! À son dernier soupir!* Those are French equivalents for English expressions and I cannot tolerate them. You must look for appropriate French idioms.'

Nevertheless he admires her intensely. The essay is strangely fluent when you consider that she has been here for only three months. But obvious rebelliousness lurks in every sentence.

'My spelling is good,' says Emily unperturbed.

He turns around to the floor-to-ceiling bookcase. However, the volume he wants take hold of is too high. He cannot reach it and hears a chair being pushed along. That must be Emily wanting to help him. She could probably do so, since she is just taller than he is, but he waves her away without looking round. Balancing high on tiptoe, with the muscles in his right arm painfully at full stretch, he manages to manoeuvre the book out from between two others.

'Let me look it up. The cat in the *Histoire Naturelle*.' He licks the tip of his forefinger and leaves agitatedly through the work. 'We analysed and discussed this essay. Then you were supposed to set your own thoughts down on paper in the same style. That was the assignment: the same style, *meess* Emily! I don't detect any biting sarcasm in Count de Buffon's work. And certainly no misanthropy.'

'You know that I don't believe in your method,' says Emily. 'When Charlotte and I imitate your writers, we lose the originality of our ideas and expression. I cannot allow that. My sister has a great creative talent and that must not be restricted. I... '

'*Meess* Emily!' Heger brings his fist down, but draws it back just before it touches the table top. 'I understand what you are trying to say. Please keep your opinions to yourself in future.'

He turns to Charlotte with a compelling look in which the fire is still smouldering.

'I... I'm not completely convinced of the advantages of your method, monsieur,' Charlotte manages to say with a great effort. 'My sister and I have a natural bent for literature, and that cannot be poured into other people's moulds.' She hesitates, but then raises her chin and says: 'You like simplicity, a sparse use of adjectives and, how do you always put it, a "merciless scrapping of what does not contribute to the story", whereas my style is more flamboyant. But I do as you wish. I am here to learn and you are my master.' She looks at him. 'My devotion is complete.'

Emily snorts audibly like a horse.

'Well, come on, off you go,' he says wearily. 'Enough for today.'

Emily leaves without a greeting, but Charlotte lingers by the door.

'Your sister should have been a man.' He clears his throat and plucks meditatively at the loose skin under his chin. 'A great navigator. That domineering will of her does not shrink from adversity or difficulties.'

'Oh, she'll undoubtedly come and apologise, monsieur!' Charlotte exclaims in alarm.

'She'd rather die than give in,' says Constantin and sees his devoted pupil with her touchingly earnest face disappear swiftly into the corridor.

*

During the evening meal the concierge comes to fetch Charlotte from the refectory. She is never that pleased to see Gertrude, because with her girlish innocence and firm bosom she is a symbol of all the temptations to which monsieur Heger is exposed. But Gertrude, with a mysterious smile, takes her firmly by the hand and pulls her along to the carré. In her dark little lodge under the stairs she produces a letter from somewhere among the folds of her skirt.

'From Emile,' she whispers conspiratorially. Charlotte again feels that ethereal, confused feeling going to her head that always seems to come over her whenever the handsome workman is mentioned. Gertrude thrusts the letter folded double into her hand and gives her a confidential pinch in her upper arm.

On her bed Charlotte unfolds the letter. There is one sheet, from the look of it a letter, and a short note in which he expresses his admiration for her knowledge of language and asks her to translate the letter into English for him. In disappointment she lowers the letter into her lap. What had she expected then? A declaration of love? As if a handsome workman would beg for a kiss from an old maid. He requires practical help from her. She skims through the letter. Thank God it is not a proposal or something similar. In her imagination she sees him kneeling before that proud wench in her patched dress and clogs who had attracted her attention during her walk through the city. Or before Little Nell from *The Old Curiosity Shop*: desperately poor, but pretty as a picture, with big dark eyes in an innocent little face.

Emile has plans to move to the little town of Green Way in the American state of Wisconsin and is asking the mayor to find work for him. His handwriting is unpractised, like that of a school child, with letters formed with frenetic accuracy on lines drawn in pencil, and his spelling is full of mistakes, but she can follow what he has to say.

She stuffs the letter between the pages of a book and decides to give it her attention later. Emile will have to wait, because monsieur is expecting another essay from her. Why do a translation, when she can write splendid sentences for her master?

She lets herself fall back on her bed. Sunbeams are dancing their way through the open windows with the waving linen curtains and conjure a magic play of light on the white beds. Monsieur. She loves him.

Downstairs in the carré Lena the nanny is ready to take the Hegers' two-month-old son out for a walk. Lena has a strange round forehead and the podgy hands and wrists of the maid who eats too much porridge.

'Isn't Prospère delicious?' she says, as proud as if it were her own baby. She holds the edge of his crocheted cap aside a little, so that Charlotte can see his white cheeks and bright eyes. Hazelnut-coloured eyes, like madame's.

Outside she sits on a block of wood, her face raised towards the sun. A pagan prayer to Helios' radiant sun chariot. *Let Claire Heger die.* Madame is healthy, but that can change. Cholera regularly rages in the streets of Brussels. And cholera does its work quickly. Gertrude has told her that monsieur was already married as a young man, but that his wife succumbed to cholera after scarcely three years of marriage. The disease also claimed the life of their son. These things happen. Madame has received an ample share of earthly happiness. She is married to an excellent man. He has made love to her and she has been privileged to bear his children. In what luxury she lives: a mansion, a magical garden, a school of her own. Not a ramshackle shed for poor people's children, but a boarding school for well-to-do ladies. Madame is so spoilt. Let there be an end to it, that's enough. Give *her* a chance. She is perfectly able to take madame's place. More than that: she would fulfil her role so much better. She may not have the outward charms of madame, but with her superior intellectual abilities she is far better suited to monsieur. Madame bores him, that is quite obvious.

She will take over the care for her husband, her children and her school. *Let him mourn.* She is healthy and young, and will wait for him. When the prescribed period of mourning is over, monsieur will marry her.

When Charlotte hears the gardener's boy coming up the path whistling a popular tune, she opens her eyes in alarm. What devilish words is she sitting murmuring here? How did things reach this point with her? Lord, Lord, save me! She must forget him. He belongs to someone else.

XVI

Close your eyes to recover from all those violent emotions. When you open them again, you are in more serene surroundings: the Palace of Ostend, in Her Majesty's bedroom no less.

Louise-Marie is half sitting up and is carefully drinking a spoonful of her hot bouillon. Her hand looks almost too weak to hold the spoon and her wrist is so narrow that she could wear the silver napkin ring round it. Her Majesty is ill—*yet again*, we can say. She is so fragile in body and mind that she is not cut out to be queen. Her little tulip head seems almost to collapse on its stalk under the weight of a crown or a tiara. Although she is a daughter of Louis-Philippe, *roi des Français*, and her upbringing in Versailles prepared her for marriage to a king, she would have preferred to enter the convent. Let us speak about this in a whisper, since she has never confessed this to her husband. Leopold is goodness itself and her three surviving children are healthy and have a pleasant appearance, so what right does she have to dream of another existence? And yet, and yet.

The chambermaid takes the bowl, still half-full, and Louise-Marie sinks into the soft pillows. Behind her closed eyelids she sees the high gate of the convent. A convent just outside Paris, which she visited with her mother when she was fourteen. It was so peaceful there. While her mother had an interview with the mother superior, she strolled through the cloister and in the garden and heard a blackbird singing, high in a fruit tree, clear and slightly melancholy. She would have liked to stay in that peaceful place, but an hour later she was sitting next her mother in the coach again, on her way back to worldly Versailles. If her father had given his consent, she would have gone into the convent. Then she would have been a nun now, *une soeur* with soft hands, growing sage, lemon balm and verbena and reading the Bible aloud in a room smelling of lavender to ladies who have come to find temporary respite in the convent. Thanks to a generous dowry from her father she would certainly have been spared teaching noisy and often very recalcitrant young girls and the distribution of bread to the poor. Oh, don't misunderstand her, the good soul! She would have ordered cartloads of bread—but would have left it to the other sisters to thrust a loaf into the hands of the toothless old woman, the old soldier who has lost his mind and the barefoot child, since she finds it hard to bear contact with the ugly, sick or poor.

Ah, the smells of the convent garden. The song of the blackbird, interwoven with the soft rustle of the trees. Her pointed face relaxes at the memory. If she is ever depicted with a dog's head in an English cartoon, the artist will definitely assign her the narrow head of the Polish greyhound. Large moist eyes in which eternal sadness can be read; ears down, like her ringlets; the long, virginal neck.

*

Leopold cannot bring himself to stay for long in the mansion in the Langestraat in Ostend. He feels like a hunting dog on a chain on a windy day. The housekeeper serves him coffee, although the woman must know by now that his liver cannot take it. He wants *tea*, camomile tea, like his mother used to have served in the nursery at Ehrenburg. He is given a cup of black tea, too strong and with a film on top. He leafs through his newspaper and throws it on the ground.

It annoys him that Louise-Marie wanted to come to Ostend.

Of course he couldn't let her travel alone, but for him there is nothing to do here. Her presence makes it impossible to meet ladies. And then this house: why did he rent it so impulsively seven years ago? At court it is called 'the Royal Palace of Ostend', but that is ridiculous hyperbole. It may have briefly been Napoleon's headquarters, but it is no more than a comfortable bourgeois house, unworthy of a royal couple. The day will come when he commissions a magnificent wooden chalet for his family, in the dunes, completely hidden from the prying eyes of curious passers-by. But Louise-Marie regards this house—or rather her bedroom here on the first floor—as a refuge, and when they arrived she immediately withdrew. She must find it reassuring that the house has so few rooms, her room is small and there is a walled garden. There are fewer staff and so fewer people come and ask what madame wants them to do. She has to rest: the housekeeper has been given orders not to disturb her. She does not eat much: bouillon, rusks, a stewed pigeon with some asparagus. No wine, but the elderflower drink that an aunt sends her from Versailles. Louise once gave him a glass to taste and he liked it. A vague melancholy seizes him. *Ma petite femme*, where are the days when you came to the beach with me?

This sombre place does not do him any good. It is not very probable that Louise-Marie will come down today. And so he might as well go out. He leaves the house to have lunch at the Hôtel La Cour Impériale. The oysters taste wonderfully of the sea and the champagne makes him light-headed, but he still cannot manage to laugh at the corny anecdotes of Mayor Serruys, whose company he endures for want of anything better. The man obviously thinks he must amuse his king like a medieval court jester.

How can he escape? Should he return to Brussels? But there

he is watched by that ever-vigilant policeman Jules Van Praet. This country irritates him. The food, the language. He longs to speak German. He lacks—dammit, he lacks a wife! If only he were an Arab; then he could take another bride. A shudder goes through him and he throws his napkin abruptly on the table, which makes the mayor tug his flaxen goatee in alarm.

Leopold pushes his chair back. It becomes clear to him what he has to do. He will go to Brussels and in a few days travel to Wiesbaden. And there he must and will see the lovely Arcadie.

*

'*Chérie*, I have to go.'

Leopold has run upstairs and entered his wife's bedroom, without giving the lady-in-waiting sitting embroidering outside the door the chance to warn her. Louise-Marie looks up from the book in her hands with a bewildered smile in her blue doll's eyes.

'Duty calls,' says Leopold. 'I shall miss you so.' The last statement is a lie. He cares about her, but like a brother cares for his younger sister, and one can easily do without that for a few weeks.

'*Je t'aime*,' he says, and while those words are still hanging in the air, he realises that this is the last time he will say such a thing to her. He kisses her lips, which are thin and completely unresponsive.

'My dear husband,' she says with genuine tenderness, but he knows that she will be relieved when he is gone. The fact is that she prefers to be alone, with a lady-in-waiting and occasionally one of her children for company. Their little Charlotte will arrive this afternoon with her nanny.

He sits up and fleetingly reads a sentence from the book on

her lap: 'Ugly as was the beating she received, so beautiful was she in the eyes of God.' She is reading another saint's life. Who is it about this time? Theresa of Jesus or Catharina of Cardona? Half-witted women who chastised themselves with whips and wore iron chains that cut into their flesh. He shudders at the religious fanaticism in which his wife loses herself. She seems to be fading before his eyes like an old print, made with poor-quality ink. He hurriedly bends forward to embrace her again, as if to make sure she really is still there. At that very moment she looks away because there is a knock at the door and his kiss lands in her neck. She does not seem to have a smell, like bones that have lain for years in the desert sand.

The bishop of Bruges is announced for a visit to Her Majesty. He is waiting downstairs in the drawing room and Leopold is able to avoid him by quickly leaving the house. With a sigh he pulls the door shut behind him with his own hands. His cases are just being loaded onto the coach and the horses have been harnessed. He is free, free! A lackey folds down the step. He is the king.

*

'Arcadie!' calls Henriette, waving with her white silk shawl from the comfortable depth of a garden bench covered in cushions under a roof of wisteria. 'Are you feeling all right? You've been looking so pale for the past few days. And last night I actually heard you coughing.'

The way her daughter is standing there on the grass—bouncing on her bare feet, legs slightly apart and arms half raised, ready to throw the ball to her sisters—she looks as frisky and vital as a young mare in a meadow full of daisies. But a person must know how to use a white lie when required.

'*Maman*,' says Arcadie casually and takes several sideways steps towards her mother as she throws the ball up and up. 'There's nothing wrong with me.'

Henriette gets up off the garden bench, which under normal circumstances she would have put off for least an hour. But the maid has just brought an urgent and especially exciting missive from the Palace, which is now hidden in a garter under her skirts.

'I think you urgently need to get away from it all, *mon petit chou*.'

She peers through her eyelashes at her lovely daughter, who seems to be moving in a bubble of soft golden spring light. Once the girl is in front of her, she pinches one cheek hard, the way one does with a weak child to put some colour into its cheeks.

'You've got to breathe in healthy air, go to the woods. Or do you know what? A cure at a spring! I could take you with me to a spa.'

'Oh, *maman*, can we come too?' cry her younger daughters in unison.

'No,' says Henriette, baring her large white teeth like a hungry rodent. 'Pauline, you're too young for the springs, and you Henriette, you know that you must get rid of that tummy before you can do any more nice things. Chase that ball a bit faster, will you?'

But there is no ball to chase after, because Arcadie is so bewildered that she is clutching it to her chest with her arms. Does her mother really want to take her to a *spa*? In the romantic novels she secretly reads spas are populated by elegant ladies and mysterious, handsome gentlemen. Oh, how marvellous it would be to go! She lets little Henriette pull the ball out of her hands and stares straight ahead. Of course it would mean that for a while she would no longer be able to meet monsieur Jacques under the big lime tree. But that can do no harm, since according to Chloé you should make boys wait; then they start longing for you and they are prepared to do absolutely everything for you. 'It's the same as with your sister and sweet things,' Chloé explained to her. 'If your cook does not have time to make *mousse au chocolat*, plump Henriette will promise her anything to persuade her.'

Arcadie coughs. And then again. In a few years' time she will definitely marry Jacques and they'll have five lovely children. But first she wants to kiss another boy occasionally.

'You see, Arcadie,' coos her mother with satisfaction, and hugs her daughter. 'You have a cold on the chest, poor dear. We're going to Wiesbaden.'

*

'What nonsense,' says Charles. He is sitting in his comfortable armchair by the fire, into which he has flopped to smoke his pipe and to rest his painful back a little. He really does not need any troublesome questions. 'Just look at our daughter! She's a picture of health. She does not need to go to Wiesbaden at all.'

Arcadie is standing in front of him with her hands on her back. For the first time her neat schoolgirl's plaits no longer suit her so well, since she seems to have acquired feminine charms overnight. In her sleeveless dress, too tight under the armpits and with a skirt that comes only halfway down her calves, she looks as delightful as a little whipped cream cake bulging over the edge of its lace paper. Henriette opens her red, full lips to protest, but cannot think of anything credible so quickly and gasps for air. She does not give up as easily as that!

'Arcadie, *mon enfant*, leave us alone,' she says theatrically. As soon as the door is closed, she sits down on the armrest near her husband, puts a hand on her heart (also the start of her voluptuous bosom) and looks at him earnestly.

'Charles, you must listen to me.' Not a trace of a smile on her face, and only a momentary seductive pout. 'Let me tell you why I really want to take Arcadie to Wiesbaden. You have a sharp eye. It's true: there's nothing wrong with her. But Charles, there is a man lurking about.'

Charles takes the pipe out if his mouth and stares at her.

'Do you mean the king?' he asks in dismay. 'Has he approached her? I had a suspicion that the man was not to be trusted around women. *Sacrebleu!*' He struggles to sit more upright and his double chins go red in succession. 'When Arcadie simply disappeared during that supper at the Palace I worried myself silly about it. He wanted to listen to her piano playing undisturbed, did he? Just an excuse to be able to ogle her.'

Henriette waves away what he has said impatiently. 'No, no, no! It's the piano teacher, that Jacques.'

Charles raises his eyebrows in disbelief. 'Surely not, he was a nice young chap, wasn't he? I thought it was strange that you dismissed him. Good references too, from our neighbours I seem to remember.'

'A rogue is what he is.' With a sigh Henriette puts the back of her hand on her forehead. 'Oh, Charles, how could I ever bring him into the house? You know I have a big heart and believe the best of people. Only when his true intentions became crystal clear did I dismiss him. It was weeks ago, but too late! Our daughter's head had already been turned: she went walking with him. Jos saw them near the bench under the lime tree. Jacques was holding her hand.'

'Perhaps his intentions are honourable.'

'Do you really think so, Charles? Has he visited you to ask for her hand? Have you received a communication from him?' She puts her hands triumphantly on her hips.

'He plans to dishonour our daughter somewhere in the woods.'

'*Mon Dieu,*' says Charles, now somewhat alarmed after all. He puts his pipe on the ashtray and stretches out his arms to his wife. 'How could I be so blind? My darling, what would I do without you?' He pulls her onto his lap, but she remains stiff.

'Don't be angry, Henriette.' He presses into the soft skin of her décolleté with his fingertip, as if making depressions in a pastry before it goes into the oven. 'You're right, my angel. There's nothing else for it. Take her with you to Wiesbaden, so she can forget that young man. But the expense, oh dear...'

'Charles, you silly man!' exclaims Henriette. 'If our daughter's name is sullied, no respectable man will want to marry her. Then we'll be liable for her maintenance. And do you want her to drag out her days in a convent?'

'No, no!' whispers Charles heatedly. 'Don't even talk about it. Arcadie has the right to a husband who adores her and she was born to be a mother. Take her to Wiesbaden. For as long as you think necessary.'

XVII

During monsieur Chapelle's music lesson madame Heger sometimes likes to come and perform a song. She stands next to the piano, arranges some curls around her face and sways to and fro to the melody until the moment has come for her to start singing. Madame is at her most beautiful when she sings, more beautiful than the young protégées standing around her: a chestnut tree in full bloom amid puny birch saplings. Her voice is somewhat hoarse and the highest notes seem to break through a mist, sometimes almost out of tune. Although she must undoubtedly hear it herself, it does not seem to bother her, which Charlotte does not think fitting for a lady. But she has to admit that it is a sign of great self-assurance: never before has she met a woman who uses her imperfections to seduce.

She hates attending these demonstrations of madame's charms, but they form part of the compulsory singing lessons. That afternoon she is standing with her sister at the back of *la grande salle*, where singing lessons only take place when madame comes to regale her pupils with a song. With its grand piano, its many-branched candelabra and its huge globe—which is hanging up on the ceiling, but which can be lowered on a heavy cable—the spacious room is slightly reminiscent of a stage set. Monsieur Chapelle is in the habit of playing the piano with great pathos, occasionally raising one hand theatrically, and then setting it loose on the keys like a stoat on a nest of mice. In the airy songs that madame prefers, he tries to control his temperament, but even the playful version of an opera by Bellini, from which madame is performing a song today, acquires a threatening edge under his fingers. In fact, monsieur

Chapelle is paying little attention to madame today, but is looking with a questioning raised eyebrow at the young ladies, who idolise him. That does not seem to disturb madame, so full is she of herself. And anyway, that afternoon she turns out to have a silent admirer. She cannot see him herself, because he is hidden in the doorway, but Charlotte notices him.

Monsieur has his usual pile of books under his arm and is undoubtedly going to his study shortly. He must have come specially to listen to his wife, since this large room is at the end of the school building. Madame sings and when she sings she is no longer the headmistress with the cool, mechanical smile, but a *chanteuse* in a salon full of gentlemen in a fug of tobacco smoke. There is an intense expression on monsieur's face. His lips slightly parted, his eyes fierce and dark; he is staring at his wife as if she belongs to someone else and he can only desire her at a distance.

Charlotte looks from madame to monsieur and back again and for the first time sees her through his eyes. Her still slightly swollen belly and breasts full of milk only make her more attractive: they evoke lovemaking, mating. She thinks she sees a dark stain on a level with a nipple—is milk leaking out? Does monsieur, in the intimacy of their bed, in an upsurge of passion, suck on her nipples? Madame's song puts her almost into a magnetic sleep and she feels a longing deep in her abdomen.

Then Emily has a coughing fit and clumsily drops her folder of sheet music on the floor, which dispels all rapture. With a furious jerk monsieur turns round and his eye lights on Emily who is gathering her sheets together on the floor. Charlotte kneels down to help her sister and when she looks up again, he has gone.

She leaves the school. Lifts her skirts up and walks frantically back and forth across the pavement in front of the establishment. What had she thought? That monsieur would give up his charming wife for *her*: a small, dark, miserable creature? What sick pride led her to harbour such delusions? In reality she is so puny that he does not even notice her, just one of the many women in the boarding school. There is nothing, nothing beyond what she has imagined to herself. That nocturnal walk arm in arm through the streets of Brussels meant nothing to him. The gate opens a fraction, and there is Emily, asking her what on earth she is doing in the street and telling her to come in.

She is no longer the same person. It's as if she has been rudely woken from a dream with a splash of cold water in her face and a dig in the ribs. May days glide past the windows and the sky remains cloudless, but she shivers. Like the other girls she wears a cotton summer dress, but if she knows that she will not meet monsieur on the stairs or in class she wraps an old woollen scarf round her shoulders. She is tired. Most of all she would like to lie down on the ground, in the sand on the floorboards. She wants to be alone, but she is not allowed that. *Oh, please leave me in peace!* During lessons she curls up small behind her desk, but mademoiselle Blanche's ruler often points in her direction. And if she has to speak, her voice sounds broken.

After lunch, in the full refectory, she suddenly feels a hellish pain in her abdomen. She has just got up, with her plate, knife, fork and mug in her hands to take them to the kitchen, when the cramp catches her unawares. The things fall on the ground with an alarming clatter. She stands there bent double, leaning on the table with one hand. Suppose she were to die—not madame but herself. Before she has written even a single story worth reading. Before she has been loved by a man. One of the girls puts an arm round her shoulders. It is Marianne, a nice girl, no older than about seventeen. Her friend Godelieve helps Charlotte sit on the wooden bench. A third girl pours her a glass of water. She does not want that attention. The tears are stinging her eyes; she is not worthy of their attention. Emily comes to see what is wrong and Charlotte feels her compelling fingers firmly round her chin.

'It's nothing,' she says. 'Time of the month.'

An excuse to escape her sister's severe judgement. But later that afternoon, when she goes to the toilet between two lessons, she sees blood in her knickers. Bright-red spots, blood so red that it seems to well up from a stiletto-sharp cut. She is not going to die.

*

Charlotte has forgotten none of the hunger with which monsieur had spied on his wife when she sees him with Suzette. This young French woman has been at the boarding school since the end of May. In the mornings she follows the lessons, but early in the afternoon she disappears through the gate with her violin case under her arm. It is said that she is very talented and is having private lessons with Charles de Bériot at the conservatory. A female violinist! Unusual, since the violin needs a master to play and tame it. With its female forms, the instrument does not lend itself to being played by a woman. But Suzette is not an everyday woman: her mass of wavy black hair gives her a southern air and it is whispered that she has Algerian blood. That head of black hair, however, is her only beautiful feature.

She is short and her skin is as flabby and dull as dough. Her eyes are too round and yellowish, and when she stands and practises her violin (while the others are still in bed), she seems to squint; she looks so intently at her bow that she becomes one with it. She has a predilection for extravagant compositions, which the girls hate, but of which Charlotte can sense the beauty. When Suzette made her entry into the boarding school, shrouded in a strange kind of cape and with three violin cases, which she wanted to carry upstairs personally, she could only admire her, although she recoils from so much female independence.

A few days after madame's performance she finds monsieur in conversation with the French girl. They are having a philosophical discussion, so profound that she would not be able follow them. After the evening meal and before prayers there are those few free hours that the boarders spend in the garden and in the refectory. Monsieur and Suzette are sitting in the refectory at the head of one of the two long tables, next to each other by the open window. She herself is reading an English novel by the porcelain stove, which is not lit, but is decorated with a flower arrangement. She does not want to do her homework, because *La Suzette* is not doing so either. The other girls are sitting bent over their text books or handiwork, and Emily is making a sketch of a half-rotten pear tree outside in the light of the setting sun. She tries to concentrate on her novel, but hears snatches of the conversation between monsieur and Suzette. And then suddenly there is that penetrating whispering behind her.

'Look at him, the infatuated fool.'

She turns round, and sees Renate pulling funny faces. She pouts exaggeratedly, like a clown wanting to kiss a girl on the trapeze, and the pupil next to Renate ducks giggling behind her embroidery frame.

'The eternal lover,' whispers Renate contemptuously, watching monsieur out of the corner of her eye.

It cannot be true, it cannot be true. Charlotte lays the book against her bosom. She has heard pupils make remarks like that about monsieur before, but she was deaf to them and saw only the master who shared his knowledge with the ignorant creatures around him. And yet! See how he looks at Suzette. See him laugh uproariously at an apt remark she makes. If only she could take his face in her hands and turn it away from that dark young woman, so that he looked her in the eyes and she could kiss him. She is prepared to accept for a while that he still cares about madame, but Suzette is a pupil. Look how he gazes at her. Suzette's voice is low and commanding with a teasing undertone. She forces herself to look at the dark girl. Is that down on her top lip? Monsieur takes Suzette's mobile hands in his to check her stream of words and to add force to his argument. Does he call *this* an extra lesson? Where is madame and how is it that she allows this? Charlotte abruptly slams her novel shut, pushes her chair back noisily and leaves the refectory.

*

Charlotte is sitting on the sill of the window behind her bed, with her bare feet on the ridge of the roof below her. It is warmer outside than she had thought possible. She runs the sleeve of her nightdress over her wet cheeks, but is careful not to wet the sheet she has written on in ink. The sky is a lovely blue that is becoming ever darker with shreds of bright pink. It will be over an hour before the others come to bed, and hopefully they will leave her in peace till then. Emily discovered this perfect hiding place on the roof when she had an attack of breathlessness, but now Charlotte is making grateful use of it.

The tears keep coming, tears of disappointment, but the

sadness is replaced by a vague hope. If monsieur previously loved another pupil and now has feelings for Suzette, there is a chance. Then he can love her too. Or he already loves her.

She tries to reread the dictation that monsieur gave Emily and her yesterday. Something about a Christian, Eudorus, who is led into the Roman arena, where he will be thrown to the lions. His fiancée has been taken prisoner by the philosopher Hierocles. The judge makes Eudorus a proposition: if he makes a sacrifice to the Roman gods, he will be released and his fiancée will return to him. Oh, the temptation! It looks as if Eudorus will succumb, but then he says loudly and manfully: 'I am a Christian.'

Choosing religion over freedom and love: that is a message that Charlotte does not want to hear now. But she sees Eudorus standing in the arena and she hears his powerful voice. She wishes she could express herself so forcefully. 'Here I am, look at me,' she would like to shout. 'I cannot think of anyone but you. I am yours!' But she cannot do that, because she is a well-brought-up parson's daughter. If she were a streetwalker—like the ones she has seen in the rue d'Argent: provocative, their décolleté so deep you could almost see their nipples, their cheeks feverish—she would address him and without beating about the bush ask him to go to bed with her. But the chance is great that monsieur would walk straight past a strumpet, and would even push her impatiently aside.

The sheet on her lap reminds her that she still has her pen. Beauty and musicality have not been granted her, but does she not have a rare command of the written word? Is her pen not an instrument with which she can threaten, wound, enchant and perhaps even seduce? She crawls back inside through the window and, in the washroom, splashes water over her face. She has four evenings left to work on a new essay.

'"Anne Askew dropped the quill with which she had almost written her signature and stretched out willingly on the rack."' Emily stops to cough, looks for a handkerchief in the pocket of her apron, and continues. '"Her eyes closed, as if she were falling asleep, and she said: 'I am a Protestant.'"' Charlotte is flabbergasted. Monsieur has not read out her essay, but has told her sister to do so. He expresses no approval and does not have one of his attacks of critical rage, which make her cry and are concluded with a few soothing words. It has to be said: he makes an indifferent impression. Sitting at his desk he arranges his papers, probably for an evening class with his Flemish workers.

'*Meess* Emily,' he says, as if he feels something is expected of him, 'you will correct *meess* Charlotte's essay. And you, *meess* Charlotte, that of your sister. That makes a change and change keeps us alert.' After which he fills the remaining half hour of the lesson with a dreary grammatical question on which Emily has asked for clarification. He regularly consults his watch, and at five on the dot he pushes some folders into his leather case and leaves the room with a muttered '*Bonsoir*' under his breath. Charlotte does not move a muscle. Her sister stands up, but she remains sitting there as if turned to stone. Then she gets up, leaves her things where they are and goes after him. There he is; he is leaving the carré and going into the garden.

'Monsieur, wait a moment! Please.'

'Yes?' He waits on the terrace and only half turns round, with a grim expression round his lips. She knows that she should let him go, but she cannot give him up.

'Monsieur, I want to offer my apologies. It was so wrong of me!'

'What are you talking about?' he asks, playing with his bunch of keys.

'Anne Askew,' says Charlotte quickly. 'In my essay I take a stand against Catholicism. But I ask you to forgive me. I had forgotten that you are Catholic.'

He looks up in astonishment and is silent for a moment, as if he needs time to remember what on earth she is talking about.

'Had you forgotten that you are staying in a country where the whole population is Catholic?' he says finally, and an amused smile makes his mouth relax. 'I cannot believe that, young lady. But I won't make too much of it. You are English and the English are impudent and superior.' He seems to be looking for a particular key in the bunch.

'Monsieur...'

'Leave it,' he says severely, without looking at her. And then he hurries out of the garden.

She stares at the closed gate. Behind her is the boarding school, burning her back. They must be serving the evening meal now, but she does not want to go in. For a moment the house is as repellent to her as the country houses where she once worked as a governess. She would like to follow her master, into the street. And if she cannot follow him, she wants to go to somewhere full of life: a market with the excited voices of traders, a cattle market, preferably with animals and farmers. Men—she wants to see men. No longer to have only women around her. She dislikes women. Apart from her sisters she dislikes all women, although her sisters may be her jailers. She turns and hurries to the gate. For a moment, just for a moment to get away from here. But there, on the pavement, monsieur is coming in her direction.

'*Meess* Charlotte!'

She does not want to see him; she cannot stand his indifference. But you cannot turn your back on your master.

'What are you doing out here? You're not dressed for a walk.' He grabs her by the arm, wants to lead her like a child.

'Why did you come back?' she stammers and makes a half-hearted movement with her arm to shake his hand off.

'*Meess!* What's this?' He sounds greatly surprised. 'I forgot a book. It must be in my study.'

'Let me come with you to the workers,' says Charlotte.

'My dear child,' he says, startled. 'I cannot do that this evening. First I'm calling in to see a colleague. What's more, Claire thinks that working-class neighbourhoods are too dangerous for her pupils at night.'

'Our difference in faith need not come between us,' says Charlotte, and trembles so violently that she closes her eyes. She feels his hand in the nape of her neck. He comes so close to her that she can feel his warmth and then pulls her firmly to him. She inhales the tobacco odour of his coat, smells his whole body in his overlong, curly, uncombed hair; his belly against her belly, his thigh against hers, his manhood—his manhood against her belly. A few seconds, a minute, she does not know—she thinks of those who might see them like this, but stays where she is. And then suddenly it is over and she opens her eyes.

'Go in now,' he says softly.

XVIII

It is as hot as Africa, which is seldom the case in Brussels. Abrasive hot air like the breath of a fire god hangs vibrating in the streets and over the Zenne. The river is syrupy and here and there floats a dead silver-scaled fish. The leaves of the oaks and beeches on the boulevard round the city are leathery and the lawns in the Warande Park are showing yellow scorch marks. The people of Brussels puff and complain, throw open the windows of their bedrooms at night and lie sweating on their clammy sheets. At night it is too hot to sleep or make love and during the day it is too hot to work, but only a few can afford to stay in the shade, and fan themselves to keep cool.

Emile the workman, his shirt unbuttoned and his braces dangling on his thighs, wet with sweat and cursing his lot, stands tearing rags to shreds for the paper mill. Soon it will be evening and he can go, but in his room under the glowing-hot tiles it is stifling.

King Leopold is posing with the ever-cool Louise-Marie for a foppish painter in the Royal Palace of Laeken. The king is longing for the moment when he can tear off his high collar and go swimming in the lake with his sons. His hand rests on his wife's naked shoulder, feels the bone under her white skin, so brittle that like the wishbone of a chicken it seems to be begging to be broken. Louise-Marie smells of lavender water, a discreet eau de toilette, and still it suffocates him like an excess of white lilies in a chapel of rest. With his free hand he strokes unseen the gold silk of the empire armchair in which she is sitting. Once it belonged to Napoleon's beautiful Joséphine, a woman lively and sparkling as a waterfall.

In dry, dusty Brussels the Pensionnat Heger is one of the rare oases. The high walls cast sheets of shade over the garden. The strawberry plants and gooseberry bushes are doing so well that the women in the school cannot eat all the fruit and the cook uses them for her famous jams and tarts. Every day after sunset the gardener waters the bushes and madame's pots of marigolds. Their water butt is the best in the city, says monsieur. He has never known it run dry.

Beneath the colossal pear tree known as Methusalem, Charlotte sits with three other boarders around madame Heger. Madame has lowered her needlework into her lap and tells them about Joan of Arc.

'So you see,' she says at the end of her story, picking up the striped smock for Prospère again. 'You don't have to be a man to make a difference in the world. Joan was only seventeen when she went into battle at the head of the French army.'

It is quiet for some while and the sunlight falls on them, filtered through the canopy of leaves. A handkerchief is given another embroidered initial, a letter from home is reread and one girl is dozing, half-resting against her friend. Charlotte is browsing in a herbal and mutters the French names of the herbs to herself. Usually she does not attend these kinds of relaxed gatherings with madame, but today she wants a favour from her.

'Arcadie Claret is only sixteen,' says Cecilia, a young woman with a conceited air and lovely grey eyes. 'She should be good and pure, but no, she is seducing our king.'

Charlotte has no idea who Arcadie Claret may be, but it is as clear as day that Cecilia is making use of the opportunity to dish up a little scandal. At these words Marianne, the girl who was lying dozing, has sat up as if stung by an insect.

'Oh, madame!' she exclaims. 'My aunt is just back from a cure in Wiesbaden and she saw the king there with that Arcadie on his arm. Everyone is gossiping about it. Our poor queen! Suppose that mademoiselle… Suppose, suppose…'

'Suppose she has a child by the king?' says Cecilia completing her sentence, and raising an eyebrow. 'That's not likely to happen. It appears *maman* Claret is a calculating lady. She teaches her daughter to fan the king's desire by throwing him the crumbs of her affection and making him wait. Like Anne Boleyn did with King Henry.' Her words express contempt, but her voice is deep with scarcely concealed admiration.

'*Pourvu que ça dure*,' jokes Marianne with a heavy Corsican accent, imitating the mother of Napoleon when she talked of her son's conquests.

'The chance is great that the liaison will break up,' says madame and she elegantly puts her hand on her heart. 'But even if it continues, the king will never marry her. Let us not forget that he is a great and conscientious man.'

Anis, cannelle, verveine. Anise, cinnamon, verbena. Charlotte tries to concentrate on her reading, but cannot. *A great and conscientious man.* He will never marry that girl. Her throat is dry, and she would most like to slip away but that is not possible. She must stay calm. Madame is talking about the king and his mistress, and not about monsieur and herself. She cannot have any inkling of that, can she?

Cecilia leans forward confidentially but before she can say anything, madame cries: '*Mesdemoiselles!* Enough of this gossiping. You're like fishwives.' The corners of her mouth move up slightly, as if she is making fun of the naivety of her boarding school charges.

The bell for the evening meal is rung. The pupils get up and shake out their skirts.

'Madame,' says Charlotte and she feels her voice tremble. 'Have you a moment for me?'

'Of course,' says madame, sewing another perfect little stitch in the cotton.

Charlotte waits a second until the other women are inside. 'Our six months in your boarding school are drawing to a close,' she finally says, 'but my sister and I would like to stay on, madame. Our studies are far from complete. I have only to listen to your elegant French to realise how much there is for me to learn!'

Madame looks at her slightly mockingly out of the corner of her eye.

'Could we stay on, madame?'

'I thought you had no money left,' she says rather brusquely.

'That is true.' Charlotte bites back the raw humiliation. 'Aunt can no longer help us. But my sister and I are not frightened of hard work. We could give lessons for nothing, Emily piano and I English, in exchange for our stay here.'

Madame's lips part slightly while she holds the smock away from her to survey the result.

She is hesitating, Charlotte knows, but she is a businesswoman. She knows an attractive offer when she sees one and won't say no.

Madame lets the thread run out of the needle and trims it with a pair of small brass scissors.

'Oh, why not? The two of you could teach four hours a day. Of course I shall have to discuss it with my husband first.' The words 'my husband' hang in the air with a strange emphasis.

'Of course, madame.' Charlotte bows her head humbly, but is inwardly rejoicing.

Louise de Bassompierre has left, with the whole caravan formed by her family, for their summer estate near Veurne. The farewell was intense, since she will not be back at the boarding school until the beginning of October. Emily can still feel how Louise's cool hand slid from hers at the gate; she can still feel her kiss half on her cheek, half on her neck. Now her friend has gone there is nothing left for her but gloom. Nothing more can delight her. The garden is too hot and there is not a book in the library that she would want to read. Belgian food, which she liked for a while (if only because Louise loves *pistolet* rolls and regularly brought her a glass of chocolate milk) she now finds too heavy. Most of all she would like to exist on just coffee and some fruit and bread, were it not that in that case Charlotte could be guaranteed to write a letter to their father sounding the alarm.

Charlotte asks why she is so wrapped up in herself.

'I miss Louise!' she feels like shouting. 'She is the only one who understands me.' But she does not shout; she does not even reply. She does not feel like talking, and apart from that her sister might make a jealous scene. She remembers only too well how envious Charlotte could be of her strong bond with Anne. It is striking, though, that Charlotte does not continually bombard her with concerned remarks. Undoubtedly all her thoughts are on Heger, that self-centred lout. She simply cannot understand how Charlotte who once created with her pen the dangerously attractive Duke of Zamorna, is now swooning over a man with a chest as hairy and broad as that of a Scots bull. Charlotte cannot stop talking about him. *Monsieur-ci, monsieur-là.*

None of it would be so bad if they let her get on quietly with studying. But since Charlotte has conceived the absurd plan of staying on here for an extra six months (without consulting her at all), she has to give piano lessons several times a week. Not to talented young ladies but to three *children*. The youngest daughters of a certain Thomas Wheelwright, an English doctor who has just settled in Brussels. The girls are receiving schooling during the vacation to help them catch up. Frances is ten, Sarah eight and Julia seven, and they are so clumsy and have such tiny hands that it is impossible to teach them anything decent. They also sit there snivelling because they would rather be playing outside, but she only wants to teach during the meal break, because otherwise she herself will miss one of her private lessons in French and German.

Emily is just explaining to Julia that she must never come to class with sticky fingers, when she is interrupted by drumming on the door. Gertrude brings a letter. The handwriting is not Louise's but her brother Branwell's, and consequently she puts the letter on the mantelpiece. She does not remember it until after the evening meal. Charlotte opens it and reads it out. Their father's curate, their own handsome, cheerful William, has died of cholera.

What Charlotte and Emily do not realise as they sink down together on a sofa and the older one seeks the younger one's hand, is that this is only the first in a series of sad tidings.

*

Charlotte cannot cry for William. Look at her sitting there on the sofa. Why should she cry over the death of a curate, when

187

as a little girl she saw the cold, bloodless face of her dead mother? And at the age of nine the silent figure of her sister Maria, as she sat there on a chair in the entrance hall to the school waiting for their father to come and collect her—with grey shadows under her big dark eyes, as approaching death is a sketch in charcoal. Maria had smiled bravely and Charlotte had kissed her pale cheek, but then had gone to the square to watch the other girls playing ball. Death had no place in the life of little Charlotte as long as she could focus her attention on something pleasant: young girlfriends at play, a young dog or cornflowers in the verge. But now and then death pushed her roughly into a corner and forced her to look it in the face. Like that afternoon her father went upstairs with her to say farewell to her sister Elizabeth. She hesitated by the door, but her father's hand was there in her back. Elizabeth lay in the bed in which Maria had died a few weeks earlier and was gasping for breath with her whole being. Her lips purple as blackberries and her eyelids shiny with sweat. The way she sank back in the pillows and she, Charlotte was suddenly the oldest, and her father said she must be strong for her brother and sisters.

Charlotte cannot cry for William, although she liked him. While putting on her nightdress in the dormitory, she tries to picture the curate. He was always good-looking, his fringe of beard neatly trimmed and his voice as cheerful as the tinkle of sheep bells. A shame that he will no longer brighten up the parsonage, and it remains to be seen what dreary character will come in his place. Poor William. Poor Anne too, although it is not clear whether he felt anything more than comradeship for her. He paid court to so many girls. Yet it is quite possible that he would have eventually chosen Anne, despite her rather dull nature, since as papa's son-in-law he would have had a better chance of succeeding him as parson. Not that William had ulterior motives—no, she does not think that, but he was quite simply inclined to choose the easiest and most pleasant option. Poor Anne. Charlotte stands in front of the mirror and loosens her plaits pensively. Her sisters are destined to become old maids. She sighs, but with a touch of relief.

XIX

Pigeons adorn the roofs of Brussels. They sit on the ridges of the mansions and palaces. They bill and coo on the narrow ledges of the church towers and on the frames of stained glass windows. Now and again a flight of pigeons alights on the worn-out roofs of the alleyways and they scratch about in courtyards where the cobbles are uneven and grubby children squat down beside them. There's not a child in Brussels that has not once fed a few crumbs to a pigeon. There's no country with more pigeons than Belgium. There's no well-to-do citizen of Brussels who can do without his dovecote; and here and there even a workman with a little money or a farmer with a sizable farm is starting to keep a few pigeons.

Charlotte observes the pigeons from her hiding place on the roof. She supports herself with her elbows on her knees and rests her chin in her palms. These domestic birds are slate-grey, some with more and some with less markings; the occasional one is snow-white. Their eyes are small and hard as pinheads. They bill and coo, trip along the ridges, two steps to the left, two steps to the right; adjust their feathers, fly away and alight somewhere else. Charlotte sits regularly on the roof, with her pen and a notebook, with her passions and moods. She sits there when the first autumn chill descends and is caught unawares by thick drops of October rain.

The days in the boarding school are like the pigeons on the roofs of Brussels. One is not so very different from the other. They come and go, silently or with flapping and chattering. In the mornings there is cautious whispering in the dormitory as people wake up, as if the dawn is too fragile for so much intensity; the wet, blushing faces over the wash basins, and then suddenly a bright laugh, a piece of soap that falls to the ground or a cry when a corset is over-tightened. A new day. A bead in a jar of beads. *Don't forget to pray.* The Lord's Prayer for her and Emily, the Hail Mary for the Catholics. *Pray.* Mademoiselle Marie already smelling of snuff at breakfast. *Don't drag your feet on the stairs!* There is the silence when Charlotte has set the class an English translation, the scratching pens of her pupils, a branch that taps against the window during a storm. And there is monsieur.

Monsieur who puts his hand round her wrist when he reads out her essay '*La justice humaine*'. The firm grip of his fingers, as if he will never let her go, and then Emily of course starts coughing. Monsieur at the bottom of the stairs as she comes down, holding her gaze as if his eyes were a trap, the jaw of a predator. There is no Suzette any longer. Or more precisely: she is still there, but can no longer count on monsieur's attention. There is madame, somewhere in the background, and apart from that there is no one but her, Charlotte. She sees how he longs for her when he looks at her during the lesson: his fingertips that feel his stubbly chin and for a moment pass over his mouth. She feels the desire in the hand round her wrist.

She waits, she waits. One last time she sits on the windowsill to be alone with her reflections, one last time before the tiles beneath her feet become too cold and too slippery. There are moments of golden happiness, and then suddenly monsieur seems to forget her; he is swallowed up by the Athénée, his wife and the books he has to read. After which he discovers her again, passes her in the corridor with his eyes glowing and lightly brushes her with his hip.

Her longing is intense and almost obstinate: it whines and claws, like a hungry cat circling your ankles while you are cooking. *Monsieur, monsieur.* Look at me. She wants to touch him, she wants to feel him.

*

'It's from the château of Koekelberg,' says Emily, looking in the drawer of the buffet for a knife to open the letter. The refectory smells of cold porridge, as the maid has not yet come to clear up the remains of breakfast. Emily calmly scans the lines. 'Martha Taylor is seriously ill. She has diarrhoea and is vomiting.'

She speaks the words so unemotionally that Charlotte would like to slap her face.

'How awful,' says Emily, giving her the letter. 'She'll probably succumb like William. We must avoid that foul disease. You mustn't go and visit Mary.'

'Oh, stop it!' Charlotte sinks down onto the long bench. With a feeling of nausea she turns away from the table covered in greasy smudges and coffee rings. Martha, such a cheerful, sweet child! It is appalling.

And this time she cries, for Martha, but also for the fact that your life can be so suddenly in danger, that you can be hit by a carriage with a pair of runaway horses or can be struck down by a dreadful disease. Man is fragile and defenceless like the mouse in the kitchen that receives a vicious blow with the broom. She must talk to Mary. She must go to Koekelberg!

Driven by the wind, a layer of clouds in light shades of grey scuds over the city. Here and there is a chink of clear sky. It is chilly, but Charlotte leaves her cape flapping loosely around her for quite a while. She has neither the time nor the inclination to look around her, she skirts the Grand-Place and hurries along the quays, although a bridge on the quai des Tourbes evokes a rather melancholy memory of the meeting with Emile. His letter, to the mayor of a small town in America, lies forgotten among her linen at the bottom of the wardrobe; she never translated it. But Emile has gone from her thoughts, because the sky grows dark and around noon, in the meadows of Molenbeek, it starts raining fiercely. By the time she pushes open the gate to the château and hurries through the grounds, she is soaked and worn out.

'You're too late,' says Mary. She descends the majestic circular staircase and her whole appearance—her hand limply holding the banister, the heaviness in her dark eyes—testifies to her sorrow. She extends both hands to Charlotte. 'Martha did not live till morning.'

The two friends wash the dead girl together. Mary opens the curtains and the bedroom fills with light. Beyond the tall windows the grounds extend in muted shades. Mary soaks a linen cloth in a bowl of lukewarm suds and Charlotte dabs the silent body, which has already lost its warmth. Martha's dear hands, her shoulders, her young belly. They put clean underwear on her and a navy-blue woollen dress. Afterwards they sit next to each other on the bed, at first too embarrassed to speak, but then—alone together for the first time in ages—Mary tells her about her plans to go and teach in Germany and Charlotte whispers passionate words about her love for Constantin Heger.

*

Despite her delightfully pretty face and delicious turned-up nose, Gertrude is transformed into an avenging angel. She brings Emily and Charlotte one piece of bad news after another. Martha has only been buried for a day and there stands Charlotte on the terrace with a letter from her father in her hands. She has come outside with Emily to escape the curious gaze of the concierge. Although the evening meal is only just over, the twilight has sucked the colours out of the world. Rain from a moment ago drips from the almost bare branches and the bluestone under her feet looks slippery.

'Is there something wrong with papa?' asks Emily in alarm. She cannot do without him. He is indispensable. Without him there is no home up there in the hills.

But it is not their father, it is Aunt Elizabeth. She is very ill: an obstruction in the abdomen.

'Oh,' says Emily. 'She often has that.'

'This time it's serious. It looks bad. We must go home, Em.'

That last statement seems to confuse Emily. Her long fingers flutter up excitedly to her breast to knot her shawl as if she is already preparing herself to leave. But she is silent. Charlotte bites on her lower lip. Dreadful letter. She does not want to go home. She wants to stay in the boarding school, because Suzette must not steal monsieur from her and madame must not have him completely in her power.

But scarcely an hour later she knocks at the Hegers' apartment. The maid takes her to *le salon de madame* and madame Heger does not keep her waiting too long. She is already wearing her nightcap and in the faint light of the dying stove embers she looks as worn out as an old laundry maid. Her dark hair seems to have lost its sheen and is tucked carelessly under her cap. So is it true what the maids are saying: has madame had a miscarriage? Charlotte has stood up and madame shows no sign of wanting to sit down.

'Poor girl,' she says after she has heard Charlotte's story. She puts her hand on her shoulder and even pulls her for a moment against her soft, maternal body. Every muscle in Charlotte wants to resist the embrace and she has to force herself not to recoil. She forces something resembling a smile and wishes madame good night. She asks Gertrude about train departure times, and the concierge hurries to the station to look at the timetable and inquire about boats.

Charlotte goes wearily and slowly upstairs to pack their cases. Emily is bound to need help.

There is Emily, sitting on her bed: her bent back and shoulders in her warm dress with the soft flower motif, a glimpse of her profile, like a pale crescent moon, and her ginger hair in a loose knot in her neck. And, leaning against her, head on her shoulder, that young girl, Louise de Bassompierre, whom she recognises from her narrow shoulders and heavy brown plait. She knows that Louise's small hand is in Emily's large thin one. She clears her throat.

*

Charlotte would never have dreamt of leaving the boarding school, have had her case taken downstairs, thrown open the window behind her bed and taken her leave of the pigeons, so that their alarmed flapping disturbed the natural order of things. Although she has known moments of great irritation in the school, she enjoys her study and her place is with her master. She would never have dreamt of leaving the boarding school, but she has no choice.

Emily and she stand with the Hegers outside the gate and the departure cannot be delayed.

'Let me take you to the station,' says monsieur Heger much

to her delight, and goes over to the rented coach to help the driver hoist the cases onto the roof.

Emily shakes hands formally with madame. She already has a book under her arm, a French work, to read in the train later, and possibly in the coach too. She is a master of detachment. Charlotte herself kisses madame on the cheek; she knows what is expected of her. She stands next to the headmistress, who still looks as pale as yesterday evening, and for the first time she feels more attractive than her.

'Madame,' she says, hoarse after a night without sleep, and then looks at monsieur.

'We must go,' he says. 'Otherwise you'll be late.'

Once out of sight of his wife he takes her hand.

'Come back,' he whispers in a commanding tone and stuffs a folded letter in her travel bag. '*Meess* Charlotte, come back to me. The letter is for your father.'

He helps her get in and takes her hand again when he is sitting next to her. She didn't imagine it. She thanks the Lord for this clear sign. He loves her and they will be reunited.

Emily sits rigidly on the other seat and stares blindly at the window, her book closed on her lap. When the coach, on reaching the place d'Anvers, sways heavily to avoid a carriage coming out of the boulevard at a foolhardy speed, she loses her composure for a moment and her eyes fill with tears. If her vision had not been so clouded, she would have seen in a flash through the window a blond girl in the other coach with scandalously full lips: the young Arcadie Claret, seated next to her proud *maman*, who has exhorted their coachman to hurry, since mademoiselle Claret is expected in a house in the rue Royale.

CHRISTMAS IN ENGLAND

XX

When she arrives in Davy's carriage Charlotte looks warily around her. The mare has difficulty in climbing the steep main street, although the animal knows the route blindfold and the flat bricks are laid irregularly to give horse's hooves some grip. The old houses, discoloured by coal smoke, stand tall and thin on either side of the narrow street and there is not a single one where you might imagine someone of consequence lives. Haworth, with its grocers, bakers and butchers; Haworth where you can buy white cabbage, brandy, candles, bread and legs of lamb, but if you ask for novels, letter paper or fashionable materials, eyebrows are raised, since for those you have to go to Keighley or Bradford. Haworth with its thick dialect, in which old acquaintances shout their greetings to her, which she answers with a forced smile. The backwardness of this place stifles her and she would say something about it to Emily if she were not afraid of insulting Davy or a passer-by with her dislike of the town. Their town, not her town. No longer at any rate. And how badly dressed the inhabitants are: the women with coarse woollen shawls and the men in shirts that are more yellow than white. Shoes, coats and hats, but equally teapots and quilts: aesthetics plays no part in choosing an item here and all that matters is suitability for the harsh life in the Pennine hills. Charlotte looks at the toes of her narrow lace-up boots and knows that her father will upbraid her for such frivolity.

The cart goes round the back of the church and there is the parsonage. Although the grey house seems to have shrunk, it still retains a certain status. Emily goes up Church Street and

Charlotte follows her hesitantly past the field of a thousand graves, so many of them already housing inhabitants she has known herself. No one grows old in Haworth; if a mother is able to keep two of her four children, she thanks the Lord.

Emily pushes open the garden gate and there stands Tabby, their old maid, polishing the brass knocker on the front door. Tabby has been very ill and for almost three years lived with her sister in a neighbouring hamlet, but now she is in better health and she is back at the parsonage. Charlotte embraces the fragile old woman and smells the scent of the cheap soap that almost everyone here uses to do the washing. A familiar smell, which she now dislikes. Did she smell of Haworth like that when she arrived in Brussels? Did that sickly, grey odour hang around her, detectable by all?

Their father comes into the hall and Tabby, Emily and herself instinctively retreat to give him room. It is as if she is seeing him for the first time: this straight-backed man with the charisma of a great leader or thinker, who had come into this world to perform momentous deeds, but was shackled by destiny to a cold church in a bleak, windy region.

'Papa,' says Emily, and leans against him for a moment, whereupon, in a rare display of sentiment, he presses a kiss on her light brown hair and extends his hand to her, his oldest, Charlotte.

Martha brings tea, toast and marmalade. Once it was Charlotte's favourite food, but now she feels more like *pistolets* and *breughelkop*. A jug of water is also put on the table, but the water is such a greenish colour that in Brussels not even the dogs would drink from it. Emily does not seem to notice the immense contrast between Haworth and the quartier Isabelle. Once she has crossed the threshold of the parsonage she has abandoned her morose silence and looks content. She drinks tea by the fire and summons up vivid memories of her childhood with their father, Branwell and Anne. Keeper lies next to her on the tiles and with her fingertips she massages the folds at the back of his neck. When the geese Victoria and Adelaide start honking in the front garden, she giggles with pure joie de vivre and goes over to the window to look at her darlings.

'Emily, can you be a little calmer?' says their father in a mildly reproachful tone, since they are in mourning.

In her mind, Charlotte sees Aunt Elizabeth sitting in her armchair by the fire. Her white hair so spiky that it gave her a boyish look; her hands so mobile, even during tea busy darning or mending, while every so often she focused her thoughtful gaze on you. She knew you better than you knew yourself. Her armchair is now in the corner by the door and her cushion embroidered with the sunny yellow broom of her beloved Cornwall lies waiting for her in vain.

When they were still in Belgium, just before the train left Brussels for Mechelen, Charlotte had received the death announcement from a panting Gertrude, who had come running up with the morning's post. By the time they arrived in Haworth their aunt had already been buried.

Oh yes, Charlotte loved her and would much rather see her appear in the doorway with a dish of her wonderful apple pudding in her hands, but death has no place in her life as long as she can fix her attention on something pleasant.

'Tell me about Constantin Heger,' says her father. 'What do you think of his method of teaching?

Suddenly Aunt Elizabeth and the jug of greenish water dissolve into thin air. Charlotte puts her hand on her father's arm. She had to promise Emily that she would not deliver monsieur Heger's letter until the third Sunday in Advent so as not to disturb mourning, but nothing prevents her from talking about her beloved monsieur.

*

God is kind, and on the second Sunday in Advent He covers Haworth in a layer of snow. A light, dreamy white coat as if thousands of sleeping lambs have descended on the town. Snow hides what is ugly and muffles what sounds shrill and rough. The freezing cold brings a fresh tingle and the snow sparkles with an infinity of stars. Snow and the approach of Christmas make even Haworth picturesque. Ivy is hung from the doorposts of the shops and when the door of a bakery opens, the smell of cinnamon, crystallised ginger and butter dough come to meet you. As evening falls, the bright voices of factory children ring out, as they sing their carols from door to door.

On the third Sunday in Advent, Charlotte is sitting at the table after lunch with her sisters and her father. Branwell is lying full length on the sofa declaiming snatches of poetry from the *Bradford Herald*, a paper he thinks highly of since two sonnets by him were published in it a few months ago.

'Marvellous that I am to become the teacher of young Edward Robinson, isn't it?' he says suddenly, putting down his paper. 'He seems a bright lad to me. And his mother, what a jewel of a woman! She made no secret of the fact that she found me *very* charming.'

'Not too enthusiastic,' says his father. 'Stay calm about it. I feel very gratified, though, about Anne and you being together in Thorp Green.'

'Papa,' says Charlotte, putting the letter on the table in front of her father, 'for you, from monsieur Heger. I apologise for not giving it to you before now. I didn't want to disturb you in your grief.'

Emily looks up suspiciously from her writing, but when her father has broken the seal with his pen knife, she bends so deeply and with such apparent devotion over her exercise book that she appears to become an impregnable fortress.

'You read it out, Charlotte,' says their father. 'My eyes are too tired.'

She feels a cramp in her abdomen.

'Sir,' she begins cautiously, translating the French into English. 'You will certainly be pleased to hear that your daughters have made quite remarkable progress in the various subjects. That progress is entirely due to their industry and perseverance. Only seldom do we have the pleasure of having such exceptional pupils in our charge.'

Her father, pleased, sits up straighter.

'I have not had the honour of meeting you in person,' Charlotte continues, 'and yet I feel sincere admiration for you, for anyone judging a father by his children cannot be mistaken. The culture and delicacy that we have found in *mesdemoiselles* your daughters inspire us with great respect for your personality.'

She cannot help smiling with pleasure, but out of the corner of her eye she sees that Emily is still writing her poem, or at any rate pretending to. Since she has been home, she has plunged with renewed enthusiasm into the creation of her fictional world.

'However, we cannot hide the fact that the loss of these two highly valued pupils of ours fills us with sorrow and concern.' Charlotte speaks somewhat louder and with more conviction. '"Their sudden departure touches us so deeply, because we have almost parental feelings for them. Their education has been suspended and they have left their assignments uncompleted, when not so very much more time was required to round everything off. Another year and your daughters would have been perfectly prepared for the future; they would have had a good education and be capable of teaching others."'

She pauses for a moment to let the words sink in properly.

'There were plans to have Miss Emily take piano lessons with the best teacher in the whole of Belgium. As you know, she has already given lessons to our youngest pupils. Miss Charlotte has also begun teaching and she already has something of the self-assured air that is so indispensable for a teacher. Another year and we would have been able to offer at least one of your daughters a position in our boarding school. In that way she would gain the independence of which most young women can only dream.'

Emily still does not look up, but surely she cannot help melting at such warm affection!

'I think we should go back, papa,' says Charlotte abruptly, longing to reach a conclusion. 'There are no hindrances. You know that for the past few months Emily and I have paid for our keep and our studies by teaching.' She speaks in a tone that brooks no contradiction, as if it is no longer her father's task to decide her fate.

Emily gets up so brusquely that her inkwell threatens to fall over.

'No,' she says. Nothing but that one rebellious word.

'Come on, Emily,' says Charlotte. 'Don't be such a spoilsport; we are well off in the boarding school. You'll have piano lessons at the Conservatoire Royal.'

Emily starts trembling all over her body.

'No!' she cries. 'No!'

So violently that her eyes bulge. She unleashes a cry like a frightened, tortured animal and stretches her hands out in front of her, fingers separated. Anne tries to embrace her, but Emily pushes her roughly away and runs into the hall and through to the kitchen.

Charlotte and the others hear the back door being slammed.

'Oh no,' says Branwell, 'she must be going onto the moors.'

Father Brontë presses his fingertips together in an attempt at self-control. A worried wrinkle has appeared between his eyebrows.

'Emily won't be bossed about,' he says emphatically, his eyes resting on Charlotte. 'You are not to do that.'

'Then she won't come with me, papa,' says Charlotte, furious at so much irrationality. 'But I'm going. *I'm* going.'

She walks into the hall, and even before she has put on her bonnet and wrapped her cloak around her, Branwell is standing in front of her. He dons his winter coat, takes Emily's cape off the hat stand and opens the front door.

Without exchanging a word they walk towards the fields behind the parsonage. Emily would never choose to make for the houses.

Snow covers the barren moorland that even in summer produces little but some undergrowth and small animals. The fresh footprints must be Emily's, but she is nowhere to be seen. She has been running.

'Emily!' cries Branwell, cupping his hands round his mouth. His ginger hair swishes around his long face and he takes off his glasses to dry the lenses. They walk on, side by side, and he gives her his arm.

'Emily is strong,' he says. 'She won't do anything stupid.'

'Branwell!' cries Charlotte, because that is precisely the fear that now seizes her: that she has disturbed Emily's precarious equilibrium and that she will wander for hours across the moors in the winter cold. She tears herself free of Branwell and starts running. Only when her lungs are burning does she walk more sedately, and then breaks into a run again. Branwell follows after her. A merlin hangs above them in the sky, riding the air current.

'Emily!' shouts Branwell at the top of his voice.

They follow the cattle track past walls built of piles of stones of different sizes, and without conferring at all, head for the waterfall. Charlotte hides her cold hands under her cloak and Branwell keeps the collar of his winter coat up. The track starts to descend and Charlotte is running again—and is that Emily down below, is it her? It's her!

The stones are slippery from the snow and Charlotte's boots are not made for this countryside. She stumbles, but Branwell grabs her elbow and for the first time in ages she is overwhelmed by a feeling of tenderness for him. He is her brother.

Emily is sitting on the boulder at the water's edge that no one sits on in her presence, because as a little girl she claimed it as her own. Her plait has come loose and her hair is hanging dishevelled over her shoulders. Her thin, angular body, in a dress with just a shawl over it, is shaking with cold. She resembles a tragic heroine wanting to throw herself from the rocks. But there is no boiling sea, there are no cliffs; there is only the waterfall, so familiar, splashing and rushing, and if you let it, washing your cares away. Branwell puts the cape round Emily and now she has been safely found, Charlotte would like to raise the subject of Brussels again.

'One word,' says Emily without looking up from the pebbles in the water. One word and you'll push me over the edge. One word and I'll separate two fighting dogs and let them bite me till I bleed. One word and I'll never eat again, not a mouthful.

Charlotte pulls herself together. Right then, she decides for herself. I'll go back to Brussels alone. You stay here.

As it happens, Emily does not even want to go to the parsonage. Not yet; she'll come on later. *Yes*, she promises, and her hands flutter like angry crows. And *no*, she won't do anything silly. She does not allow Charlotte to tie the ribbons of her cape.

*

It is as if a sea monster is romping about with the ship. It pushes it along with its scaly head and regularly strikes the stern with its agile tail. Bulging, obsessed eyes, and with its head just above the black water it bursts into a roar. The ship surges high on the waves and then falls back with a jerk. Only the constitution of a true seaman can resist such a rough dance with the sea.

Charlotte is sitting in her bunk in the bowels of the ship, although she would like to be in the fresh air, but the waves are breaking on the deck and a sailor ordered her below with an oath and an irritable gesture. On the bunk above her a woman is lying groaning. Her little daughter is dabbing her forehead with a damp cloth. A number of girls of about thirteen walk arm in arm from side to side of the ship and giggle at every swerve and lurch to ward off the fear and the nausea. Wave after wave after wave.

There is no one Charlotte knows here who is aware that she has no relations in the male quarters. She is on her way to Brussels alone. Although she should be strengthened by her father's blessing, she stares miserably at the bottom of her metal bowl. She is just a soul longing for love.

IN THE TRAP

XXI

Although the bells of Saint-Michel and Sainte-Gudule have just struck four o'clock with a dull echo, outside the window the capricious shapes of the garden are bathed in blue darkness. Wind breathes icily on the glass.

'I love you,' says monsieur Heger. He is sitting rather slumped back at his desk, his hands loose in his lap. A gloomy grin passes over his face.

'What did you say?' asks Charlotte softly and she feels her lip trembling. His words would have made her burst into rapturous inward exultation, had it not been for the fact that he speaks them in the company of a third person, which is at the least strange. She is sitting in monsieur's heavy armchair, with in front of her on the desk his silver inkwell and a pile of pupil's homework that she has carefully pushed aside. He himself and Maurice Chapelle, like pupils, are sitting on the other side of the desk in ordinary chairs. When she returned to Brussels madame Heger asked Charlotte to give her husband and the music teacher a couple of hours' English tuition per week.

During their first lesson monsieur Chapelle explained to her in broken English that he is monsieur Heger's brother-in-law. Or rather: the brother-in-law of his late wife. News that left her speechless, particularly because madame gets on so well with the music teacher. So isn't she jealous of the woman who preceded her in her husband's bed?

'I love you,' murmurs monsieur again and he seems sincere: his narrow eyes, his pouting mouth. And then, teasingly slowly and in French: 'Don't you understand, *meess* Charlotte? These are the only English words I know.'

Whereupon he starts beaming at what he himself obviously finds a witty pleasantry, while Maurice Chapelle starts giggling and leans on his brother-in-law's shoulder almost in tears.

She could hit monsieur, here and now, with all the passion that wells up in her. How many feelings possess her: lust, hope, love, tenderness and jealousy; some of them like velvet, others slippery and chilly as a fish or viciously sharp like a trident. She looks away from the men in confusion, goes over to the blackboard and writes in chalk the first lines of poetry that occur to her:

For long ago I loved to lie
Upon the pathless moor;
And hear the wild wind rushing by
With never ceasing roar.

A poem by her sister Anne, but it is Emily that she sees in her mind: her tall, thin body in a flannel dress lying full length on the damp peaty soil, one hand resting on the moss.

She turns to the men and blindly sets them the task of translating the verse for the next lesson. Her inner chaos paralyses her and she wishes that she could lie down on a bed, like a child wrapped in a warm shawl.

*

'*Ma chère mademoiselle* Charlotte!'

There comes madame Heger down the corridor, with her bunch of keys jangling from a silk cord round her waist. She is once again her old buxom self but her cheeks are cherry red and she is a little out of breath.

'You don't have any lessons this afternoon, do you? Would

you do something for me? Lena has a day off and I need to go somewhere unexpectedly.'

She lays her hand on Charlotte's arm.

'Of course it's not your task,' she says with beautifully acted modesty, 'but would you look after my children for a little? I really cannot entrust anyone else with the task, *ma chère*. Claire is staying with my sister so it's only Marie and Louise. Prospère is asleep. If he cries, you can give him some gruel. The kitchen maid can make it.'

Her smile is sweet and fat as butter candy, but her brown eyes are cool. Without waiting for Charlotte's reply she hurries off somewhere else with her bunch of keys, her hips swaying in too enchanting a rhythm to be really decent. Who, oh who could refuse madame anything?

*

Marie and Louise are sitting in the large drawing room. Louise is trying to tie a pink ribbon round the porcelain head of her doll and is murmuring motherly words to her.

'*Mademoiselle*,' she says, as Charlotte kneels down beside her.

'Have you come to have tea with me?' And she pours fantasy tea into a tiny cup painted with blue flowers the size of peas. While Charlotte pretends to sip her tea, Louise tells her that she has a friend, Simon, really, *mademoiselle*, and he is so small and sweet and is allowed to sleep in her dolls' bed. And once Simon got lost and found himself in the kennel of the neighbours' nasty dog with its purple tongue, and then, *mademoiselle*, papa went and got him. Papa was the only one who believed her!

And she offers Charlotte a biscuit, invisible on a plate, while she takes a real biscuit from the dish on the drawing room table. What an imagination the child has!

Marie is sitting sulking with a thick lower lip in a deep arm-chair and now and then peers at them out of the corner of her eye.

'She is angry because *maman* and Lena have gone and you've come to look after us,' says Louise in a know-it-all tone, and her sister sticks her tongue out at her so far that it must hurt. It dawns on Charlotte that Marie has monsieur's narrow eyes, and frowns just like him. For a moment she is touched, but only for a moment, because she is just as much madame's child. Madame who entrusts her children to her.

Louise lugs in the most beautiful picture book Charlotte has ever seen, so heavy and so big that the little girl can scarcely lift it. It is the fables of Jean de la Fontaine, illustrated with pictures in soft watercolour shades.

'This is the first volume,' says Louise proudly once she has handed the book to Charlotte and creeps onto the sofa next to her. She puts her thumb in her mouth and says, stopping sucking for a moment: 'You don't have to read them all.'

Charlotte leafs through the book with pleasure and runs her fingertips over the prints. The frog in spring-green grass filling itself with air and the ox with its stupid eyes. The flattering fox, a fleeting gold, and the raven, its beak the shade of oranges.

'"The cricket chirped day and night while it was summer,"' Charlotte reads, and Louise snuggles up to her with her warm little body. '"While Mrs Ant the neighbour crept busily up and down through the grass."'

Suddenly Marie comes up to them and pulls Louise's thumb out of her mouth.

'Dirty,' says Marie, '*maman* says you mustn't do it, it's dirty.'

And Charlotte is given such a contemptuous look that she almost has to laugh. Louise is obviously used to such outbursts by her sister, as she reacts with a resigned sigh and puts her hand on the cricket with its painfully thin limbs to indicate that Charlotte must go on reading. She does so, and Marie stands and listens rather bashfully. Just as the freezing wind comes and the cricket searches frantically among the bare bushes for larvae and blades of grass, a couple of piercing cries sound from upstairs.

'That's Prospère,' says Marie accusingly, as if the English *meess* has left him up there. 'He's hungry.'

'Then I'll go and get him.' She carefully lays Louise, who has half dozed off to sleep, down with her head on a cushion.

'Be a good girl now, Marie, and ask the maid to make some gruel for Prospère.'

Marie evidently does not feel like obeying, because she stands there as stiff as a garden gnome, and then seems to have second thoughts and runs down the corridor to the kitchen.

When Charlotte stands at the bottom of the narrow staircase, she hears Prospère burbling to himself. In her mind's eye she can see him playing with his little fingers. The stairs lead to the upper storey of the school, with the oratory and the dormitory on the right and on the left the rooms reserved for the Hegers' use. She comes here occasionally to collect schoolbooks or pencils from the library at the end of the corridor. One door is ajar: could this be monsieur's bedroom? And madame's, if they share the bed every night. Her curiosity is great and she peers inside.

She looks straight into monsieur's eyes and she gasps as if she were confronting a rearing horse. Monsieur! His eyes, dark with astonishment, his hair thick and messy around his face. The shades in the room are sober and dark—grey, wine-red, a dull gold—and his body shines in the cold fingers of daylight that grope their way in between the curtains. Broad, muscular shoulders—naked—, his belly white and fleshy. The skin of his chest is soft over a mesh of contained power. A length of thigh. Strong as a man who works outside: a boat hauler who at the end of the day has bathed in the river and wades to the bank. And yet: her master. His eyes assume a yearning expression and try to hook her like an anchor, catching somewhere between her ribs. He holds a linen shirt in his hand, which he was obviously about to put on, and it is hanging over his private parts.

She knows that she should walk on. Looking back she will remember how quickly it all happened and how little time there was for reflection. He drops the shirt without taking his eyes off hers. She sees him: a man so much more masculine than her brother Branwell, whom she once saw walking about the house with no clothes on in a drunken bout. So much more masculine than the emaciated, greenish-skinned old man from Stubbing Lane whom she washed before his burial. This is the man who should be hers. She sees his manhood out of the corner of her eye. Her desire grows with his and makes her want to cling to him. It is that feeling, its animal intensity, that makes her break the spell. She tears herself free, which causes a stabbing pain in her breast, and hurries down the corridor to the stairs, almost stumbling over her skirts.

When she returns to Louise in the downstairs drawing room, the maid is just coming in with a plate of gruel, followed by Marie who has wheedled a piece of dry sausage out of her and is now chewing on it fiercely.

'Marie,' says Charlotte mechanically, 'your hands are greasy.'

The maid raises her eyebrows and looks at the gruel, which makes Charlotte realise that that she has entirely forgotten the existence of Prospère. She cannot go back. She must go back!

At the bottom of the stairs she hears monsieur talking tenderly and teasingly to the little boy. Then the door of the carré slams shut and fiery ladies' heels resound on the tiles in the corridor. *Madame est de retour.*

XXII

The Heger boarding school is like a beehive, with madame as the queen, the teachers and pupils as worker bees and monsieur as the valiant drone who sees to the fertilisation of the queen. That construction has worked wonderfully well for years, but now threatens to collapse, because a worker bee has taken it into her minute head to depose the queen. Completely unnatural behaviour, which can only be due to the fact that she has flown over from Albion and is unfamiliar with the morals here. Although we must admit that the intense pheromone which the drone secretes in her vicinity is not conducive to female peace of mind.

The day after Constantin Heger showed his naked body to the young lady from Yorkshire, the Brussels carnival, colourful, evil-smelling and chattering, erupts like a brood of excited cockerels with combs and wattles the colour of raw flesh, shiny yellow wings and silver-green tail feathers from a crate in the market. Since English Charlotte and French Suzette have never yet experienced a Brussels carnival, monsieur Heger wants to take them into town with him that afternoon.

'Excellent idea, *chéri*,' says his wife without any concern when he informs her of his intention in the morning over breakfast. She spreads a spoonful of grape jelly over her bread and butter. She is happy, she loves life. Why shouldn't she? She is queen.

Outside it is freezing cold, with an icy grey sky like a bell jar over the world, but monsieur is striding with a young woman on either arm towards the streets and squares where drink and pleasure boost one's body temperature. Our company has not donned fancy dress, though it must be said that Charlotte's appearance has undergone a few subtle changes since her return from Yorkshire. Her faded brown cape hangs in her wardrobe in the dormitory and she wears a dark-blue cloak, which she had made from a model in *La Gazette du Bon Ton*. And there is more: the thin plaits in a low loop on either side of her face have disappeared and striking short ringlets dance against her cheeks (in her wardrobe there is a lock of hair twisted in a handkerchief, which she hopes to be able to give to monsieur soon). Moreover, in a doorway on the landing of the boarding school this English parson's daughter lost her suspicious, timid fox's look. After all, she thinks she is loved.

'The word 'carnival' must be derived from *carne vale*,' lectures Suzette with the downy moustache, out of breath from monsieur's stiff pace. 'The farewell to the flesh and all things of the flesh. Or are you thinking of the combination of *carne* and *valere*, in the sense that the flesh rules?'

Monsieur replies, but it is not completely clear whether he is talking about bacon and cutlets or the pleasures of the flesh. They have found their way right to the Grand-Place and the noise sweeps over them like a wave. Carnival! Slatterns perform a dance of joy to the beat of a drum; up goes the hairy leg and up go their long shirts, dirty and at buttock level rubbed with mustard.

Who'll come with us to Verapa?
we'll all swap work for wine,
we'll eat and drink and take our ease,
and fall asleep like swine…

There comes a Domino with four tankards of beer, his face white with flour set in the darkness of a deep hood. He dances like a devil in hell fire, the beer splashes over the rim and his comrades, Dirty Dollies in sheets, take the tankards from his hands and the Domino farts so loud that he must have eaten cabbage for three weeks in preparation. And Charlotte wants to leave. How disgusting all this is; she does not know this, does not understand it, being a child of the hills, where the greatest tumult is the howling of the storm. She hates it here and lets her arm slide out of monsieur's, but he grasps her hand firmly and says loudly in her ear: 'You're safe with me.'

The Fool is a woman in a tight-fitting suit and with a grin full of rotten teeth. A swarm of Dominos, inflamed by her pendulous breasts, attempt to catch her with a net. Suzette is dragged along to join a swirling dance by a Pierlala; his hat with its red pompoms and white coat are stiff with mud, but there is a crease in his trousers and his shoes are of shiny calf leather. There is the band—'Back, back!'—and behind the cornets, drums and trumpets comes a throng with garish masks made of rags, wood, paper and daubs of paint, in tablecloths and Harlequin costumes. Below the knee you can usually see who is hiding under all that finery: a beggar as king with a crown and scabby legs, a girl in clogs as a knight, and her wooden sword flies out at a monk who is trying to grope under her chain mail. And then the smells in the cold air, the beer and all that meat, so much meat—'It has to go, it has to go!'—because Lent begins at midnight: suckling pigs on the spit, sausages with thick blobs of lard. Knobs of butter in the pan; a woman frying pancakes and in another stall the butter is melting in the waffle iron. The piles of sweet pancakes have no time to grow with all those clutching fingers and hungry mouths. Tall wooden giant's legs make their way through all the commotion, and just look: it is a girl up there, a gypsy child with an anxious old woman's face, and her brother goes round collecting the money.

Give in to your senses! A man kisses a woman and then another woman, and the women laugh. The immorality, the godlessness! And yet, safe with monsieur Charlotte dares to look around. How great the temptation is to abandon her resistance and let herself be carried away by sensual pleasure.

Suddenly she sees Emile. There he stands, like an unspoilt child in a shaft of pale light in the middle of an arena, his eyes so light and magnetic and yet no one seems to notice him. He is handing out pamphlets. His is muttering, most probably in Flemish, but this is not a good moment for angels or heralds. A young farmer, with a syrup-covered waffle in one hand, takes a pamphlet with his free hand and then drops it onto the cobbles. A neatly dressed lady (a seamstress or nanny) holds his pamphlet and looks up at his face, so handsome, but is then pulled away by her young man. Even Charlotte has no time to talk to him, since monsieur takes her arm, and she is the faithful dog on the master's leash. Suzette cries full of passion that she will capture the colours and sounds of this folkloristic event in a stirring composition for piano and violin.

*

A stone's throw from the Grand-Place, in the exclusive patisserie Chez Nina in the rue de la Madeleine, Henriette Claret and her beautiful daughter Arcadie are sitting down to an extensive *goûter*. They have been shopping that afternoon and Jos, the coachman, has just taken two hatboxes containing really delightful bonnets, one for Arcadie and one for her *maman* with him to the coach. In the patisserie with its long buffet, Venetian glass candelabras and waitresses in black dresses and starched white aprons, there is a smell of freshly-ground coffee beans, spiced *speculaas* biscuits and vanilla. With a cake platter of sweet confections on their round marble table this should be a truly pleasurable moment, but either the éclair has disagreed with Henriette, or the conversation with her daughter is not proceeding as she would wish, since she is rather upset as she peers into her *café au lait*.

In nineteenth-century narratives there is nothing easier than turning the clock back. You simply put the slides you've just used back in the magic lantern. Let's see what surprised Henriette Claret in *The Curious History of Arcadie Claret*. There we have Arcadie, immortalised on the glass plate in a few delicate brush strokes. She is sitting at the cast-iron table with a marble top and her fingers are touching the ribbons of her bonnet, ready to untie them. In the top left-hand corner you see Jos with the hatboxes and a waitress who is holding the door open for him. The next slide is projected and there it says in letters with lots of curlicues: '*Maman*, can I open my lips when the king kisses me?'

No wonder then that we find Henriette somewhat flabbergasted. She peers into her *café au lait* and does not know what to answer, although she is not often lost for words. Still, she could have seen this question coming. More than that: there are bound to be questions that go even further. It is her job to answer them before they become pressing; she should have anticipated even this one! Oh, how virginally young Arcadie looks, with her childish pout and her big eyes without red rims or bluish shadows.

'You are talking about the lips of your mouth, aren't you?' whispers Henriette leaning forward so that her heavy bosom is almost hanging in the dish of pastries.

Arcadie's eyelids flutter like butterflies in surprise and she does not look up at her mother, but unbuttons her satin gloves with feigned concentration. Her cheeks acquire a light red blush, as if she has just drunk a couple of mouthfuls of sweet mulled wine.

'Well, answer me,' says Henriette.

'*Mais oui, maman*,' lisps Arcadie, not knowing what other lips her mother may mean. She glances timidly around her to be sure that no one has heard her talking about something as risqué as *kissing*. Both the lady and the long-haired Irish hound at the next table are staring at her with interest and with their ears pricked. The waitress who comes to pour more coffee seems to absorb every detail of her dress and her mother's hairdo. They are being recognised! It looks as if *le tout-Bruxelles* knows about their friendship with the king.

'Have another one, *mon petit chou*,' says Henriette, holding out the dish of delicious pastries to her daughter, but Arcadie shakes her head and strikes the edge of the table top restlessly with her white gloves.

There is no moment that you cannot brighten with a delightful piece of cream cake, Henriette reflects, as she lets a mille-feuille slide onto her plate, but that is a piece of wisdom her daughter has yet to understand. Oh, what on earth is that child worrying about? It must undoubtedly be wonderful to be kissed by Leopold. In Wiesbaden she was able to admire the king at leisure, while he was walking ahead of her with Arcadie. The man has long, straight legs, and splendidly firm buttocks. Admittedly he is fifty-two and Arcadie not yet quite seventeen. *Can she open her lips?* A momentary flash of something approaching panic goes through her. Is he really a dirty old man then, as Babette insinuated?

'You mustn't let him under your skirts,' Henriette hisses. 'And he mustn't take off his trousers. It's far too early for that.'

'*Maman*,' whispers Arcadie in alarm. 'What on earth are you talking about?'

'He hasn't deflowered you, has he?' Henriette's plump fingers close forcefully around her daughter's wrist.

This is too much for Arcadie. She has no idea what her mother is talking about, but it's bound to be something dirty. She shakes her hand free with a certain rebelliousness, pushes her chair back and hurries to the cloakroom.

People are staring in Chez Nina; malicious tongues are wagging. Henriette can feel the looks of the customers and staff burning into her skin like hot splashes of butter. She hears the excited whispering and the half-smothered mocking laughter. An elderly lady, resembling a fat cat, has her narrow, shifty eyes fixed on her.

How badly that woman is dressed, thinks Henriette, trying to boost her confidence, as a badly-dressed woman cannot affect her. Her dress looks like a horse blanket. *Mon Dieu*, compare that with herself, in rich red satin with gold braid. She slides her hand into the muff on her lap to stroke the warming ermine. Those women are envious; it's as simple as that. Arcadie and she now belong to the world of the great: they mix with kings and princes—oh well, with one king in any case. The nobility will be simply obliged to admit them to their circles if they wish to be on good terms with Leopold. And then the bourgeoisie will follow suit.

Where has Arcadie got to anyway? Henriette would most like to go to her, but it's better to remain sitting calmly, if she does not want to attract even more attention. She stirs sugar into her coffee and spoons cream from the jug. The image of her daughter looms up in her thoughts. Those curl papers give her a luxurious bunch of curls. Or is her hairdo just a little *too* luxuriant? Isn't she really too young for that dress of stiff purple shot silk? And then those shoes with heels she can hardly walk in…

Her Arcadie, her pride, her darling!

Henriette is actually seized by a moment's doubt. She can still retreat. She can tear her girl out of his arms. She can play the mildly indignant mother who is protecting her daughter and is anxious to save His Majesty from a foolish *faux pas*. Charles has a sister in Switzerland and perhaps Arcadie should go there. Charles would totally agree with her. But as soon as Henriette takes a bite of her mille-feuille and the sugar layer breaks between her teeth, her thoughts become languid and her cares melt away in the creamy filling. Oh, oh, oh! Chez Nina really makes the best pastries in Brussels.

Send Arcadie to Switzerland and insult the king? She knows damn well that she will not do it. It is for Arcadie's own good that the king will kiss her. There are fathers who marry their daughters off for a few sheep or a field of potatoes. Charles wants Arcadie to marry a military man or a country doctor. Henriette resolutely wipes a blob of pudding off her upper lip. She is having none of all this. Arcadie is meant for the king. This is the chance for the whole family to raise its social status. Charles will of course be given a noble title; their sons will wear magnificent uniforms, and Henriette and Pauline will marry young men from the best families. It is a hard task for a mother to tear a daughter from her bosom and present her to the king. But she must think of the prosperity that will be Arcadie's.

Her eyes fill with tears at the thought of her self-sacrifice. Yes, she will have to surrender Arcadie's childish innocence— but not too quickly. Little by little. Arcadie must make His Majesty wait, just as Anne Boleyn made the king of England wait.

Babette told her the story of that King Henry and the wonderful Anne—what a seductress. Arcadie will stand at the altar with her king, but she will not be beheaded—oh, how ghastly! She hastily replaces the image of Arcadie on the scaffold with Arcadie as a medieval princess in a tiger skin cloak and with a jewelled crown on her blond locks. Who knows, she may one day, in the radiance of her youth, take the place of the sickly Queen Louise.

When Arcadie comes back to the table, smelling of the rosewater that was in a flacon next to the wash basin, an actual tear rolls down her mother's cheek.

'*Maman*,' she says, moved, and puts her arm round her mother's shoulders. 'You mustn't cry.'

'He's allowed to kiss you, child,' says Henriette with a tremble in her voice, in anxious anticipation of her daughter's reaction. To her happy bewilderment Arcadie starts smiling broadly, as if she has just been given a fluffy white dog with a checked ribbon.

'*Merci maman*,' she says, taking a sugared almond from the dish with the coffee and letting it slide along her young red tongue between her full red lips.

*

When they leave the patisserie there is a huge commotion in the street. There is the rolling of drums and the pavements are full of people.

'Oh, no, the procession is coming!' shrieks Henriette. 'I'd completely forgotten about the carnival.'

She looks around her to see what has happened to their coach. Jos is on the pavement across the street, cap in hand, but has been distracted by two lewd girls with painted faces like heathen savages.

'Jos!' cries Henriette, grasping Arcadie by the sleeve in order to cross the road with her. It is at that moment, just as Arcadie sets foot in the street and ruins her silk shoes in horse manure and the drummer almost stops for the officious Henriette, that she is seen by Charlotte Brontë, a rather colourless young woman with sagging ringlets who is standing waiting on the pavement on the arm of a gentleman.

A young, fresh face, a beauty you seldom see, and Charlotte recognises her. She knows at once: this is the girl from the beach. The girl she saw in the hotel in Ostend. The memory has faded, but the envy went too deep to let go of the girl entirely. Those laurel green eyes, the generous mouth, the pure complexion. How richly she is dressed—a princess. She would like to ask monsieur who she is, but she does not, because she does not want to call his attention to a beauty beside whom her own modest attractions pale.

For a moment she looks sideways at monsieur and she would like to kiss him on the cheek. She laughs, laughs, although the grey cold bites at her fingers and toes and she would like to be lying in a warm bed with this man.

He pulls Suzette and her into a café with him. He drinks beer and Suzette accepts a tankard. Charlotte refuses and asks for water, but the landlord laughs at her.

'Calvinist!' shouts monsieur in her ear, so loudly that it hurts her eardrum. 'Prim protestant.' His breath is warm and sour; the skin of his cheeks seems flabby and he has to look for support for a moment, which he does by putting his arm round the waist of a pretty red-haired waitress. Just as Charlotte is thinking about walking off and disappearing in the throng outside, monsieur says something to Suzette and the Frenchwoman leaves with a sullen face.

'I've sent her to the conservatory,' shouts monsieur. 'Her violin lesson begins in an hour and she has to get her instrument.'

Unexpectedly they are alone: monsieur and the young woman who yesterday saw his naked body and could not sleep for wanting him.

Meat, meat—there is so much meat. In the street slices of pâté on bread are being sold, and even slices of pâté without bread.

Forty days' fast, but first eat like animals. Monsieur buys her a waffle with syrup. She slurps a cup of hot chocolate milk and feels happy. He says that she is beautiful and writes wonderfully, and sways to and fro. He dances round with her and this is no longer a drunken dance, but a dance of lovers. He pulls her half behind a stall and his fingers grip her upper arms, and he kisses her, full on the mouth. The kiss seems to last an eternity, and then they are back in the street and his hand slides out of hers. Suzette stands in front of the stall looking at them with a hard line round her mouth.

'Monsieur,' she begins in a humble tone, yet with something adder-like in her dark eyes. She met another pupil from the conservatory in the crowd, and no, there are no lessons, because this is the last day of the carnival.

The three of them walk back to the boarding school, no longer arm in arm. At first the commotion muffles the silence between them, but then it grows quiet and it is clear that they have nothing more to say to each other.

XXIII

Whisper a secret to a woman and you entrust it to the wind. A chill gust sweeps the secret of the kiss into the carré. It circles up in a vague murmur to the bedrooms and swishes into the classrooms in the folds of the skirts. It sways into the garden on the sigh of a laundry maid, rustles in the wheelbarrow full of frozen leaves and dances in the hem of Gertrude's woollen cape.

Listen to me, I've got something to tell you... Listen to me... It mumbles softly down the corridor, swirls round the corner and so reaches madame, who pencil in hand is going through the housekeeping book with the cook. It blows lightly in her neck, and sends a shiver down her enchanting back. The headmistress has an ear for secrets: the secrets of the young women entrusted to her care, the secrets of the teachers and those of her husband, because she is not so stupid as to trust a man just like that. She feels, she hears, she knows. Suzette complaining of a cold that she caught on Mardi Gras. How icy the day was and how she was sent away and afterwards could not find mademoiselle Charlotte and monsieur again. They had disappeared.

'What do you mean disappeared?' asks mademoiselle Blanche with her oblique nostrils flared like a frightened hare.

'What do you mean disappeared?' asks madame in a light tone, as she sharpens her pencil. It won't be as bad as all that. Tell me, it must be a misunderstanding. I trust my husband *and* mademoiselle Charlotte; she's a parson's daughter.

In the dormitory Suzette sits on her bed in the company of the gossip Renate, with the drapes closed. 'Behind a chocolate milk stall,' confides Suzette to her new friend. Secrets need friends. 'I'm not exactly sure what they were doing there,' she adds for the sake of honesty, 'but I have strong suspicions.'

She peeps between the drapes into the empty dormitory, because no one else must know her secret.

'On my word of honour,' swears Renate, kissing the Virgin Mary on the medallion round her neck.

*

Charlotte sits at table in the refectory and picks at her salt fish and carrots with vinegar. Lent has begun, but what does she care? Her heart is pumping young, red blood and she feels as agile and strong as a wild cat. Mademoiselle Blanche is nibbling a piece of dry bread and stares at her.

'Why that inner joy?' she wants to know, and her little mouth wrinkles benevolently, although her sniffing sounds more contemptuous.

And Charlotte bursts out laughing, her first laugh in the boarding school, and how funny that Blanche looks with her hare's snout, and how happy can someone be! A series of women's eyes looks at her in astonishment, and it's quite possible that Suzette whispers something to her neighbour, but no one can touch monsieur and her. It is love.

Later, when darkness has fallen, she goes into the garden and dances pirouettes among the pear trees, round and round and round and she wraps her arms around herself and eagerly breathes in fresh, greenish air. In her pocket is a carefully folded note that she found among the pages of the novel *Paul et Virginie*, which monsieur put in her desk, on which is written in powerful, inspired pencil strokes: *Je vous aime, Charlotte*.

Finally. She is no longer alone.

XXIV

Spring comes.

A spring that begins cold, with ferns and palm leaves in white ice on the windows. In the garden rebellious little Marie tries to crack a frozen puddle with a stone. The milk cart rattles shrilly in the morning. Itchy woollen shawls and cracks in hands and feet.

Charlotte shivers as she slides out of bed in the morning, but she has love. Monsieur rubs her swollen red hands warm behind the door of his study, presses a kiss on the inside of her wrists. *He is warmth.* That's how she will always remember him: his arms, his muscular biceps. He holds her tight, brushes her hair out of her face, caresses her nose with his lips. Caresses that are new to her and that she did not know her body would react so willingly to. She does not ask him about the future, but is confident that there is a future for them. And Jesus said: 'Go ye... According to your faith be it unto you.' She has faith, and the Lord will help them. True love has a chance. What Claire Heger and monsieur have is no more than a business arrangement: a headmistress who needed a husband and a man who after the death of his wife and son was left alone and desperate and could be persuaded without much effort to rest on a soft marriage bed.

Charlotte stands in the dormitory and hears the bells ringing outside, but she refuses to listen to the wise words that her father sends out into the cosmos in his Sunday sermon: his exhortation to temper one's desires, reminding people of their duty. She opens the window, which makes the pigeons flutter upwards like snippets of paper against the backdrop of the church towers. Appealing to God is not the privilege of the clergy. She folds her hands and prays for her happiness.

Spring arrives, and for as long as it lasts, it is heaven on earth. Lent is over and with it go the cold and the hunger that must not be assuaged. In a garden full of blossom she is given presents for her birthday by several of her pupils: a sketch of the boarding school, a few dried flowers in a card, a poem on the spring.

He loves her. His notes in her desk, between the novels that he gives her, among her exercise books. As soon as she opens the lid of her desk, the aroma of his pipe hits her. He loves her and even writes full of praise about her essays. She has always known that he admires her writing style, but he obviously found that difficult to express.

In a boarding school full of women it is impossible to love a male member of staff in secret. Too many eyes, too much jealousy and women's intuition.

His eyes seek hers during a walk with all the female teachers and pupils to a farm in the country. The young ladies in their cheerful cotton dresses, their rosy cheeks, radiant eyes, and she is his chosen one. He pours a bowl of milk for her, comes up to her with his hands full of radishes to let her taste, calls her to come and look at the cows.

He puts his foot under her dress during the English lesson in his study. Slumped far back in his chair in order to reach that far, and it makes her laugh; she cannot help it, she bursts out laughing, and monsieur Chapelle does not understand why, looks inquiringly and with a surprised smile from her to monsieur and back. Their love is so beautiful—surely he cannot take offence at it?

She meets monsieur in a back street near the Zenne, stands

waiting for him after a note between the sheets of an essay. He pushes her against the wall, lets go of her hurriedly when a man in a cart comes by, and then kisses her, presses against her, wants to possess her. *Je vous aime, Charlotte.* He puts his hand under her skirts and feels how wet she is. He is her master, she is his.

And then spring is over. He writes that he must speak to her, in his study. The tone of the note is dry. She does not know what to think, but faith is not dead in her, however often it has been dashed in her young life. Has he found a solution; does he want to elope with her? That's impossible, that's forbidden. And yet she would do it. Right now, right now, monsieur.

*

Monsieur places his palm against her cheek.

'Don't be sad, *mon amour*, but you cannot give Maurice Chapelle and me English lessons anymore. She prefers that you don't. I… How shall I put it…? I won't have so much time for you for a while.'

'Not so much time,' Charlotte repeats tonelessly.

Mon amour. He runs his thumb over her lips, as he announces a distance between them. He hesitates, wants to give a less banal explanation, but changes his mind.

'I'm sorry,' he says, and while she is still looking for words to formulate a question, he opens the door, which creaks treacherously, and goes into the corridor.

*

'Rest assured, *mademoiselle*,' says monsieur Chapelle and his gushing friendliness betrays his regret. He has taken her aside as she came into the classroom with the other young ladies. 'English is definitely a useful language.' He leans his thin frame against the piano, with his long legs stretched, and runs a little finger over his thin flaxen moustache. 'On that island of yours they can communicate with it and in America too it is extremely popular.' And with an apologetic smile: 'But you will have to admit that English is totally unsuitable for writing songs in; it is not melodic. Moreover, we have little opportunity for speaking English in Brussels. So what point is there in learning it? Let me concentrate on the language of music.'

Whereupon he leaves her to welcome madame Heger, who has just appeared in the doorway. And oh, how lively madame sounds, and she has a new song.

'Madame has a new song!' exclaims monsieur Chapelle to his pupils and they let out enthusiastic cries. Charlotte slips out of the class, does not know where to go and returns discouraged to the dormitory. A performance by madame is more than her frayed nerves could stand.

*

Her heart is a tired muscle. She lies in bed and sees monsieur, feels his palm against her cheek. 'I'm sorry,' he said and walked away from her. How naïve she was to assume that their romance could stay hidden from madame. Claire Heger is not an *imbécile*. Behind that amiable smile there lurks a sophisticated spy. An experienced headmistress knows all about intrigues and courtships, has informers and reads letters.

It is well-known that during the lessons madame snuffles around in the dormitory to 'inspect' the wardrobes. She herself has realised for some time that Gertrude checks the wash to see who has had her period and who has not. Monsieur's billets-doux could not escape madame's attention for long: probably she goes through the contents of her desk.

Charlotte sits up in bed, her arms around her knees, and stares into the dark. Madame sees a danger in Charlotte's association with her husband, and perhaps that is more of a favourable sign.

If only there were some one she could talk to. If only she could, like the other women here, tug a friend's sleeve and crawl into bed with her to confide a secret and ask for advice. Tears are running down her cheeks and she is too disheartened to wipe them away.

Em, I miss you so.

With her sister she had formed an island in the boarding school, a capriciously shaped island, and apart from Louise de Bassompierre none of the women had been able to clamber ashore. She herself had not made friends with anyone, not with any of the chilly, foolish and superficial Belgian girls and teachers. She had not spoken to them and now they don't speak to her, the eccentric, proud Englishwoman.

XXV

Charlotte walks hurriedly through the garden of the boarding school, her head bent, her face hidden under the brim of her bonnet. She leaves the garden and lets the gate swing shut behind her. The rue d'Isabelle is deserted and yet there is an air of expectation. This first September day is dazzlingly sunny. She lingers for a moment and looks round at the gate. She can go back to the dormitory and lie in bed there, with the sheet pulled up high. She can say that she is not well (that would not be a lie), but she cannot stand it any longer within the walls of the empty school. Everyone, apart from the cook, the maid and herself went to their families for the summer holidays two weeks ago, something she cannot afford.

So it will have to be the streets of Brussels, the streets of this strange city with which she can find no connection. She gathers her skirts and goes up the steps to the park. There, among the statues, and around the basin with the water lilies in it, young ladies stroll with their beaux, and an older, greying couple, arm in arm, united in more mature love.

On the terrace of the pleasure gardens a mother is leafing through a newspaper, while her sons are spinning their tops. Near the bandstand a couple are lying in the grass under the lime trees. He is reading aloud to her, most probably a *poème*, and she is lying with her eyes closed, surrendering herself unashamedly to the sun and to his voice. Charlotte cannot stand their happiness, and wants to go. The borders are still full of blooming plants. The summer is a time of blossoming. For her too, for her too! In her bosom there is a bud pushing with all its might, but being smothered and doomed to fade.

It is busy on the quays—market day—and she walks among the stalls, ignoring the cries of a bald, fat chap extolling meat knives and looking at the ground so as not to see the fresh, contented faces of the housewives and maids. The smell of melons is sweet on the air and a little further on there is the revolting smell of rotten fish. A farmer singing the praises of a heifer, the restless neighing of a horse, a lady with a black veil giving her coachman instructions. And everywhere the sun: the sun that warms and caresses even the hard, deathly cobbles into soft cushions, and strokes her face with soft hands as if it wants to console her. But she does not want its tenderness and is like a resentful child turning away from its mother. She refuses to accept any tenderness that does not come from monsieur. A boy drops a dish full of eggs, a woman pulls along a sheep on a rope, and her mind wanders, lost.

At the Marché aux Grains she stops and does not know what street to take. Oh, if only she could go to Mary, but Mary is no longer at the château of Koekelberg. After Martha's death Mary lived for a while with a family she knew in the rue Royale and last month she left for Germany, where she is teaching at a boys' school.

She turns round and round. Where to then, tell me, where to? To Martha's grave in the Protestant cemetery. Surely there must be something familiar about a cemetery; after all she spent her whole childhood among the graves. Along the quays and through the city to the rue Royale. Once outside the Porte de Louvain the road begins to climb. The atmosphere becomes oppressive and she feels a bead of sweat running down her back. She is not certain of the way to the cemetery, because she forgot to bring a map and Emily is not at her side, but she has time: no one will miss her in the school. Her hot food will get cold at her place at table in the refectory and the indifferent maid will scrape the plate into the dog's bowl.

She sits on the grave and tries to think of Martha. Young, happy Martha dead in her coffin, pale and threadbare like a dress hanging forgotten on a washing line for years, a prey to the elements.

And she loves him. She loves him.

'Monsieur,' she murmurs. 'Monsieur!'

The sun is everywhere and the hours just will not pass. The hands of the clock on the medieval church seem to crawl as if they are being held back by evil powers. Her only consolation is that if she exhausts herself sufficiently, the night will finally bring her a few hours of oblivion. She walks back to town and although she feels tired and there are blisters on her feet, the way is too short for her. She rounds the corner of the rue d'Isabelle and there is the boarding school. The day has been exhaustingly hot and darkness shows no sign of falling, but she does not want to go in yet. The school is her prison and until her pupils are back and her presence is required, she prefers to stay away for as long as possible.

A booming of bells catches her attention. It is the hypnotic voice of the church of Saint-Michel and Sainte-Gudule calling the faithful to vespers. She does not know what possesses her, but she hurries towards it, along the rue de la Chancellerie and up the many white stone steps to the church. Next to the porch a beggar puts out his hand towards her and she gives him a coin, not for his salvation, but for hers.

How cool it is in the church. A few women are sitting praying with rosary beads between their fingertips. She wished she could sink down onto the flagstones, but she goes and sits at the side to wait until evening prayers are over. In a deserted corner of the church confessions are being heard. Confession! She is a sinner and has to tell her story. Someone must listen to her. A working-class woman approaches the confessional; she tidies her greasy hair by smoothing it against her skull and straightens her apron. Can the priest see her then? Isn't confession anonymous?

She can still change her mind: she can go back to the streets where no one knows her. However, she remains seated and waits. The woman emerges from the confessional with the trace of a smile on her lips.

She gets up, scarcely knowing what she is doing. The tradition is alien to her: how should she address the priest? She creeps into the confessional, lets the red velvet curtain fall behind her and is almost overpowered by the smell of incense, pipe tobacco and old sweat. Just enough light enters to be able to make out vaguely the face behind the wicker grille.

'*Mon père*,' she says and the blood rises to her head. 'I have sinned.'

'Are you a foreigner?' asks the priest severely, obviously surprised by her accent.

She answers in the affirmative, and adds that she was brought up as a Protestant. He wants to know if she is still a Protestant and she nods, which he appears not to see, so she clears her throat and whispers: '*Oui, mon père.*' He says that in that case she cannot confess and tears well up in her eyes. If he dismisses her without letting her tell her story, she will be close to despair. She tells him this and begs him to listen to her.

'*Ma fille*,' says the priest tenderly, making her almost choke on her tears. 'Confess and let this be your first step towards the true Church.'

She tells him everything, in a furious tempo. About the safe but oppressive life in her father's house and how she escaped from it. How she thought she would be able to enjoy freedom in Brussels, but allowed herself to be shut up in a boarding school. The priest's face comes closer to the grille: she feels his breath on her cheek.

'Tell me what your sin is.'

'I love someone.'

'There is nothing wrong with that.'

'He is married.' Well, that was it, she had said it.

'He is married and has children with the woman.'

'Then you must stamp out those feelings. You must tear them out of your mind as if they were thistles in a flower garden. Pray to the Lord and ask Him for help. Pray to the Holy Virgin. I can teach you how to do that.'

He gives her absolution, although she is lying, because she cannot mend her ways; she has no intention of leaving Belgium and distancing herself from monsieur.

When she leaves the confessional, she sees that the priest in his black cassock is also coming out. She looks around, but there is no one else waiting. The church is empty. Everyone is outside, in the sultry evening.

The priest is young, but his face already has the plump, slack contours so typical of the clergy of this religion. He takes her hand in his hands, but his grip is limp.

'You must come and see me, *mademoiselle*,' he says, 'tomorrow morning in the presbytery on the rue Montagne du Parc.' They will talk about her sinful thoughts and he will help her resist the urge. Catholicism, the truth faith, will bring peace to her heart.

She says devoutly '*Oui, mon père*' but she knows that she will never visit him. Imagine him with his kind words and consolation tempting her to become a Catholic!

Once outside, she still does not know where to go. She wants to rest in the arms of the man she loves. It would not matter at all to her if that was under the open sky, if he left everything for her and they were both as poor as the wretches who slept in porches. But monsieur is where he is. On the coast on the terrace of a white villa: he with his pipe, madame with her embroidery, Louise patiently teaching little Claire hopscotch. He must surely be thinking of her and counting the days until he can return to her.

*

That night in the boarding school she descends the staircase. Her candle casts a ghostly light on the stairs and her pale feet. There, under the stairs in the carré, is the concierge's little lodge. The door gives way. This is the cupboard containing cough syrup and other medicines. The cupboard is locked, but she knows where the key is: in the smallest drawer in Gertrude's desk.

She squats down in front of the cupboard and through the glass sees the laudanum. Two of the familiar little bottles with the cork. A couple of drops help against headache, cramps, diarrhoea and attacks of melancholy. She can empty them both. Or would that make her vomit? It is bitter stuff; perhaps she must mix it with sugar.

In the morning she will not be able to remember how long she sat there, but she must eventually have gone back upstairs.

*

The school fills up again as suddenly as it emptied. Coachmen and servants carry cases, boots and boxes full of books upstairs and from the classrooms and the drawing rooms comes the sound of the animated voices of worried mothers and their lively daughters, who in their new autumn clothes look like pert pheasants. A few tears are shed, but 'It's not for long, *mon petit chou*, we'll soon come and take you out for a Sunday!' Charlotte receives the girls in her group, as from this year on she will have her own class which she will teach in French and English. She avoids madame Heger and waits for her master. Only after the gate has been shut for hours and madame comes to inspect the dormitory to ensure that there are no ribbons or shoes lying around under the beds, does she dare cautiously to inquire whether monsieur is back home and whether he will resume classes tomorrow.

Madame does not look at her and straightens the sheet on a bed with critically raised eyebrows.

'My husband has gone to the Athénée Royal to welcome the boys,' she says, briskly plumping up the pillow.

'You will find the timetable in the refectory tomorrow.'

Her voice sounds controlled and when she looks round the dormitory and claps her pretty hands as if to herald the new school year, Charlotte sees the inconceivable: the full rounding of her belly.

*

'Victoria!' cheers a young man in a grey overcoat and he throws his top hat in the air so enthusiastically that it leads one to suspect that he is an ardent admirer of the young queen in the coach.

The crowd along the rue Royale consists mainly of locals:

mothers with prams, teachers, schoolchildren and officials who have been given a half day off. But English shouts also ring out.

'God save the queen!' screams a group of English schoolgirls frenziedly, waving red, white and blue ribbons.

It is repugnant to Charlotte that there can be so much joy and colour in the world, when she herself is so heavy-hearted. She screws up her eyes against the bright sunshine. A carriage with dignitaries from the English court drives past and is followed by Queen Victoria's open carriage. The coach drives slowly and so close to the pavement that Charlotte has the feeling that she can get in just like that. Victoria is sitting next to her uncle, the Belgian king Leopold, whom she is visiting for a few days, and how she is enjoying herself! She bares her little white teeth in a smile and waves her plump, blue satin hand. An energetic lady, dressed fairly dully, with nothing discernibly royal about her.

She has love, Charlotte knows, she has her Albert. It consoles her somewhat that the Victoria of the portraits, with the thick, dark hair, the mouth small and moist as the trembling snout of a fawn and the startled blue eyes, is very little like the real Victoria. The young queen has a receding chin, heavy eyelids and is—yes, actually a little fat. She is the most powerful woman in the world, but she has not been granted beauty either.

The cheers, the flags and her little queen on a visit, and yet there is not a friend in the whole city on whom she can rely. *Be strong, Charlotte.* Her fingers clutch Mary Taylor's letter in her coat pocket. *Let go of him, Charlotte, leave Brussels.* But she is asking for the impossible. After Victoria and Leopold's carriage come the cavalry of the royal guard in their white uniforms. When the first commoner's coach follows, Charlotte disengages from the crowd and is about to cross the road.

'Whore!' a shrill woman's voice suddenly cries. 'Dirty whore!'

Charlotte turns in alarm and her shoulders hunch involuntarily. A coarse wench, dressed in rags, throws a piece of cobblestone at a young lady in an open carriage that is stationary in the traffic jam. The stone ricochets off the edge of the door. Is it her again? The attractive young lady does not cringe, but keeps her eyes focused defiantly and proudly on her attacker, while her mother next to her in the coach, her face contorted with fear, pushes in front of her daughter in an attempt to shield her.

'It's that whore Arcadie Claret!' cries the wench. 'She makes love to the king while our queen lies in bed ill!'

The girl from the beach.

XXVI

Their shuffling bare feet on the wood and their arguing over a lost earring, the cloud of talcum powder that has to disguise their body odour as the week goes on, their lamentations about the stove that does not draw properly. And everywhere—in the washbasins, on the floor, in the porridge and even baked in the bread—their long hairs that have fallen out in infinite shades of brown and blond, and occasionally thick and black. So many women and yet Charlotte feels lonely. She is like a prisoner waiting in her dungeon for her release, if it ever comes. A pigeon descends onto the windowsill and with its beady eyes peers impudently inside. Charlotte is cold and wants to get a shawl from her wardrobe, but remains sitting on her bed, paralysed by her grief.

*

She occasionally sees monsieur: in the corridor, in the classroom, in the refectory. He is in hectic conversation with mademoiselle Sophie or mademoiselle Blanche, leafing frantically through his papers, hastily pouring a dash of milk in his coffee. She is no longer given private lessons and during the classes in French literature he does not read out any of her essays. He still corrects them, but where the margins were once full of comments on style and content, now he notes solely the spelling mistakes, and she makes fewer and fewer of those. She waits for a word from him, but how long can you wait for a voice in a desert of silence?

In desperation Charlotte withdraws evening after evening

to her classroom and writes an essay that monsieur will really not be able to ignore. It is the plea of a poor painter to a baron, with a request for support. *My Lord,* her pen scratches across the paper, *I would not ask you for help if you were only rich and powerful. But you are my equal in intelligence and my superior in experience and virtue.* With stiff, cold fingers she lays the essay on monsieur's desk. *Excuse my temerity, My Lord, but I am bold enough to say I have genius. You can help me escape obscurity and wretchedness and help my talents to blossom.*

A week or so later she finds the essay in her desk. It contains no more than a correction here and there, scarcely legible, because monsieur pressed so lightly on the pencil. The moment has come when she must do something impulsive (it is in her nature and in bad times she can no longer control herself). That morning she gives an English lesson to her regular group of pupils; what madame calls her 'select group of clever pupils', a designation that greatly surprises her, since she believes that none of the Belgian girls here in the school excels at anything whatsoever.

'Tell me about your Sunday, Joséphine,' she asks in English. The girl brushes her chin with the end of her plait and gawps at Charlotte as if she has just spoken Arabic.

'Tell us what you did on Sunday afternoon. Just a few sentences, it's not that difficult.'

Joséphine rolls her eyes upwards and jerks her shoulders in boredom. She still says nothing and something like anger starts to well up in Charlotte, a feverish rage that drives out the chill in her body and mind with whiplashes.

'Very well.' Charlotte opens her book and says briskly: 'None of you will be going into the garden shortly, but you will stay here and write an essay on what you did on Sunday afternoon.'

'Oh, *mademoiselle* Charlotte,' cries the beautiful Aimée, 'please don't do that to us!' Undoubtedly she wants to go to the forbidden path in the garden during the break to catch a love letter from her admirer thrown out of a window of the Athénée Royal.

The girls whisper rebelliously and no one seems to be about to take up their pen. Godelieve, a Flemish girl, starts coughing ostentatiously and Charlotte dislikes her stupid appearance and inane eyes, which only brighten when she is plotting mischief. Godelieve coughs until everyone is looking at her and then shoves a dictionary provocatively off her desk with her elbow. It falls to the floor with a thud.

For a moment Charlotte is nonplussed by such impertinence, but then she snaps.

'You will all also be missing lunch. Write a detailed account of everything you have done on Sunday afternoons this autumn.'

Every sound, ever breath seems suspended: this is too much. The only worse punishment Charlotte could have devised would have been cancelling Sunday leave—a punishment even madame Heger has only ever imposed once, and that on a pupil who had kissed a workman in public at the Grand-Place. Godelieve, obviously shocked, picks the dictionary off the floor.

During the morning break Charlotte goes to get a glass of water and drops into the kitchen to tell the cook that her pupils will not be eating. That causes some commotion, since 'Oh, it's such wet, shivery weather' and 'The girls need their soup!'

On her way back to the class, in the pocket of her apron, she touches Mary's last letter with her fingertips. Mary writes that she must leave Brussels. *At once, Charlotte. You're heading for unhappiness if you stay.* Mary is most probably right and she should leave, but she cannot face it now. She must fight for what she loves.

When noon arrives, she also becomes hungry and she is unable to concentrate on marking the piles of schoolwork in front of her. The girls are bent over their desks, writing a punishment exercise, which as she knows only too well, was intended purely to cool her rage. But so what? Does she not have any right to feelings? Is she as a teacher a soulless being only able to dictate soporific texts, spy on her pupils and like a ventriloquist's dummy say what madame wants her to say?

Godelieve is bent so far over her writing that her nose is almost touching the page. She should talk to the girl's parents about glasses; why hasn't she done that yet? And how pale Alexandrine looks! Fasting won't do her any good, as she has been having dizzy spells recently. A vague tenderness for her pupils surges through her and she regrets her stupid punishment. On second thoughts, Godelieve may not be a simpleton at all; didn't she recently write a poem in English, about a litter of new-born kittens it's true, but really good and touching?

The life of these girls is as flat as the Flemish polders. Everything is decided for them and one or two years after leaving the school they will become mothers, married off to the son of a business associate of papa's, or an older man with a noble title. Or, if they are lucky, married to the young man of their choice, as long as he is well-to-do and of good family.

Perhaps their lives aren't all that bad. Perhaps her own life is chaotic, a chain of wrong decisions?

For the first time she regrets not having made friendships at the boarding school. That would certainly have been possible with the older girls and the teachers.

And it is the tenderness welling up in her that makes her

long for monsieur, and she knows that she can no longer be separated from him.

Just before the end of the lunch break and before mademoiselle Sophie comes to teach history, she summons Aimée to her desk and gives her a folded letter.

'Take this message to monsieur Heger in the Athénée Royal. At once.'

I want to see you, monsieur. Come to me tonight at eleven o'clock in my classroom.

*

She has hope. He will come, he will take her in his arms and no longer talk in vague terms.

During the meal in the refectory that evening it is as if she has bubonic plague, she is so universally avoided. The kitchen maid has even 'forgotten' to make tea for her, despite having done it for her since her first evening here in Brussels, as she cannot tolerate coffee in the evenings. After the meal Charlotte grabs her coat, mutters something to Gertrude about visiting an acquaintance and leaves the school. She goes and sits in the church of Saint-Jacques-sur-Coudenberg and looks at the devout old crones who come to pray there at this late hour. When even they have gone home, she makes an attempt to read a silly French novelette that she confiscated from a pupil during the lesson. Her hands are clenching with cold. She stays there until the women of the boarding school have almost certainly gone to bed. Every second Tuesday in the month monsieur has a meeting of the Saint-Vincent de Paul Society and comes home at about eleven. She bows her head, moved by the thought of him: she knows him as if he were her husband.

As she walks along the school's path she sees a gas lamp still burning in the carré and in the small drawing room, but madame will soon be going upstairs now. She is heavily pregnant and the birth is expected in December.

At a quarter to eleven she herself is standing by the window of the classroom, with a candle next to her on the windowsill. She is not wearing a shawl, since she wants to make an elegant impression, but the stove has gone out and it is chilly. A street lamp casts a golden light on the garden path to the carré: the gate, the bare trees, the path. And there is monsieur (how well she knows him!); he slides the narrow beam in front of the gate and comes up the path. He sees her and with a lively expression on his dear face he raises his arm slightly in greeting. Unbelievable that she once suspected that this man hit his wife, simply because of his virile aura. He is a good person. A few more moments and he will be with her. It is taking rather a long time, but he must be first hanging his coat in the cloakroom cupboard. It is taking a long time. She stands by the door and holds the door handle, but does not dare open it: she does not want to see the empty carré. It cannot be that he is not coming. Finally she goes back to the window, opens it and leans far out in order to look at the windows on the right. The light in the carré has gone out and in the small drawing room it is also dark.

Later she feels the door of Gertrude's lodge: it is locked.

*

'You wished to speak to me,' says madame Heger with a sigh. She sounds hoarser than usual and takes a handkerchief out of her sleeve. November is particularly damp and chilly this year, and various residents of the boarding school have caught cold.

'But before you speak, *mademoiselle* Charlotte, I would like to ask you something.'

Charlotte has not slept the previous night and has not had breakfast either. She feels terrible, but sits as straight as she can on the soft sofa and keeps her hands folded in her lap.

'Why did you punish your pupils so severely?' asks madame. 'Because Joséphine couldn't tell you in fluent English that she rode her pony through the park on Sunday? Withholding food is a physical punishment, *mademoiselle*. It may be current in the schools of Yorkshire, but here we are gentler.'

'Gentleness in education makes pupils soft, lazy and disrespectful,' says Charlotte, but her voice does not sound very convincing. Hasn't she herself always pleaded against schools like Cowan Bridge, where she and her sisters were served food that had gone off?

'Are you saying that I am not respected? In my own school?' Madame sniffs and blows her nose. Pregnancy has made her puffy-faced, with blotchy red skin, but she is still far too handsome to arouse pity. Anyway, how could Charlotte feel any pity for the woman carrying monsieur's child? She does not answer the question and concentrates on the winding stalk with pale red flowers in the Persian carpet.

'*Bon.*' Madame clasps her hands. 'What do you want to speak to me about? Is it about that fuss in your class yesterday?'

'I wish to tender my resignation, madame.'

Voilà, you've won. Let me go now.

The flowers unfold against a royal blue background.

'It's not clear to me why you are doing that,' says madame, true to her hypocritical personality, 'but I will consider your request. Please look at me.'

Charlotte looks up reluctantly and madame turns out not to be such a virtuoso actress, since her whole being exudes relief.

'Your studies are completed, *ma chère*,' says madame and she unexpectedly and surprisingly gracefully sits down beside her on the sofa. 'It seems to me a wise decision to go home and set up a school.' And in an indulgent tone, edging still closer to her: 'Don't be resentful. Single women can find great fulfilment and satisfaction in serving others.'

Madame's mercy, madame's wisdom: like a common kitchen knife thrust between her ribs with a single shrill, furious cry. Charlotte stands up brusquely and is about to leave the drawing room, but the door swings open and there is monsieur.

'*Meess* Charlotte! What are you doing here?'

She tries to walk on without a word, but he grabs her by the arm.

'What is going on? Sit, sit!'

He gives her a push towards an armchair, but she refuses to sit down.

'*Mademoiselle* Charlotte has tendered her resignation,' says madame.

'Resignation? But that's complete madness! You didn't accept it, I hope.'

'I'm considering it.'

'We cannot do without *Meess* Charlotte here in the school. In fact, in a few days she'll be coming with me to the Flemish workers. It struck me this afternoon how useful she could be to me there.'

And Charlotte, who thought she was dead, feels something like life stirring in her again and drinks in his words thirstily.

Madame tucks her handkerchief in her sleeve and stands up.

'Oh, is that so, Constantin? I think it would be better if we discussed this privately.' She rocks her way to the door, one hand under her belly, and opens it wide. '*Mademoiselle*, I'll let you know my decision. You may go.'

*

Madame is to give birth that same evening—prematurely, it seems—to a daughter who does not weigh enough and who it is said will not survive: Julie Marie. Monsieur leaves the side of his wife and their new-born daughter as little as possible. Monsieur Chapelle is kind enough to take over the evening classes at the Vieux Marché from his brother-in-law, although it must be said that the rough workers send shivers down his spine. And Charlotte? Charlotte waits.

XXVII

She comes downstairs and there he stands, deep furrows in his forehead and a single furrow between his eyebrows, as if carved in wood with a sharp stone. A pensive look, his strong hand round a baluster.

It is the second half of December and monsieur is finally going to take her with him to the evening class. Her ringlets have sagged at the end of the day, but she has put on a freshly starched dress and is holding her dark-blue cloak over her arm.

'Come on,' says monsieur rather flatly. He takes the cloak from her, but just as he throws it round her shoulders, madame comes into the carré, her head shrunk in her pale, flabby skin, but with her rattling bunch of keys and with the cash book at the ready.

'*Chéri*, are you really going?' she asks in a friendly tone. She is like the exhausted hero who even after an arduous campaign advances once more heroically onto the battlefield with his sword drawn. 'Oh, I see that *mademoiselle* Charlotte wants to accompany you, but I'm afraid it won't be possible.'

This time a sword is planted, with the most amiable of smiles, in her heart.

'*Chéri*, I must write urgently to that English nanny who offered her services,' says madame and she ties the scarf solicitously round her husband's neck, though he immediately loosens it a little.

'It must be done this evening,' she continues, 'because then our neighbour, who is going to London, can take the letter with him.' And then to Charlotte: 'You *must* help me, *mademoiselle*. My English is so abominable.'

Charlotte feels a strange, dizzying heat rising to her head. The carré and madame with her cherry-red shawl and her brave eyes disappear behind a misty haze.

'My heart is going to break,' she murmurs, and casts an entreating glance at monsieur. It cannot be that these few hours with him will be taken away. He opens the garden door and gestures to her to go out.

'Not now, Claire, please,' she hears him say, and then they are together on the garden path. Trembling all over, she walks to the gate. Oh, don't let madame come after them!

Monsieur slides the narrow beam from the back of the gate and there is the street, but she is shocked to see Gertrude waiting on the pavement with her basket.

'Help her carry it,' says monsieur curtly and walks on ahead.

*

She has scarcely sat down next to Gertrude, on a chair against the wall at the back of the parish hall when Emile is standing in front of her. The class is just about to begin, but he makes no move to look for a place at one of the tables.

'Can I sit next to you?' he asks, and even before she can answer he has put a chair down next to her. Gertrude nudges her conspiratorially in the side and whispers: 'You've hooked one, girl. He's a much better bloke for you.'

Charlotte is reasonably indifferent to who or what is sitting next to her, but then she sees monsieur trying to catch a glimpse of her between the heads of two workers and reads the surprise on his face when he notices Emile next to her. Perhaps he will become jealous; perhaps he realises that she won't wait for him for ever.

'Why haven't you come with Heger again until now?' asks

Emile in an emphatic tone, his breath on her cheek. 'I was so looking forward to seeing you.'

'Shush,' says Charlotte, 'monsieur Heger is beginning. What are you doing here anyway? You'd do better to sit at the front.'

'Listen, I've got to speak to you,' says Emile imperturbably. Although his trousers are worn out and his dialect betrays his lowly origins, he exhibits calm self-confidence. 'It's important, for me, but for you too.'

She nods, more to get him to be silent than in assent. A worker at the front of the room is reading aloud falteringly from *L'Observateur*, a Brussels newspaper. Emile turns his hat in his hands and she sees the dirt under his fingernails, but then she looks to the side and meets his hypnotic, light-eyed gaze. If a physiognomist were to read this man's facial features without knowing his background, without seeing the heavy shoes and blue cotton neckerchief, he would definitely conclude that he came from a noble family and knew Classical literature.

'I'll wait for you by the bridge,' says Emile, 'the bridge to the islet. D' you know where that is?'

She does not reply and he pushes his thigh against hers.

'Charlotte, d' you know where that is?'

She is no longer a *mademoiselle* for him; he has appropriated her.

*

On the way back to the boarding school Gertrude falls behind. Of course she is standing somewhere under a lean-to kissing her Jef, who has worked his way up to foreman in a grain merchant's and seems to have serious plans for her.

Fine, chilly raindrops are falling in a dismal cadence.

Monsieur Heger leads Charlotte to a deserted quay. The

water of the canal seems black and their breath steams in the darkness. He does not pull her to him or kiss her, but after a painful pause, in which he seems to have forgotten exactly what he is doing here, he takes her hand—which is wet and cold, since in her confusion just now in the boarding school she forgot her gloves.

'You don't love me anymore,' says Charlotte and she shivers as he runs his warm lips over her fingertips.

'No, no, it's not that,' says monsieur, but when she tries to snuggle up to him, he tenses his muscles nervously. 'Not here, Charlotte, suppose someone sees us.'

'You don't love me anymore.'

'Yes I do, really I do, and you must stay in Brussels. I need you, I cannot do without you.' His voice falters with emotion and in the half-light she thinks she sees his eyes gleaming moistly. 'For months I have been trying to temper my feelings for you, but I cannot. I want to have you with me, but we must be discreet.'

She does not dare give her dream for the future a name, because it is scandalous. If she cannot marry monsieur, she is prepared to live in sin with him. But such a relationship is so associated with infamy that it cannot be put into words; and if you were to try, the words would sound shameful here on the quay in the dark. Even the question she asks she ought not to ask.

'Do you mean… Do you mean that you do not choose me?'

He shakes his head in desperation. 'What are you talking about? I have a family, Charlotte.'

Madame Heger with her sanctimonious courtesy and her over-soft hands looms up before Charlotte and she loathes her.

'Why didn't you come to my classroom that evening?'

He looks away from her in embarrassment, peers at an empty crate bobbing about in the water, but then an imperious look comes into his eyes and he grabs her wrists.

'Claire was waiting for me. Can you not understand that? That does not mean I don't love you, I do. I want you to be mine.'

'Why should you? I'm no beauty, I cannot sing or play an instrument.'

'Oh, you little witch, how you are ranting. You and I, we're one, don't you know that? I long for you and you fascinate me. Whole worlds flow out of that pen of yours, worlds that are foreign to me. Endless possibilities. And that stubbornness, that English stubbornness—I want to break it.'

'Say it then. Say you choose me.'

'We can see each other regularly outside the *pensionnat*. I can arrange something, a room in town.'

She feels the grip of his hands loosening and rage flares up in her.

'Listen to what you are saying! How is it possible, monsieur? What you are proposing to me are the crumbs from your table. The sweet bread is for madame and I'm allowed what is left after she has eaten her fill. You don't want me, but nor do you want to lose me to someone else. Am I supposed to stay as a kind of slave? Who do you think I am? The fact that I do not possess riches or beauty does not mean that I have no feelings.'

She tears herself free of his grip and pushes him away.

'You won my heart with all those fine sentences from celebrated French writers. You listened to me and retrieved me from the darkness; you seduced me with your warmth and built castles in the air for me. And now you are blowing them away, away. "What are you talking about, Charlotte?" What am I talking about, monsieur? About your lies. You're breaking my heart.'

Before she realises what she is doing, her hand flies out and she hits him full in the face. With a cry of astonishment he recoils and she moves away, first with quick steps, then running, but the cobbles are slippery and as she turns the corner, she slips, falls full length on the ground and grazes her knee, tearing her stocking.

She stumbles on and does not know the way; darkness envelops her. It is dangerous here, as she knows from Gertrude: they attack you, or worse. She does not care anymore, she is already dead anyway.

There on the bridge stands a ghostly figure and it comes towards her. She panics, but then she recognises Emile.

'Charlotte, what happened?'

She wants to go on, run, but she is exhausted and remains standing in front of him. He takes off his neckerchief and tries to rub the mud off her chin, but she takes the cloth and dries her cheeks.

'Come 'ere.' He puts his arm round her. 'I'm so glad you came. Come on, you're chilled to the bone.'

*

''Ere it is,' says Emile.

The working-class café has promising bronze light behind the misted-up windows and in the pane above the door there is a name etched that with the best will in the world Charlotte could not pronounce. With her damp strands of hair, her chin grazed and her skirts covered in mud, she would rather not be seen. But the gentle pressure of Emile's hand in her back and the thought of a fire and hot soup make her give in. When she enters the smell of blood sausage and apple comes to greet her.

Good, dry wood is crackling in the hearth. Emile says something to two men with big moustaches sitting by the fire in their blue linen work smocks; he points to her, with her wet hair and dirty clothes. They immediately make room by the fire. If she really were a beautiful young woman, they would definitely have bowed to her playfully and inquired about the accident that had befallen her. As it is, they simply nod in sympathy.

'Sit down,' says Emile, 'and take your wet coat off. I'll be back.'

She has seldom had the experience of someone caring for her in this way, and it warms her heart.

A woman with black curls, worn loosely up, and scarlet painted lips sings a song in a strange mixture of plebeian French and what must be Flemish. The audience cheers and the waitresses serve tankards of beer. And whoops, the singer is dancing around with a young soldier, his eyes glazed with drink beneath his greasy hair.

''Ere,' says Emile, putting a towel around Charlotte's shoulders and a glass on the table. 'Drink up.'

'Brandy, that's far too strong for me,' she protests, but when she has rubbed her hair dry, he pushes the glass towards her and she sips at it. The brandy leaves a pleasant warmth in her chest. Emile arranges her cloak on a chair in front of the stove and sits opposite her on a stool.

A steaming bowl of pea soup is set in front of her. The red-haired waitress with the ample bosom stares shamelessly at Emile's noble face, but he does not deign to look at her. The girl reminds Charlotte of the waitress whom monsieur had playfully grabbed round the waist at carnival. She cringes at the memory, for that day he kissed her for the first time and she was so hopeful.

She eats the hearty soup and, like Emile, dips her bread in

it. She does not understand why, but more tears come and fall into her soup.

'That's all right,' says Emile. 'Let 'em come.'

She looks timidly around her and produces her handkerchief.

'You've got to let that Heger go,' says Emile. 'Surely a sensible woman like you does not want an affair with a married man.'

'Why on earth are you poking your nose in?' she asks fiercely, but he goes on: 'Do you want to fall pregnant by him then and be thrown out in the street, a disgrace to your family?'

In her horror she drops her spoon onto her bowl and splashes of green stain the bodice of her dress. Emile again hands his neckerchief and looks at her from under his eyelashes.

'Listen to me, please. I've got a proposal.' He puts his hands on his knees. 'Let's go to America together. Not to Verapas, 'cause that colony of Leopold's seems to be a big disappointment, but to Wisconsin.'

She stares at him in bewilderment.

'Wait, Charlotte, listen. An uncle of mine is in Wisconsin and it's good there. Come with me. I ain't been able to save much, but I'm an 'ard worker and I 'ave my talents. More and more farmers are movin' north and I want to set up a seed business. We can start small. You're not a factory girl but a person of education. You speak English and French, and you're not frightened of 'ard work. This is our chance of freedom. You're a liberated woman, Charlotte.'

Liberated? A woman who would willingly run away with a married man? If she did not feel so wretched, she would burst out laughing.

'Liberated, yes,' Emile maintains. 'Otherwise what are you doing in Brussels? You're not afraid. I want us to go together.'

'That's ridiculous, I scarcely know you.'

It begins to dawn on her how absurd her presence here is. Suddenly she gets up, grabs her cloak off the chair and wraps it round her.

'Thanks for the soup.'

She forces her way to the door, which is not easy, as a string of guests is just arriving: merry workers with beer and gin on their breath. A man with tough white hair growing out of his nose and ears brushes past her and gives her a drunken wink. Outside, she wants to get outside. She opens the door and the dreadful cold immediately creeps under her clothing. It is no longer raining and she feels the urge to run away.

'Charlotte, be reasonable!'

She turns round. A lock of hair falls onto Emile's forehead that she would like to push aside tenderly, but on second thoughts would not. Emile takes her by the elbow and walks a little way with her to a quiet street.

'You don't feel anything for me, Emile. This would be just a useful arrangement for you. Why don't you choose yourself a pretty wench?'

He does not reply, but pushes her gently against the blank wall of a warehouse.

'I want *you*,' he mumbles in her neck. 'Marry me, Charlotte. Let's leave 'ere together.'

The rough wall and his fingers intertwined with hers. For a moment it seems that she will lose herself in his embrace, but he does not press his body against her like a man who wants to possess a woman. His mouth is not lustful like that of monsieur.

'Emile,' she whispers sternly, 'let me go.' And when that does not seem to get through to him, she repeats her words with a scream and struggles fee.

'Whoa there, whoa there,' he says, putting his hands up.

Before she starts running, she turns round to him once more. There is disappointment in his intense, light eyes—or is it indignation?

*

That same evening she slips her letter of resignation under the door of *le salon de madame*. This city, this Brussels, is driving her crazy: she must get away, she is too tired to go on fighting. Once in bed she tries to sleep, but cannot, and at about four she comes downstairs, shivering with weakness and cold. Gertrude's lodge is not locked and she carefully takes a bottle of laudanum from the medicine chest.

XXVIII

While Charlotte lets herself be carried away on the sweet waves of opium, being united in the middle of the night in a passionate embrace with monsieur Heger and giving birth to a chubby baby son, it starts snowing outside. White flakes swirl down, so soft, so still, swaying softly like feathered seed. By dawn the squat towers of the church of Saint-Michel and Sainte-Gudule have caps on and the houses are tenderly tucked in. In the garden the branches of the pear trees have been covered in flour as if from an enormous sieve and on the wall sits the white cat with the black bib that wants to come and drink its milk, but is too frightened to leap into the soft ice-cold depths. Outside the walls of the boarding school, up the many very slippery steps to the rich district, a slight and insignificant girl of about sixteen, shrouded in rags, sweeps the snow from the pavement in front of the mansions along the park. Her uncombed hair falls like a white cascade down her bony face. At the other end of the city, on the quai des Poissonniers a dun-coloured mare slips on the icy cobbles and in her fall pulls the other horse in the team with her, causing their cart full of bricks to topple over.

Only the most stupid and youngest women in the boarding school, those who have no knowledge of the inconveniences that a fall of snow entails, are delighted when the curtains are opened onto the downy white world. Cries of rapture ring out. 'It's snowing! It's snowing!' Oddly enough mademoiselle Charlotte is not woken up by the commotion. She does not get up with the others, but lies in bed motionless, on her back and with her mouth slightly open.

When mademoiselle Charlotte does not appear at breakfast at seven o'clock, Louise de Bassompierre offers to look upstairs to see whether she is unwell. It is not clear whether that is the case, as the teacher is in a deep sleep. When the morning lessons begin and madame Heger is consulted about what mademoiselle Charlotte's pupils are to do in the meantime, she comes to check on the situation personally. Accompanied by Louise she goes upstairs to the dormitory, in her haste lifting her skirts higher than is decent.

Ô ciel, the thought goes through her, surely that wretched Englishwoman hasn't harmed herself? Scandal must be avoided at all times.

'*Mademoiselle*, get up!' says madame, shaking Charlotte by the shoulder with the same ferocity with which the maid is beating the lumps of snow out of the doormat outside. When her exhortation turns out to have no effect, she sends Louise for a basin of water and a flannel.

'Thanks, Louise, and now go downstairs.' She does not need any witnesses.

Mercilessly, madame presses the cold wet flannel on Charlotte's neck; Charlotte groans in her sleep and tries to push her away with her hand. She is still wearing her dress, crumpled and with green spots on the bodice.

'Open your eyes,' orders madame and she pinches her patient so viciously on the cheeks that the fingerprints will be visible for hours. Were it not for the fact that she did not want to make the bedding wet she would empty the whole contents of the basin over her. 'Open your eyes, I'm telling you.'

Just as with one of those expensive dolls with the new-fangled moving eyes, Charlotte's eyes open as soon as she sits up a little.

'Oh, of course, I might have known.' Madame looks at her

intently. 'Your pupils are as small as grains of salt. Oh, how foolish you are!' She sighs. 'Well, your condition is not too bad in the circumstances. Sleep it off.'

Once she is downstairs, madame tells the girls in the first classroom that their teacher is a little unwell and needs rest.

'*Mademoiselle* Charlotte is going home to set up a school with her sisters, but it makes her melancholy to have to say goodbye to all of you.'

'Really?' asks Godelieve with a guilty look.

'Oh, girls, make something nice that she can take home as a souvenir,' says madame. 'A self-portrait—or no, make a sketch of each other. Godelieve, perhaps you can write a poem.' Then she closes the door and hurries to the carré, where the domestic staff have gathered to collect their weekly wages shortly.

'Gertrude,' madame hisses in a whisper at the concierge, pulling her by the sleeve towards the small lodge under the stairs. 'Remove all the laudanum from the medicine chest at once.'

*

Later that day, when Charlotte reluctantly returns from peacefully bobbing about in a pond covered in water lilies, she feels a cool hand on her forehead.

'Drink some tea, *mademoiselle*,' says the young woman at her bedside.

The tea is strong and sweet, and she recognises Louise de Bassompierre. 'How long have I been asleep?'

Louise smiles. 'An eternity. But you are awake and well, that is the most important thing.'

When Charlotte is lying back on her pillows, she notices that

Louise is holding a letter in her hands.

'What's that?'

Louise bows her head and her fingertips involuntarily stroke the paper.

'A letter, *mademoiselle*. For your sister Emily.' She has gone red. 'Would you be good enough to give it to her when you go home?'

'Oh child, my sister has long since forgotten you.'

Charlotte throws back the covers and puts her feet, still rather shakily, on the ground.

'With all due respect, I think not,' says Louise and she picks up a framed print off the floor. 'Emily gave me this before she went, you see.'

Charlotte holds the print on her lap. It is a pencil sketch of a fir tree struck by a storm or lightning, undoubtedly by her sister.

'Emily will get your letter,' says Charlotte, 'but believe me: you were out of her heart the moment she set foot on English soil.'

She is startled by the cruelty of her own words.

*

The train, the train. It thunders through the dreary flat land, the white meadows hemmed with fishbone trees. Silent villages that seem abandoned. The air is a rare cobalt blue and here and there a star is still twinkling. There is almost nothing as lonely as travelling by oneself at a holiday time and knowing that one will not be home by evening. On this first morning of 1844 Charlotte is actually more than alone, as madame Heger is sitting opposite her. Like a watchdog the headmistress will take her to the packet boat. Madame is knitting, something in expensive wool for one of her children. The clicking of the knitting needles and her busy hands. She regularly holds the item away from her to examine it. So they travel together from Brussels to Ostend: the young woman who loves a married man and the worldly-wise lady who knows how without too much upheaval she can nip a flirtation of her husband's in the bud. In Charlotte's mind's eye, in the reflection of the wet window, monsieur Heger is travelling with them. A dressing gown with an Oriental motif over his pyjamas. How his hands were shaking early this morning in the carré when he gave her his own copy of *Les Fleurs de la Poésie Française*. In presenting her with her certificate, carrying the seal of the Athénée Royal, he kissed her just by her ear.

'I shall miss you so,' he whispered hoarsely.

*

The harbour of Ostend is a watercolour in brown and grey tints: the ships, the quayside and the melting snow.

Charlotte extends her hand with a stiff arm to take her leave of madame.

'It is better like this,' says madame. 'Build a life in your native country, *ma chère*. That's where you belong. We'd prefer it if you never came back to Brussels. Do you hear me? Never.' She gives a sharp tug on Charlotte's fingers. '*Au revoir, mademoiselle.*'

'Oh, for heaven's sake leave me be,' cries Charlotte. And she hurries up the gangplank onto the packet boat.

BANISHED

XXIX

Shame on the emigrée who returns home without a travel bag bulging with gold coins and a desirable husband from the distant country on her arm. Charlotte, the parson's daughter, is back home. Roll up, roll up! Her heart in pieces and no ring on her hand.

The wind hits her in the face as she walks up the steep main street of Haworth. Two factory boys, their caps defiantly back to front on their heads, lug her trunk. She turns up her collar and prays she does not bump into anyone she knows. Once she raps the brass door knocker of the parsonage, Emily opens up.

'Em,' stammers Charlotte. 'Em.'

She starts sobbing and wants to fall into her sister's arms, but Emily recoils from so much pathos. Slightly irritated, she gestures to Charlotte to stop crying and go into the living room.

Her father is sitting writing by the window and looks up. It is as if there is a milky skin over his pupils.

'Who was that at the door, Emily?'

'It's me, papa,' says Charlotte and crouches down beside her father. He lays his hand on her wet cheek.

'Oh, my prodigal daughter. Are you sad, dear child?'

'Yes,' she says, and then she lies: 'Saying goodbye to my pupils was hard, papa.'

How can she tell her father, who preaches abstinence and self-control, that she loves the husband of another woman? *Thou shalt not covet your neighbour's house, nor any thing that is thy neighbour's.* Her father in the pulpit, his proud stance, his inward eye focused on the path of righteousness, his words echoing among the high arched vaults.

*

Brussels, 1 January 1844
My dearest girl,
You are on board the ship that is taking you further and further away from me. And I sit in my study, light my pipe and think of you. Your image looms up before me in the light of the gas lamp. There you are, my little witch. Restrained and passionate. Subservient and yet stubborn. You love me and yet you left me.
This afternoon I dined with my children and some members of my family to celebrate the New Year. I wasn't feeling well, but did not want to spoil the tradition and the festive mood. Marie and Louise read out their New Year's letters and I tried to concentrate on their words. But my thoughts were elsewhere. I miss you, Charlotte.
When I went down the corridor past the refectory just now, I thought I saw you bent over your writing at the long table. My girl, immersed in some reverie or other, pondering on what fantastic story she would write for me next. I wait for your essay but nothing comes. My desk is covered in essays and exercises, but nothing is worth reading. How impoverished I feel since you left this morning. No one looks at me as you did, with your big brown eyes.

In just a little while you will be back in your familiar surroundings. You will find consolation with your father and the rest of the family. This is how it has to be, dear girl. Don't be afraid. For a woman like you, with all your gifts, there is definitely a wonderful future in store. Be prepared to enjoy it. Remember your master in Brussels now and then. Your master who has lost his most promising pupil and lives only for a sign from her.

With all my love,
Constantin Heger

*

Haworth, 26 July 1844
To Constantin Heger
Monsieur,

It is not my turn to write, but it is so long since I heard from you that I will venture to do so anyway. Forgive me for sending you all too sentimental a letter this spring. But after your letter of the beginning of January—which expressed such affection and gave me such hope and joy—you gave no further sign of life. That causes me immense sorrow. But monsieur, I have nothing to reproach you with. And rest assured: this letter is controlled in tone.

Dr Wheelwright's wife told me that recently you have been looking tired. That causes me concern. Are you, as in previous years, preparing a play with the pupils? That requires a great deal of commitment from you. In addition, the examinations will be beginning soon and afterwards the prizes will be awarded and presented. The end of the school year is an arduous time and you will undoubtedly be having to give up many of your free evenings. I find it such a shame that I shall not be able to see the play. I am sure it will be splendid yet again, as you have a great talent for direction.

Monsieur, it would give me such pleasure to receive a letter

from you. If you are too busy to write to me, I will under-
stand. Nevertheless I hope that you will make some time
for your favourite pupil (am I still that?). The letter can be
short, I don't ask much of you. But I think almost every wak-
ing moment of you and a letter from you, however short,
would give me new strength.

Oh monsieur, I am frightened that I will forget my French if
I cannot correspond with you. You will say that I can write
to a pupil or one of the teachers, but none of them uses the
French language with such panache as you. You are my
master.

Will you give my regards to Madame? You see how reason-
able I am.

Adieu monsieur.

'Am I disturbing you?'

Her father comes in, his thick spectacle lenses steamed up, though he does not seem to notice. His ageing body is still strong and he knows exactly where he can put his feet here in the house without bumping into anything. And yet he hesitates, just for a fleeting moment and misses the arm of his chair with his hand. A blind giant. In a while he will be operated on by a doctor in Manchester, but the cataract must first mature.

'I'm writing a letter, papa. It must be ready by twelve o'clock, so that Davy can take it to Bradford. Just in time for Mrs Wheelwright, as she is travelling back today.'

'Aha, another letter to Brussels!' He sits down at the table and folds his sinewy, deeply veined hands. His beard has been trimmed and his nails filed, which makes an almost dandyish impression on Charlotte. Monsieur was so much more masculine with his tousled hair and his badly shaved cheeks and chin.

'You are very loyal to your friends there,' says her father.

There is a mildly joking undertone in his words, but his expression is serious.

'Write out my sermon this afternoon,' he says. 'I assume you'll be finished with your letter by then. And, tell me: when are you finally going to set up the school?'

Charlotte suppresses a sigh and puts down her pen.

'Let's abandon the idea of renting a school building, papa. We can start on a small scale in the parsonage, as you suggested. It would make a big difference to the costs. If Emily, Anne and I share a room, there will be room for a couple of girls.'

'Get on with it then, Charlotte. You urgently need a task to concentrate on.' He gets up and gropes around for the church key, which must be somewhere on the table. Charlotte pushes it towards his searching fingers. As soon as her father has closed the door of the living room behind him, she presses her fist on her heart in an attempt to relieve the feeling of oppression. She dips her pen in the ink.

Why is it that all I am able to do is say goodbye to you? Fate can be so merciless. Yet the day will come when I travel to Brussels again, monsieur, I am sure of it. I shall find a way of seeing you again, if only for a moment at the gate.

Adieu,
Charlotte Brontë

*

Haworth, 21 October 1844
Monsieur,
You have not written to me, and that makes me sad. Not that I blame you for anything: naturally you have a busy life. In the absence of your company or your letters I seek consolation in the volumes you gave me. I have picked them up and reread them so often that the pages are coming loose and that the bindings are becoming frayed. For that reason I am having them rebound. One by one, so that I do not have to do without them all at once. To my great sorrow the bookbinder has no linen in the greyish yellow shade in which Paul et Virginie *was bound. Worse still, he actually has no yellow linen at all and so I have chosen a soft green for all the works.*
Every book evokes memories in me, monsieur.
Last May you gave me a little German bible. Surely you cannot have forgotten that spring, our spring? I read and reread Schiller's Testament, *because I once found it in my desk with a note from you between the pages. How happy I was then!*
On my way back to England I almost wanted my ship to sink and to drown like Virginie. But I am alive in my father's house, and from what I can deduce from what Mrs Wheelwright writes about the boarding school, you are also still among the living. Permit me then to shake off the sadness from my shoulders and to believe in life again. Write to me, please. I am sending this letter with a good friend who is travelling to Brussels. Can I ask you to send your answer to me with him? He will be staying there for a few days, so you have ample time. Give me reason to smile again, monsieur. I haven't laughed for months. Without some joie de vivre I shan't be able to set up a school either.

I wrote to you in May and July, but there was no reply. Perhaps my letters are not reaching you? Give me a sign of life, please.

Adieu,
Charlotte Brontë

*

Haworth, 9 January 1845
Monsieur,
I shall die if you do not write to me. How long will you go on torturing me with your silence? I cannot sleep, monsieur, and suffer from headaches. I toss and turn at night and see your face in front of me. Oh no, it does not fade: I remember every line, every shadow, and could sketch you at will.
Monsieur, shall I come to Belgium? Is it because you think it is impossible for us to see each other again that you no longer wish to correspond with me? I could see you at the gate, or better: in a place where we can speak at leisure. Do you remember, that back street? You cannot have forgotten. I beg you: send me word.
And if you no longer want me, if you have no more love in your heart for poor Charlotte who was once your favourite, then let me know. Better an excruciating pain than this nagging doubt. I don't know how I would survive if you were to refuse me your friendship, but people are so much stronger than they feel. Probably I shall become a burnt-out woman, from whose dull eyes you can see that she was once for a moment able to warm herself at love's flame, but was then chased back into the freezing cold. No more stories would flow from my pen, monsieur. Without you I am nothing. À

bientôt. *I no longer have the heart to write adieu. I long so intensely for the sound of your voice, for the friendly pressure of your hands.*

Ever yours,
Charlotte

*

'She's the one for me.'

Branwell is lying full length in an unbuttoned white nightshirt on the couch in the living room, his eyes shining and bloodshot, his skin waxy pale. This is how the lifeless body of Shelley must have looked, washed up on a deserted beach in Tuscany. But Branwell is not dead and indeed he speaks his words of love theatrically. His disconsolate appearance is due to an evening with a bottle of gin in the Black Bull.

'Branwell, how can you?' Charlotte manages to say with difficulty. 'What idiocy to fall in love with your employer. Mrs Robinson is so much older than you. Oh, God. Does her husband suspect anything?'

With a touch of narcissism, Branwell brushes a long lock of hair away from his face. 'Robinson is a fool. He does not know a thing. This summer I'm travelling with the family to their summer residence in Scarborough. Lydia and I are really looking forward to it.'

'Branwell, what will come of it all?'

'One day we shall be together,' he says hoarsely. 'You'll see. I know: you all think I'm a failure.' His voice rises in imitation of his sisters. 'Branwell cannot even paint a decent portrait. And his poems—ha, they're worthless compared with our masterly stories and poems. And I bet you think that I was dismissed from the railways for stealing money from the till.'

He looks for his glass under the couch. There is still a little water or gin in it and he drinks a mouthful.

'Do you really think that I didn't know that each of you is writing a novel? You exclude me from your plans, because I am nothing but a bungler, a pathetic creature. That's what you call me, isn't it? Only Lydia sees what I really am. She thinks I'm a valuable person. She adores me.'

'Oh, be quiet!' Charlotte puts her hands over her ears, but then she hears her brother's voice, muffled as if by a wall of water: 'And you then, are you so unsullied? You're suffering from severe melancholy—a broken heart, it seems. Has that Brussels schoolmaster got something to do with it by any chance?'

*

Her hands are trembling and the paper is blank. Why can't she be indifferent, like Emily, and let the past rest? Louise de Bassompierre's letter lies forgotten and unanswered at the bottom of Emily's writing case, while Charlotte still longs for a few lines from monsieur in his brisk, rather untidy handwriting. Next to her lies the manuscript she has been working on for the past few months. It deeply disappoints her, while Emily has written a great work, as wild and disconsolate as her beloved moorland hills. Powerful and pitiless as the wind that rushes across the undulations of the landscape. If there is no reply, this will be her last letter and her mourning must come to an end.

Haworth, 25 November 1845
Monsieur,
Forgive me for writing to you again. For over six months I have forbidden myself to take up my pen with that end in

mind. A calvary, since while I am sending you letters, I feel linked to you. So I cannot stand it any longer...

*

Her letter, two folded sheets closely written on both sides, lies in the rather coarse hands with stubby fingers of Constantin Heger. The gas lamp, the aroma of his pipe and these sublime, sad words from overseas put him in a melancholy mood.

Charlotte! He had not thought he would hear any more from her.

'Constantin.'

His wife's voice. How she watches over him, his Claire! She has come in noiselessly in her satin slippers. Her dressing gown is hanging open: the décolleté of her nightdress. He knows her so well. Her smell warm as cinnamon, the weight of her breasts. Why does he now suddenly think of Suzette? Her violin playing today... What a mysterious young woman she is, and that long, black hair, so soft, and his fingertips running along her naked arm.

'The letter,' says Claire. 'I want the letter, give it to me.'

He holds the letter under the table top out of her reach.

'You're not going to reply to her, are you?

'*Mon amour,*' he says seriously. 'I haven't written to Charlotte Brontë for an eternity. It hurts me that you should ask that question. I gave you my word. Don't you trust me?'

'Give me the letter.'

He lets go of the letter with something resembling a groan, and she tears it up, not in fury, but with cold determination. The snippets fall into the waste-paper basket. She runs her hand momentarily through her husband's curly hair and then leaves his study.

It is bedtime and Constantin Heger turns out the gas lamp. He puts a bulky book by Rousseau under his arm and is already on his way to the door, but then he changes his mind, puts the book back on the table and kneels down by the waste-paper basket. He carefully takes out the snippets of the letter and stuffs them into an envelope. The following day in his study in the Athénée Royal he will devote himself to sewing them back together. In that way he will be able to read and reread Charlotte's words and delight in the adoration he elicits.

XXX

59 Boundary Street, Manchester—a modest, respectable boarding house. On the first floor Charlotte opens a window wide. Although it is a dry, fairly warm afternoon in August, the sun is hidden by a brown pall coming from the chimneys of the cotton mills. Charlotte leans with her palms on the windowsill and looks at the terrace of narrow, red-brick workman's houses opposite. Below boys are playing knucklebones and a few old people are sitting on kitchen chairs next to their front doors. Charlotte puts her writing things on the side table by the window. In the next room, where heavy curtains dim the daylight and muffle the noises from the street, her father, almost seventy, lies resting. A few days before, his left eye was operated on by Doctor Wilson, the famous eye surgeon. The operation went satisfactorily and most probably her father—with glasses—will be able to read again. But before they return to Haworth he must rest in bed for at least a month. There is a bandage over his eye and at the moment he is sleeping. Charlotte would like to be allowed to nurse him herself, but on the instructions of the doctor her father has employed a nurse, an exaggeratedly obliging woman who relieves her of all care. As a result she has a month ahead of her without the pressure of responsibilities. A month in which she has an unexpected amount of time to herself. She sits down and knows what she has to do. This is a golden opportunity to start a new novel.

There was no possibility of taking a walk that day. We had been wandering, indeed, in the leafless shrubbery an hour in the morning…

In this industrial town, enveloped in brown fog, at this side table by the window, Charlotte throws off her submissiveness. Her grief has given way to melancholy, her melancholy to rage and her rage to the decision to tell a story that is extraordinary. She no longer feels the need to write to Constantin Heger.

Charlotte is musing. She forgets to be bored and forgets to take tea to the nurse and her father. She is the little girl at Cowan Bridge boarding school again, having to say goodbye to her big sister. Maria is sitting on a chair in the entrance hall to the school waiting for their father to come and collect her—grey shadows beneath her big tired eyes, since approaching death is a sketch in charcoal. Maria smiling bravely. Charlotte kisses her on the cheek, but then goes to the square, to watch the other girls playing ball. *Maria, I will call you Helen, Helen Burns.*

She stirred herself, put back the curtain, and I saw her face, pale, wasted, but quite composed: she looked so little changed that my fear was instantly dissipated.

While Charlotte muses, while the ghosts from her past assume new contours, colours and names, in Antwerp harbour Emile the workman and his young wife board the sailing ship 'Infatigable', which will set sail for America at first light.

While Charlotte muses, Arcadie says goodbye to her father in the library of the Campagne Claret. The following day she will leave on a tour of Switzerland and Italy with the king. 'Look after yourself,' says Charles Claret, his voice trembling with emotion. 'Oh child, I had a different future in mind for you. What's more, you're bringing shame on our family, although your mother thinks differently about it. It hurts me, but I don't want to hear any more news from you.'

'Not even if you become a grandfather later?'

'Not even then,' he says and turns away from her.

Charlotte has no knowledge of the adventures of Emile and Arcadie. In her mind's eye she sees the girls of the Pensionnat Heger strolling through the walled garden. Slate-grey pigeons flap upwards against the backdrop of the church towers. She is walking arm in arm with her master through the rue d'Isabelle and his face appears in a patch of yellowish gas light. *Monsieur, be Edward Rochester for me.*

He had a dark face, with stern features and a heavy brow; his eyes and gathered eyebrows looked ireful and thwarted just now.

And she herself? She will be called Jane. Not a heroine possessing beauty and wealth, but a poor young woman with modest charms, like herself. Not an Arcadie who dances on the beach in calf leather bootees. Jane Eyre will be her name, and her boots will be worn and dull. But she will triumph.

Charlotte dips her pen in the ink.

Afterword

For the essays written by Charlotte and Emily Brontë in Brussels, I based myself on *The Belgian Essays* by Sue Lonoff. I translated them freely from the French.

The letters of Charlotte to Constantin Heger and the letter from Constantin Heger to Charlotte are fiction. However, they are similar in tone and content to the actual letters.

For more information or to receive our newsletter,
please contact us at: info@worldeditions.org.